Paula was magnificent. Standing knee-deep in the water of the sparkling mountain lake, Jack held her at arm's length, admiring the perfect symmetry of her nude body. She blushed and smiled softly.

"You're beautiful," he said with an earnestness that embarrassed her somewhat. "Absolutely beautiful."

He took her in his arms and kissed her. She responded eagerly, her mouth moving sensuously, her tongue probing, stimulating, arousing. He lowered his hands, lifting, moving slowly, firmly.

"Oh, yes," she murmured softly. "Oh God, yes . . ."

THE
DENNECKER CODE

by

J. C. Pollock

FAWCETT GOLD MEDAL · NEW YORK

For A. L. Hart—a very special man who may or may not be aware of it.

Between the idea
And the reality
Between the motion
And the act
Falls the Shadow

—T. S. Eliot

PROLOGUE

Berlin—April 10, 1945

The air raid sirens filled the predawn air throughout Berlin, sounding the all-clear, moaning and fading to an eerie silence as the last of the Allied bombers droned westward, away from the beleaguered city. The Lichterfelde district had been hit heavily that night, but the SS offices had miraculously escaped all but minor, superficial damage.

SS generals Richard Gluecks and Karl Dennecker stood at the entrance to the courtyard behind the main office of the Economic and Administration Headquarters. Gluecks raised his short, powerful arms high above his head, arched his back, and stretched, relieving his cramped muscles. The two men had spent the night working in their offices, attending to last-minute details. This was to be their final day in Berlin.

The early-morning air was cold, and a light drizzle fell, having a bracing effect after the long hours in the dank, smoky offices. Dennecker stared blankly across the courtyard, deep in thought. He was not as sanguine as his companion; he had no confidence in the future.

He glanced down at Gluecks and smiled wryly. Germany was crumbling around them, and this bull-necked, arrogant boor considered it just another adventure; he had actually heard him humming and singing to himself in an adjoining office as he destroyed files and documents—his allegiance and honor discarded with them.

Dennecker turned up his collar, shrugged deeper into his

black leather overcoat, and tugged at the peak of his cap, bringing it lower on his forehead to shield his eyes. He started across the courtyard toward the garage area at the rear of the compound, his long even strides forcing Gluecks to take two steps to his one to stay abreast. A hollow, staccato quick-step echoed across the wet, glistening cobblestones as Dennecker picked up the pace.

In each of the two open bays of the garage they were approaching was a two-and-a-half-ton truck with canvas covering a ribbed frame. The trucks were generally used for troop transports, but the two generals had allocated them for their own purposes.

Gluecks gestured toward the trucks. "Who would have thought, Karl, when we rode triumphantly through the streets of Paris in a Mercedes," he said, "that in a few years we would be fleeing Berlin in a truck, running for our lives with our tails between our legs." He shook his head and let out a short, gruff laugh. "Quite an unexpected turn of events, wouldn't you say?"

Unexpected only by an unobservant fool, Dennecker thought, but kept it to himself. He merely nodded briefly. They stepped inside the garage to get out of the rain. Dennecker opened the top flap of his overcoat and reached inside his tunic for his cigarettes and lighter. "Where will you go?" he asked.

"Northwest, to Kiel," Gluecks replied. "I have friends there who will help me until I can make arrangements for passage to South America. And you, Karl?" he asked, watching Dennecker's expression closely. "Have you decided?"

"I'm not certain," Dennecker said, less than candidly. "I have access to a small villa in Bavaria, near the Austrian border. I may stay there temporarily." He saw no reason to go into specific details—with Gluecks, it could be unwise. Although their conspiracy involving the contents of the trucks bound them to an alliance, he felt that the bond was tenuous at best. Gluecks, if captured, could be expected to bargain for his life with whatever he had at hand. The less he knew, the better.

The two men had worked together for the past three years in the section that administered the concentration camps, and neither had any illusions about their fate in the hands of the Allies. Anyone connected with the camps would, if caught, be arrested as a war criminal. They hadn't deluded themselves as some of their peers had; some had been infected by the rampant chimera, believing they could reach an accommodation with the allies, offering their services for the next battle, against the real enemy: the communists. Surely it would only be a matter of time before the Americans and the British realized that they must destroy the Bolsheviks, the reasoning went. Dreamers, Dennecker thought. Foolish dreamers.

Dennecker and Gluecks were certain that they were already on the wanted lists; when the full horror of the death camps became known, they would be hunted down with a vengeance. Their escape routes had been carefully planned to take them to areas away from the Russian armies. If they were to be captured, they preferred to take their chances with the Americans or the British.

According to the latest available maps, the routes they chose would keep them out of danger. The British had not yet reached Hamburg, so Gluecks would have no difficulties getting to Kiel, and the Americans were just crossing the Rhine, with the exception of a few advanced armored units that had spearheaded a drive to the Elbe. With the Russians on the banks of the Oder, that still left a corridor at least a hundred miles wide open to the south for Dennecker.

The morning light was fast approaching; a grayish-white streak lined the horizon. Suddenly, off in the distance to the east, an ominous mechanical thunder broke the damp stillness—the muffled sounds of artillery rumbling its warning. The Russians had resumed their daily pounding of the German positions on the west bank of the Oder. The remnants of the once invincible German army were understrength, disorganized, and widely scattered; and when the Russians began to cross the river in force for their all-out assault on Berlin, there would be no stopping them.

Dennecker shivered, less from the cold than from the thought of the fate moving slowly, inexorably toward Berlin. He tossed his cigarette into a small puddle outside the garage and watched the glowing ashes instantly disappear. If only the battle and the torment would end that quickly. But he knew that the conquerors would savor the spoils of their victory, revel in their retribution. They would give what they had received and worse.

Gluecks gazed apprehensively in the direction of the foreboding sound, his thoughts occupied with his own dilemma. "The end is near, Karl," he said solemnly. "It's only a matter of days." He took Dennecker's hand in a firm grip. "It's best we leave now, before the city is fully awake. Perhaps we'll meet again," he said, with a grin and a shrug. "Who knows what the gods have in store for us?" He opened the door of the truck and stepped up into the cab. "Have a safe journey and better days, my friend."

Dennecker watched as Gluecks drove off, feeling an unsettling, profound sense of loss. It wasn't caused by Gluecks leaving; that was symptomatic. It was the end of the fatherland as he knew it, as he had helped shape it. In his mind's eye he saw himself and Werner—Werner, blown to bits at Stalingrad—strolling on the Kurfürstendamm, swelled with pride, resplendent in their uniforms, the death's head on their caps telling everyone that they were the elite. Germany was invincible, they were the wave of the future, heralding the thousand-year Reich. How long ago had it been? Four . . . five years? God! It seemed a lifetime. He stood motionless, lost in memories, his stern, handsome features silhouetted by the growing light in the east.

An abrupt change in the rhythm of the detonations brought him quickly back to the present; the tempo of the barrage had increased—more intense, more brutal. He walked to the rear of the truck and tied the canvas flaps securely across the back.

The huge truck rumbled noisily over the cobblestones as he drove to the gate at the entrance to the compound. The SS sentries saluted smartly as he drove past. He wondered if they knew, with his departure, that they were guarding an empty building.

Once outside the compound, he turned left, toward Berlin. One brief stop and then . . . he had ridden with the hounds; now it was time to run with the fox.

ONE

Aspen, Colorado—October 1979

Jack Callahan came out of the post office, squinting in the bright sunlight as he shuffled through the mail he had just retrieved from his box. Mostly bills and advertisements, the usual, until he reached the bottom of the stack: a light-blue envelope with a dark-blue border; definitely not commercial. He was about to open it when he heard a familiar disturbance coming from where he had parked. He looked up and saw Boomer standing in the back of the open jeep, woofing and growling menacingly, his head cocked back, lip curled, hackles up, and eyes bloodshot—sure signs of a Rottweiler about to go off.

"Easy, Boomer," Callahan called. "Easy." The huge black-and-rust dog glanced in his direction, then back to the man in the Bermuda shorts with the camera hanging from a strap around his neck. Boomer sat, changing to a less threatening posture, as Callahan approached.

"That's a mean dog," the man said, backing away. "I only tried to pet him."

"He's not mean, just selective," Callahan said good-naturedly, getting into the jeep. Boomer hopped forward into the passenger seat. Jack rubbed his head. "Good boy, Boomer."

"'Good boy' for what?" the man said antagonistically. "For almost attacking me?"

Callahan chuckled and looked at the short, fat man in amusement. "No. 'Good boy' for obeying me and not attacking you."

"He's a damn vicious dog," the man continued. "He should be kept on a chain; a stupid, belligerent animal like that can be dangerous."

Callahan bristled. "Look, Mac. I apologize if my dog upset you, but he wants you to pet him about as much as I want to continue this conversation. Now have a nice day and a pleasant stay in Aspen." It was a dismissal, not a friendly farewell.

The tourist, deciding that the tall, solidly built owner was as formidable as the dog, turned on his heels and continued down the street. Jack opened the letter and smiled with a deep sense of satisfaction as he read.

> Hi Callahan,
>
> Not knowing how many vacationing skiers a ski instructor dates each winter, I'm not sure you will remember me.
>
> Last February, you extended an invitation for a fall camping trip; perhaps it was the dinner, the cozy fire, and all the wine, but I considered it a firm offer.
>
> If you are otherwise occupied, I'll understand and manage on my own. In the event that you are not, I arrive in Aspen October 2, 2:45 P.M., on Rocky Mountain Airlines.
>
> Hope to see you. My best to Boomer.
>
> Paula
>
> P.S.: Tried phoning, a dozen times; no answer.

Jack remembered her well; he had met her at the Center, after skiing, three days before her ten-day vacation was over. He had had dinner with her that night, and the others as well, and hours of warm companionship and interesting, lighthearted conversation, lying in front of the fire at his place. With her, he hadn't been caught up in the race to the bedroom, although he had to admit he had had the overwhelming desire on their last night, but she hadn't given the right signals. She had been a comforting presence: intelligent, witty, but no competitive instincts to allay; a cut above anyone he had dated before, and far removed from the one-night stands and occasional transitory "roommates." In fact, he recalled, she was the only woman with whom he had ever felt unsure of himself.

She was in her late twenties, five years younger than he; a free-lance journalist, she had told him: purposeful, independent, striving toward a goal. He was complacent, typical of many of Aspen's dislocated souls—an aimless spirit with shallow purpose; an underachiever. Their personalities were antithetical; he was a self-contained cynic with an impenetrable carapace, few friends, and no confidants, "a man who keeps himself to himself." Paula was ingenuous, warm, vivacious, and utterly charming. Callahan considered himself outclassed and, quite frank with himself, had never expected to see her again. He was, to say the least, pleased with the opportunity.

He suddenly realized that today was Friday, October 2. He glanced at the postmark; the letter had been mailed eight days ago from New York City. It had probably been lying in his box all week. He had to change his habit of picking up his mail sporadically, not to mention not answering his phone when he was reading.

"Company, Boomer," he said. "An old friend coming to visit." Boomer cocked his head to one side and furrowed his brow, the tip of his tongue protruding from his muzzle in a comical expression that always amused Callahan. He often talked to Boomer, fully aware that the dog couldn't understand all of the words, but knowing that he did understand the sense and mood of most of what was said to him. Jack believed that the more you talked to your dog, the broader his recognition vocabulary became, and Boomer understood more than most dogs whose owners underestimated their abilities.

Paula's flight arrived in less than two hours. Callahan put the jeep into a tight U turn; Boomer sat bolt upright in the seat, eyes forward, ears flapping in the wind, shifting his weight expertly, maintaining his balance and composure; he was a seasoned rider.

Callahan sped through the east end of town, following the main road toward Independence Pass. A few miles past the last heavily developed area, he turned off the highway onto a short, steep gravel driveway leading to a small house on a knoll set back in the woods. The charming white stucco-and-timber chalet-style home had large picture windows facing down the valley, with a clear view of the surrounding mountains. Jack had bought the house and five acres four years ago, and even at Aspen's inflated prices, it was worth every penny. In the rear of the property, the National Forest

Service owned the land up to his boundary; in the front, he owned to the highway; across the highway, a government-designated elk preserve ensured his privacy. His closest neighbors on each side were obscured from view summer and winter by the dense aspen and spruce forest. It was a secluded and idyllic spot—nirvana to Callahan.

The interior of the house was small and compartmental: a kitchen, with a card table and two chairs jammed into a corner; a living room, with floor-to-ceiling books on two walls, a sofa, and two director's chairs; and two small bedrooms and a bathroom. It had the ambience of a bachelor's house—casual abandonment. Jack kept it relatively clean, but he wasn't compulsive about it, as was evidenced by the four-day stack of unwashed dishes in the sink, a mound of dirty laundry tossed in a corner of the guest room, a layer of dust on the furniture, and a blanket of Boomer hairs covering the carpet and sofa.

Boomer hopped on to the sofa, settled himself, and watched the unusual hurried activities of his friend. Jack moved quickly, dusting the furniture, vacuuming the carpet and sofa (Boomer promptly returned to his spot), rinsing the dishes and stacking them in the dishwasher, stuffing the dirty laundry into a closet, and making his bed. He walked from room to room looking for obvious clutter, and noticed an overflowing ashtray in the living room on the raised hearth in front of the fireplace where he had been reading the night before. He dumped it in the wastebasket next to the kitchen table, raising a cloud of dust, necessitating a second dusting of the table. He downed a glass of milk, threw together a ham-and-raisin-bread sandwich, giving Boomer half, and headed for the door.

"See you in a little while, Boomer." Boomer grumbled his displeasure at being left behind, and curled tighter into the corner of the sofa.

The De Havilland Otter, clearly visible against the brilliant blue sky, banked into a steep descent to the floor of the valley, leveling off just short of touchdown. Callahan stood at the entrance to the baggage-claim area and watched the cumbersome plane taxi to the terminal. The flow of people was light this time of year, a trickle compared to the peak season's inundations. The crowds wouldn't return until Thanksgiving, when the lifts opened.

Paula was near the end of the line of passengers: a few business types, some youthful, fresh-faced job hopefuls, and an amalgam of casually dressed locals returning from a day in Denver, or a brief off-season trip home to touch base with parents, or to appease vindictive, avaricious ex-wives.

Callahan smiled to himself as she exited the plane. Her shoulder-length hair, raven black and iridescent in the high-altitude sun, framed her delicately boned, well-proportioned features. Her eyes appeared black from a distance, but Jack remembered that they were a deep—infinitely deep—haunting blue. She wore no makeup, and her skin had the warm satin ivory glow and texture of alabaster. A pair of tight-fitting corduroys hugged her long shapely legs, tapering into the tops of knee-high leather boots, and a well-tailored blouse and vest accented her trim waist and full, firm breasts. As she walked across the tarmac, with an effortless grace, she tilted her head back and lightly tossed her hair, an extremely feminine and appealing gesture.

Jack had forgotten how beautiful she was—or actually not forgotten, but erased the images, a defense mechanism he had learned to employ against things he considered beyond his reach. He watched her approaching, captivated by her. She was a sensual, alluring woman with a piquant loveliness that brought rushing back to him the desires aroused when he had held her in his arms. He felt a stirring, and shifted his weight to the other foot.

As she entered the terminal, he moved toward her hesitantly, not certain how to greet her. Paula eased the awkward moment with a warm smile and a tender kiss on the cheek.

"It's good to see you, Callahan," she said cheerfully. "I wasn't sure you'd be here."

"I considered it a responsibility," he teased, amused by her casual use of his last name; she had done that since the moment of introduction. "I couldn't imagine you managing alone in the mountains."

Paula grinned, casting a sidelong glance. "I'll trade on that, if it means you're taking me camping."

"I'm looking forward to it," he said, taking her bags as she reached for them. He stared at her for a brief moment, unnoticed, reminded of another of her pleasing lineaments: her voice. Like everything else about her, it seemed to have been chosen especially for her. It was deep and sonorous, at

15

times almost husky, depending on her mood and intonation, yet always feminine and provocative.

She slipped her arm through his as they left the terminal, making it seem as though it had been only a few days, not seven months, since they had seen each other. She brushed lightly against him as they walked; again he felt the stirring.

Paula had seen Aspen only in the winter, and on the drive back to town—top removed from the jeep, windshield down, her hair buffeted by the rush of cool, dry air—she had a panoramic view of Aspen's autumn grandeur. The deserted ski slopes were lush green strips, coursing their ways with varying degrees of pitch and roll through the shimmering, golden aspens and silent, immutable spruce, awaiting the inevitable early snows and first exultant skiers. And all around her, the vaulting skies were pierced by the snow-capped peaks and crowded by the massive shoulders of the Rockies, enclosing the sheltered valley with a timeless sense of security. She was enthralled with the surrounding beauty. In all her travels she had seen few places to rival it.

"God, Callahan. It's beautiful."

Jack smiled and nodded. "Wait until you get up into the high country."

Paula smiled contentedly. "When do we start?"

"Tomorrow morning."

"I'll be ready," she said enthusiastically. "I'm a little short on camping equipment, but I can pick up a few essentials in town if you point me in the right direction."

"No need for that," Jack said, making a tight turn on to the main street. "I have enough for a battalion."

Paula pointed to a lodge they were approaching on the right. "I have reservations there. May we stop for a few minutes so I can drop off my luggage and freshen up?"

Callahan was taken aback by the statement; the disappointment, almost childlike, and totally out of character, was clearly visible. "You're not staying there!" he said more imperatively than intended. "I mean . . ." He gestured an apology and softened his tone. "I have a guest room you're more than welcome to."

Paula, surprised by his reaction, quickly assessed the tenseness of the situation. She squeezed his hand affectionately. "That's very thoughtful, Callahan. I accept."

*   *   *

Boomer held his sit-stay as Jack had commanded when he opened the door. Ears raised and forward, eyes narrowed, his stub of a tail up and still, he appraised the unfamiliar intruder, Paula leaned forward and clapped her hands. "Hi, Boomer. Aren't you going to say hello?"

Boomer cocked his head to one side, then the other, still uncertain.

"Ah, Boomer," Paula cooed, with an affected sadness. "You don't remember me; I'm hurt."

Callahan watched, amused, knowing it was not likely that Boomer would have forgotten someone who had spent a considerable amount of time attentively scratching his chest in front of the fire and romping with him in the snow. Boomer was thinking; the tendrils of his memory reaching. Jack saw the moment of recognition.

Boomer lowered his ears, pulling them back, flat against his bowling-ball head. His eyes grew round and wide, and his stubby tail vibrated rapidly. Jack released him from his command, and Paula got a friendly Rottweiler greeting.

Boomer bounded forward, slamming into her, sending her sprawling onto the sofa. He jumped up next to her and flopped into her lap, demonstratively licking her hands and face with alternate swipes. She wrestled playfully with the 130-pound whirling dervish. He rolled onto his back, pawing the air, growling and snarling in mock battle as Paula rubbed his chest and tugged at the ruff on his neck.

Jack took the luggage to the guest room. Spying a pair of jockey shorts he had missed on his sweep of the rooms, he tossed them under the bed, out of sight. He smiled inwardly at the sounds from the living room, amazed at the way Boomer had taken to Paula; he tolerated very few people, being overtly belligerent and antagonistic to most. Jack saw him dash past the hallway, into a corner of the kitchen, then run back to the living room with his two-foot-long rawhide bone in his mouth—he wanted a tug-of-war. Paula's melodic, almost brassy whiskey-baritone laugh filled the house.

They had dinner at a restaurant Paula had enjoyed that winter. It was a quiet evening, the pace unhurried; the locals had the town to themselves. After dinner they spent the rest of the evening sorting through the camping equipment and packing the backpacks. Boomer whined and pounded his

17

front paws on the floor when he saw his doggy-pack come out of the closet.

"He carries his food," Jack explained. "It's one of the rules—everyone carries his own weight," he added with a mischievous grin.

Paula let out a short snort of a laugh. "I'll manage, Callahan."

Jack wasn't sure she could handle a full load, and, not wanting to take any of the enjoyment out of the trip for her, he put most of the heavy things in his pack. He showed her a map, pointing out where they would be going and the route they would take: up the front of Ajax Mountain and down the other side into the wilderness area, taking the jeep most of the way, then backpacking a few miles, up a few thousand feet, to a remote lake where they would camp.

TWO

Morning had spent hours at the lower elevations by the time the sun crested the jagged peaks towering above the quiet high-country meadow. A golden haze spread slowly over the fading grass and tenacious autumn wildflowers as a light blanket of frost succumbed to the radiant warmth. At the south end of the meadow a primordial mist rose from an urgent stream that flowed along the edge of the forest.

The old man, jolted fully awake by the icy water, toweled his leathery face dry and ran his hands briskly through his silver-gray short cropped hair. He looked considerably younger than his seventy-five years; his muscles were still toned and resilient, his carriage was still erect—the rewards of the right genes and years of outdoor life. He had stern, handsome features, with facial lines and creases that suggested he was an authoritative, disciplined ascetic.

He folded his towel neatly, draped it over his shoulder, and started along a path to a cabin set back in the woods. Out of the corner of his eye, he saw something move. He stopped abruptly, and stood motionless, his eyes fixed on the spot where he caught the movement—a predator's eyes, alert, calm, dispassionate.

An elk ventured cautiously out from the trees to the edge of the stream, a short distance from where he was standing. Twitching his ears, aware of the old man's presence, the huge animal lowered his massive head, adorned with a magnificent rack, and drank his fill, then turned and sauntered off, his tawny hide occasionally dappled and highlighted by shafts of sunlight penetrating the shaded forest.

The old man's time in the high country was nearing its end. In a few weeks he would have to return to town, before the heavy snows came. For the past three years, since retiring from the Aspen Ski Corporation, he had spent his summers photographing and cataloguing wildflowers and lichens, an avocation that seemed out of character, but one he had found to be restful and rewarding. The old abandoned miner's cabin, situated on land owned by the National Forest Service and leased to the Ski Corp, was one of his perquisites upon retirement. With the consent of the Ski Corp, he had renovated it, making it comfortable, though austere, and used it for his summer sojourns in the wilderness.

He carefully arranged his camera equipment in the large leather carrying case, making certain to include the closeup lens needed to photograph the lichen on the rocks around the lake he planned to hike to that day. He made a sandwich, placing it in one of the outside pockets of the case, and left the cabin, stopping briefly at the stream to fill his canteen before setting out on the trail.

By midday he had reached the lake, a challenging climb for even a well-conditioned and experienced hiker. It had been a constant uphill trek, eighteen hundred feet above the meadow, on a moderate to steep incline. The old man had maintained a slow, steady pace, switchbacking on the steepest grades. But it had been a long and difficult climb.

He was perspiring heavily and felt enervated and lightheaded. He tried to will away the fatigue as he usually did, but this time it was more persistent. Ignoring it, knowing it would soon pass, he began examining the boulders strewn along the shore of the lake. He found one, partially shaded by a large spruce tree, with a colorful array of lichen. Slipping the leather case off his shoulder, he removed his light meter and camera, affixed the closeup lens, and assiduously measured for the proper exposure. Perspiring more heavily now, the perspiration blurred his vision as he attempted to focus the sensitive lens.

Then it struck. Suddenly, savagely—like a sledgehammer slammed into his chest, wielded by some powerful, angry, unseen force. He staggered from the impact, dropping the camera; his knees buckled, and he fell to the ground, limp and immobilized. His breathing was raspish, quick and shallow; the pain unbearable—crushing. Yet he made no sound. His eyes were wide, expressive, defiant—beseeching; not upward for some ill-defined heavenly salvation or indentured reprieve, but inward, as though appealing to an inner strength, an indomitable warrior spirit held in reserve to be conjured up for the final battle. But there was no response; no deliverance, only the increasing, excruciating pain. Then slowly it began to diminish. A soothing calm descended; a gossamer veil of peace, of freedom, of release.

Beside a mirror lake, under a fragrant spruce, below the snow-capped peaks, beneath a brilliant autumn sky, it ended— quietly.

THREE

Boomer sat complacently in the back of the jeep, happy to be underway. Paula could have sworn she had heard him pacing the house all night. The jeep road began at the bottom of the ski runs, near the center of town, at first taking the mountain in wide sweeping traverses. It was the same mountain Paula had skied that winter, and she recognized some of the runs she had taken with some degree of incertitude—they seemed even more formidable without their soft, cushioning mantle of snow. She looked apprehensively at the sheer drop-offs along sections of the narrow dirt road as they climbed higher and the grade became steeper. At times it was unnerving, but the view of the mountains and the town—almost four thousand feet below them when they reached the top—was spectacular.

The road down the back of the mountain was no more than a rocky trail, just wide enough in spots to accommodate one jeep. Jack handled it with an expertise gained from familiarity and experience. Paula had a few anxious moments, but enjoyed the adventure. Two thousand feet below, as they entered a broad alpine meadow, the trail widened and flattened.

"At the far end of this meadow," Callahan announced, "we leave the jeep and hike the rest of the way."

Paula stared at the steep terrain rising up from the meadow and pointed to the area Jack had indicated on the map. "Is that the mountain we're going to climb?"

"That's it," Callahan said.

Paula smiled weakly. "It looked a lot easier on the map."

"It's not that bad," he reassured her.

Paula was surprised by her stamina. It was a hard climb, but she kept the pace Jack set, without pressing. Her pack wasn't as uncomfortable and burdensome as she had anticipated; she suspected that Callahan had had something to do with that. Boomer was in his glory, leading the way, oblivious to the pack strapped across his broad back. Occasionally he would get too far ahead, and as Paula and Jack would approach a sharp bend in the trail, they would see him peering around a tree or rock, making certain they were still with him. Reassured, he would bound happily out of sight.

Three hours into the climb, Callahan stopped and stood on a rock promontory twenty yards up the trail from Paula. He called back, "Come and take a look."

Paula closed the distance and stood beside him. The lake was a hundred feet below them, enclosed by jagged peaks, and sheltered in a shallow, grassy bowl dotted with boulders and scattered clumps of spruce trees. From where they stood, the land began a gentle declension to the shore of the lake.

"It's beautiful, Callahan. Absolutely beautiful."

Jack pounded in the last of the tent pegs while Paula arranged a barrier of rocks around a fire pit Callahan had used on previous trips. Boomer trudged along the water's edge, patrolling the shoreline with a territorial swagger, claiming an occasional rock or tree. He was fifty yards or so from the campsite when something entered his field of vision that alerted him. Stopping short, he gazed intently at a large spruce tree, raised his head, stretched his neck, and winded laterally. Seconds later, certain of his identification, he bellowed a deep, guttural warning that echoed off the mountain and out across the lake.

Jack turned in the direction of the sound and saw Boomer, tensed and threatening, stalking slowly toward the large spruce. "Easy, Boomer," he called to him, and took off at a dead run, with Paula close behind. Boomer held his place until Jack reached him, put him on a down-stay, and approached the tree.

The old man appeared to be sleeping in the shade of the spruce, but instinct and experience told Callahan he was dead. Kneeling beside the body, he felt for a pulse and confirmed his judgment. By the general condition of the body, Jack estimated he hadn't been dead more than a few hours.

Paula moved closer, hesitantly, understanding the significance of Jack's demeanor.

"He's dead, isn't he?"

Callahan looked up somberly and nodded. "I'm afraid so."

"Did he fall, or ..." She paused, mildly shocked and distressed.

"I don't think so," Callahan said. "There's not a mark on him, and it doesn't look as though there are any broken bones. I think he just died of natural causes."

Paula noticed the camera bag and equipment on the ground. "Do you think he's a tourist who hiked here from town?" she asked, regaining some of her composure.

Jack shook his head. "No. I know him, or at least I know who he is. He spends his summers up here in a cabin near the meadow where we left the jeep. His name's Dennecker. He managed Ajax Mountain for the Ski Corp until he retired, a year or so after I started teaching."

"He looks so peaceful and calm," Paula said softly. "As though he were sleeping."

Callahan smiled to himself, remembering some of the stories about the old man. "He was a tough old bird. He didn't retire until he was seventy-two, I believe, and then only because they threatened to fire him. He ran that mountain with an asperity that was legendary."

Jack recalled an incident he had witnessed. A doped-up hotdog skier was running out of control, recklessly bombing the mountain on an exceptionally crowded day, endangering the other skiers. Dennecker came swooping out of nowhere at breakneck speed, caught the culprit from behind, dove on him, and brought him down, sending both of them careening down the slope for a hundred yards or so before they came to a stop. He grabbed the young man by his hair, pulled him to his feet with one hand, and slapped him silly with the other—to the applause of a growing group of skiers who had stopped to watch the spectacle. He further humiliated the shaken and astounded fellow by taking his skis and forcing him to walk down the mountain. He was at that time in his early seventies, at least fifty years older than the man he had thrashed. Jack smiled again at his vision of the old man putting on his skis and heading downhill, as though it was all in a day's work.

"What are we going to do with him?" Paula asked, realizing the difficulty of the situation.

"I'll have to carry him down to the jeep," Jack replied, "then take him back to town. There's no sense in both of us going," he told her. "I'll leave Boomer here with you." He glanced at the late-afternoon sun, calculating the time involved. "It'll be dark by the time I get to town, so I'll grab a few hours' sleep before I start back. I should be here by noon tomorrow." He gave Paula a thoughtful look. "Unless you'd rather not spend the night up here alone."

"That doesn't bother me," she said. "Not with Boomer at my side. But I really do think I should help you carry him down to the jeep."

Jack shook his head. "It'll be a lot easier if I do it myself, believe me." He picked the old man up, effortlessly, and carried him to the campsite. Taking a dark-green nylon tarp from his pack, he spread it on the ground and placed Dennecker's body in the center.

Paula watched with interest the way he handled the old man—with a professional indifference, as though dealing with death was not alien to him.

He folded the tarp around the body and tied it snugly. For a brief moment he flashed on a gray, rain-soaked morning at a Special Forces camp in the hills along the Vietnam-Cambodia border. Just back from patrol, he was watching what remained of two of his friends, fellow Green Berets, being loaded onto a truck in body bags. He shuttered the thought away, and checked the knots in the rope. Picking up the wrapped and bound body, he placed it over his shoulder, balancing it at the midpoint and gripping it behind the kneecaps. He handled the old man gently and with respect, but otherwise displayed no emotion.

"Be careful, Callahan," Paula said, still disquieted by what had occurred. She smiled weakly, and in an effort to diminish the awkwardness of the moment, added, "It's not that I'm overly concerned with your well-being, but it just struck me that I don't know where the hell I am."

Jack laughed, and gestured toward Boomer. "Stick with him, he knows the way home." Boomer began to follow him. Jack pointed a finger, and stared at him, holding eye contact. "No, Boomer!" he said sternly. "You stay; I'll see you tomorrow." Boomer hung his head low and returned to Paula's side.

*   *   *

The trek down the mountain was slow and arduous; he almost lost his footing twice, while crossing the rock slides. He distributed the work load evenly by shifting the body to the opposite shoulder every fifteen minutes, and he rested frequently. By the time he reached the jeep, he was exhausted; his muscles ached, particularly his calves and the backs of his thighs. After gently placing Dennecker's body in the back of the jeep, he stretched out on the grass to rest before continuing the journey. He left the meadow as the chill night air descended.

The headlights of the slow-moving jeep illuminated the narrow dirt road and the sheer rock walls as Callahan cautiously made his way up the back of the mountain. When he reached the plateau at the top, the view was spellbinding. He stopped the jeep, leaned back in the seat, propped his feet on the dash, and smiled contentedly as the quiescent, scenic panorama took its effect.

The skies out here were seen as few places on earth saw them: pristine and inviolate, not filtered through a gauze of pollution and haze. Above, an onyx canopy, dotted with countless sparkling pinlights, extended outward for unfathomable light-years. Below—four thousand feet below—was Aspen, tucked securely in among the ancient, enduring mountains, a diminutive lambent jeweled strip, far removed from anything the founders of the old mining town could have envisioned. Home to the creative, towering intellects of the Aspen Institute; summer home to the exquisite talents of the International Music Festival; and, conversely, a haven for the largest cocaine traffickers in the country. Jaded, tolerant, pluralistic; it was a playground for the wealthy and bored—a sybarite's paradise.

Callahan had found contentment and peace of mind here, concepts that only a few years before had been empty abstractions to him. Aspen had no rigidly structured society, and none of the endemic stresses of city or suburban life. No one cared who you were or what you did, providing it didn't interfere with his own life. Jack glanced over his shoulder to the back of the jeep and wondered if the old man had found his peace here, too.

It was well past midnight when he reached the Aspen hospital. Tired and aching, he carried the body inside and placed it on the emergency-room table.

"What the hell is that?" the nurse demanded, looking distastefully at the dusty green tarp. "Get that filthy thing off the table."

Jack shook his head. "That 'thing' is a body, lady," he said wearily to the tall, slightly overweight, matronly woman looming in the doorway. "I found him up in the mountains. His name's Dennecker; that's all I know. Whatever you want done with him is your problem; I'm going home and get some sleep."

"Wait, please," she said, in a more subdued and considerate tone. "I'll get the EMT. He'll need the details for his report."

Jack stared at her for a moment, then nodded and plopped down in a chair.

The emergency medical technician entered the room a few minutes later, his clothes rumpled, eyes bleary—obviously he had been aroused from a sound sleep. He removed the tarp and gave the body a cursory examination while Jack told him how he had found the old man.

"Bear with me, Mr. Callahan," the soft-spoken, affable young man said. "By regulation, I have to call the police, and I'd appreciate it if you'd wait until they get here." Jack agreed and slumped back in the chair while the nurse called the central dispatch.

Callahan considered the Aspen police force a ludicrous joke; it had all the investigative abilities of a group of children on an Easter-egg hunt. The wide-eyed callow kid standing before him in the denim jacket and pants was no exception. He seemed impressed with his badge and gun, and weighted with his authority. Unruly tufts of long straggly hair dangled from beneath the cowboy hat perched atop the bland, nondescript face.

One of Aspen's finest, Jack thought, watching him remove a note pad and pen from his jacket. He repeatedly clicked the uncooperative pen; the tip wouldn't remain extended, retreating inside the casing each time it touched the pad.

"What were the circumstances surrounding the discovery of the victim?" he asked, in a quasi-official and offensive manner.

Callahan stared blankly at the feckless caricature, suppressing a smile. "You won't need the pen," he told him, with a hint of sarcasm. "I found him; that's all there is. I simply found him under a tree—dead."

The radio attached to the young cop's belt squawked and

told him that the coroner was on his way. He fumbled with the controls to reply and dropped the pen and pad.

Callahan walked toward the door, chuckling to himself, only to hear the red-faced kid call after him officiously, "Don't leave town; I may want to question you further."

"Oh, shit," Jack muttered, and burst out laughing.

FOUR

The shrill ringing shattered the silence in the master bed-room of the sumptuous Georgetown home.

Moaning a soft protest, the naked, buxom blonde reached across the man lying beside her, her eyes closed, feeling for the telephone on the nightstand. She lifted the receiver and brought it to her ear, stretching the cord across the man's chest. Before she had a chance to speak, the phone was pulled roughly from her hand and the mouthpiece covered.

"Goddammit!" the man snarled, in a hoarse sleepy voice. "I told you never to answer the goddam phone."

The blonde mumbled an incoherent complaint, rolled over, buried her head in a pillow, and drifted back to sleep.

The man glanced at the clock. It was eight in the morning. Forcefully clearing his throat, he answered the call.

"Senator, I'm awfully sorry to be disturbin' you this early on a Sunday mornin'," said an unfamiliar apologetic voice, "but you said to call you anytime anything important happened."

"Who is this?" the Senator asked gruffly.

"Bill Wilson, from Aspen," the caller replied, with a high-pitched twang.

Senator Hill squeezed his eyes tightly shut, then opened them wide. He searched his sleep-clouded memory, and made the connection. Wilson—sheriff's deputy—Pitkin County—paid to keep him informed on Dennecker—told it was a national security matter. "Yes, Bill, what is it?" he asked, in an overly

29

friendly and familiar tone that belied the depth of their relationship, but indicated the importance the Senator placed on the subject.

"The old man? Dennecker? Well, he died yesterday," the deputy reported in a singsong voice.

The Senator stared blankly for a moment, then a smile spread slowly across his face. "Oh, that's a shame. I hope he went peacefully."

"The coroner says it was a heart attack. He was found in the mountains, no more than a few hours after he died, it looks like."

"Thank you for the call, Bill," the Senator said. "It's appreciated."

There was a brief hesitation on the other end, then the deputy spoke. "I . . . ah . . . guess you won't be needin' me anymore." The extra one hundred dollars a month would be missed.

"No, I won't, Bill," he said, knowing what the man wanted to hear. "I'll send along a little bonus to ease the separation; you've earned it."

"Ah, that's not necessary, Senator," he said, unconvincingly.

"I insist. You've done a fine job." There was no further protest.

The Senator hung up, took a deep breath, and exhaled audibly. Finally, after twenty-four years of that kraut son of a bitch, it was over. The feeling of release didn't come in a rush; it was building slowly.

One of his few mistakes—a mistake that had resulted in a protracted Damoclean insecurity—was finally over. In an instant, in the time it took for a heart to fail, his house of cards was transformed into a solid fortress. A gnawing, subliminal fear was gone, replaced with the firm conviction that he was again in control—perhaps a few loose ends, but nothing he couldn't handle. He looked again at the clock. It was 8:10—5:10 in Phoenix. John Cook would want to know.

He glanced at the blonde curled up on the far side of the king-size bed. Dumb shit. If she had answered the phone and it had been Janet calling, he would be in the middle of divorce proceedings within a week. As he swung his feet over the side of the bed and stood up, a dull ache at the back of his head, and a slight dizziness, reminded him of last night's party. Tying his velour robe around his bulging midsection,

30

he went downstairs to the study to make the call from his private phone.

John Cook shook the sleep from his head in a matter of moments and activated the scrambler on the phone as the Senator suggested. He was pleased with the news of Dennecker's death, but didn't share the Senator's enthusiasm or acceptance of it as a panacea.

"Was anyone with him when he died?" Cook asked, considering the possibility of a deathbed revelation.

"No. He was found in the mountains, alone."

"Good," Cook replied. "I'll send someone up there this morning to check his house in town and the cabin in the mountains, to make certain he didn't leave any damaging legacies."

"He's *dead,* John!" the Senator said emphatically. "There's no one left who can touch us now."

Cook wasn't convinced of that, but decided not to broach the subject now. "It's a major step in bringing this mess to a conclusion, Tom, but I'll save my celebrating until I have all the facts."

"Have it your way, but I think we're home free."

"Did you call the judge?" Cook asked.

"No. I'll call him now. By the way," the Senator asked, remembering another matter, "did you get a handle on those cost overruns?"

"The report will be on your desk tomorrow morning."

"All right, John," he said cheerfully. "Call me if anything turns up in Aspen, but I believe we're out of the woods on this one."

"We'll see, Tom," Cook replied. "I'll be in touch." He doubted the Senator's assessment, knowing from experience that complex problems seldom ended that cleanly. There were usually residual complications that demanded careful attention— immediate attention.

Cook was a determined and fastidious man, with a brilliant analytical mind and a frightening ability to recall the slightest details from incidents and conversations long forgotten, or never noted, by others. Dennecker's death was significant, but not necessarily the end of their problems. From what he knew of Dennecker, and that knowledge was considerable, the old man was more than capable of plotting a final reckoning, a posthumous retribution. The machinations of *his* kind were legend.

Cook showered and shaved before placing the call to the security section at the plant. The officer on duty at Central Control was not surprised to hear from him, even at six o'clock on a Sunday morning. Cook was married to his corporation—almost literally, since his divorce, four years ago—and a seventy-hour week was the rule rather than the exception. The security officer told him that he would locate Candellari immediately and give him the message.

Cook was finishing his breakfast when the housekeeper showed Candellari to the swimming-pool patio. With the easy strides of a quick and agile man, he approached the table where Cook was sitting.

Cook motioned for him to sit down and poured another cup of coffee. "Is your helicopter rating current, Phil?"

Candellari nodded. "Yes, sir."

"I have something for you to do this morning," Cook said, dabbing meticulously at the corners of his mouth with a linen napkin.

Candellari listened attentively, his hard eyes riveted on his boss. He was a tall, slender man, with well-defined but subtle muscles. A sense of strength, out of all proportion to his size, emanated from him. He had black curly hair and a narrow, hawkish face bolstered by a strong chin and facial muscles along the jawline that rippled with each change of expression. The overall impression was one of alertness and self-assurance.

Cook had hired him ten years ago, as a special security consultant. Candellari had had impeccable credentials, fitting every paradigm of need: former fighter pilot, ex-CIA, and an extensive background in industrial espionage. He was competent, efficient, and completely loyal. Although familiar with the Dennecker problem, he didn't know, nor did he care to know, any of the details.

"I want you to take one of the helicopters and get to Aspen as soon as possible. Dennecker died yesterday, and I want his cabin and house sanitized before the local authorities get around to it. Bring me anything that even remotely resembles an official document: personal papers, photographs, letters. Dismantle the places if you must, but make certain that there isn't so much as a grocery list left."

"I'll take Charlie Halek with me," Candellari said, glancing at his watch. "I can be underway in less than an hour."

Cook reacted to the mention of Halek's name. "You keep that sanguinary malignant dwarf in tow," he warned. "I don't want him going berserk and drawing unwanted attention to us."

Halek was Candellari's right hand, paid out of his own substantial salary, and justified to Cook by his willingness to take direction and do absolutely *anything* he was told to do.

In one of his few attempts at humor, Candellari had told Cook that he had found Halek in a cave and removed a thorn from his paw, and they had been inseparable ever since.

Having met Halek, Cook had found no humor in the story; he believed him to be the only person he had ever met who actually derived pleasure from inflicting pain. He was a short, powerfully built man, with the arrogant look of a bully, and dark-brown glowering eyes that dominated a face set in a perpetual psychotic grin. Choleric, volatile, sadistic, but brutally effective, he was the perfect foil for the sangfroid of Candellari.

"I'll see that he understands the situation," Candellari assured him, getting up from the table.

"Report to me the moment you return," Cook instructed.

FIVE

"Hey, Jack!" the all-too-familiar voice bellowed from across the street.

Callahan knew who it was without looking.

The small, wiry disheveled figure crossed the street with a rhythmic strut, as though in tune to some inner music, puffing on a joint, heedless of the traffic; he stopped halfway across and gave the finger to an irate horn-blower.

Jack knew that the man approaching him, familiar with his habits, staked out his favorite restaurants when in need of a free meal or a few extra dollars. His timing and location were perfect this morning; Jack was on his way to the Wienerstube for breakfast, before heading back into the mountains.

"You're right on time, Jack," Popcorn said, looking more sallow and sequestered than usual. "Seven o'clock on the nose; like a fuckin' train."

Callahan laughed. Harry "Popcorn" DeStephano was an outrageous, irreverent reprobate, insane, or simply in touch with a different reality, depending on how you were inclined to view his bizarre, anomalous behavior. Jack was one of the few friends he had—possibly the only one.

"You wouldn't care to join me for breakfast, would you?" Jack asked with a knowing look.

Popcorn grinned and put his arm around Jack's shoulder. "You know what I like about you, Jack? Nothin'. You're a nothin' goin' nowhere fast," he told him, adding a boisterous laugh.

Callahan chuckled and shook his head. He was accustomed to the constant raillery and clowning; it was Popcorn's way of coping. He was a harmless character, enduring a Sisyphean existence, trying in vain to make some sense of his life. He had come back from Vietnam with a Silver Star, a Purple Heart, a steel plate in his head, and scrambled brains. A small disability pension paid the rent and kept him in grass and Quaaludes, and, on occasion, cocaine. His days were divided equally between lucidity and incoherence, and Jack believed it was only a matter of time and circumstance until he stepped irretrievably through the looking glass into an autistic nightmare.

He had met Popcorn—or more precisely, rescued him—three years ago when he had pulled off him a 230-pound local cowboy who was in the process of beating him to a pulp. Popcorn had decided that the cowboy's gleaming new motorcycle was community property, and just as he started the engine and was about to take it for a spin, the cowboy lifted him from the seat. The incident would have ended at that point had Popcorn not called him a fat hick cocksucker, whereupon the cowboy began pummeling him into the sidewalk. Jack physically restrained the incensed man until he calmed down. Popcorn, his face bloodied, his shirt torn to shreds, calmly went to the curb and kicked the motorcycle over on its side. It took Callahan another ten minutes to talk the enraged cowboy out of killing him, finally convincing him that the little squirt was obviously deranged. Once released from Jack's bear hug, the cowboy went to his scratched and dented motorcycle and was almost reduced to tears. Jack took Popcorn by the arm and hustled him away. "What's your name?" Popcorn had asked. Jack told him. "You're a good man, Jack," Popcorn had said, placing an arm around his shoulder. "If you play your cards right, I'll let you hang out with me."

The breakfast Popcorn ordered was enough for three people. Jack suspected that this was his first meal in days.

"I seen ya goin' up the mountain yesterday with Boomer and some new 'stuff' in the jeep," Popcorn said, cutting into a stack of pancakes.

Jack told him about Paula, the camping trip, and Dennecker.

35

"Oh, yeah. I know who he was. Lived in one of them old Victorian houses in the west end, snotty old bastard, used to work for the Ski Corp." He gulped down a glass of milk and started on the eggs Benedict.

"One of these days you've got to come up in the mountains with me," Jack said. "See what you've been missing."

"I don't go for that outdoor shit, Jack. It ain't good for ya; fuck up your lungs."

Callahan laughed. For the past two summers he had tried to get Popcorn into the mountains, hoping a taste of it would get him involved in some less destructive activities, but Popcorn never left town, not even to ski. He had chosen Aspen for its tolerant attitudes and relaxed drug laws, giving him easy access and no hassles, whatever his preference.

Popcorn finished eating, leaned back in his chair, and let out a loud, forced belch, drawing disapproving glances from around the room. "Thanks, Jack. I don't know what I'd do without ya. . . . Speakin' of doin' without," he added, with a sheepish look, "can ya loan me some bread?"

Callahan gave him twenty dollars, saying, "Save it for food, will you, Popcorn?"

"Sure, Jack, sure," he said, looking away. "How long ya stayin' in the mountains?"

"A few days," Jack replied, getting up from the table.

"I'll see ya when ya get back, okay?" Popcorn hurried out the door and down the street.

Jack knew how the twenty dollars would be spent.

Circling high above the meadow, just beneath the surrounding craggy peaks, the helicopter chopped rhythmically at the air; the rapid, pulsating vibrations echoed outward, then resounded back and forth across the clearing below, amplified and held captive by the impenetrable rock walls. Banking at precarious angles, the agile craft swept the perimeter twice before hovering briefly and settling to the ground.

Callahan stopped the jeep where the narrow trail broadened and entered the meadow—a few hundred yards from where the black-and-silver Bell Jet Ranger touched down. He went unnoticed by the two men who stepped out, ducked under the still-rotating blades, and headed toward Dennecker's cabin.

He removed the binoculars from the glove compartment

and watched as they stopped to talk at the edge of the stream. The tall, lean man appeared to be instructing the short, stocky one, who moved from view behind a cluster of spruce when his companion entered the cabin. Callahan scanned slowly to his left and trained the binoculars on the helicopter. He didn't recognize it as belonging to any of the local flying services, and it was the wrong color and markings for Army Search and Rescue, or the state police.

He couldn't quite rationalize the vague, visceral suspicions that set him on edge; perhaps it was something as innocuous as the way they walked, or gestured, or the way the shorter man moved quickly out of sight. He didn't know, but over the years he had learned to acknowledge and follow his gut instincts—they had saved his life, and the lives of others, on more than one occasion.

Getting out of the jeep, he moved swiftly and quietly through the forest, skirting the edge of the meadow. Once across the stream at the far side, he went deeper into the woods before turning and working his way toward the cabin, approaching it from the rear. He paused, kneeling at the base of a large tree, a few yards behind the cabin, and tried to locate the position of the short, stocky man.

The blow came suddenly and silently. Callahan crumpled and dropped limply to the ground, having no knowledge of what had hit him, insensately enveloped by the instant and total blackness.

Charlie Halek raised the log high over his head, poised for a second, more devastating blow.

"That's enough, Charlie," Candellari shouted from the back door of the cabin. "He can't identify us."

Halek stared blankly for a moment, disappointed by the interruption. He lowered the thick chunk of firewood and tossed it off to the side.

"Go back to the front of the cabin and keep an eye on the helicopter," Candellari told him.

"Okay, Phil," Halek replied, grinning. "This sucker won't wake up till tomorrow." As a vicious afterthought, he kicked Callahan solidly in the groin; the force of the blow lifted the unconscious, flaccid body off the ground.

As the waning late-afternoon sun receded behind the tallest peaks, casting splintered golden rays and pyramidal shadows across the surface of the lake, Paula's concern deteriorated to an erosive uneasiness. Her imagination ran the gamut of possibilities, from unexpected delays to mechanical breakdowns and fatal accidents. It was not in her nature to panic, even in the most difficult situations, but she did experience a twinge of anxiety at the thought of being left alone to find her way out of the mountains, and began to regret her willingness to remain behind. Even with her limited knowledge of Callahan, she was certain that he was not the type to take his responsibilities lightly—something had happened to him.

Boomer was curled up on the grass, next to where she was sitting, his head in her lap, sensing her disquietude, and in his instinctual, primitive way relating it to his own inchoate discomfort over his friend's prolonged absence. He was inordinately edgy, alerting to the slightest sound.

Paula had enjoyed the dog's company; he was not merely protection, but an attentive, affectionate companion. He was a truly inquiline creature who, she was convinced, had no idea that he was a dog. He had followed her inside the tent the previous night and slept at her side; the grumbling and snoring were at first distracting, then reassuring in their steady, primal rhythm. She awoke that morning to find him staring intently, his huge head only inches from her face, waiting for her eyes to open—the signal for his day to begin. When she unzipped the tent flap and looked outside at the early-morning light, she realized that Boomer had subtly hurried the moment.

It had snowed sometime during the night, and a light dusting covered the ground. A heavier accumulation had settled on the peaks, and a prevailing wind sent lacy wisps spiraling upward—a harbinger of winter's impending silent cloistering of the high country.

The snow melted quickly, shortly after sunrise, and after breakfast Paula, with Boomer ambling along at her side, had walked the shoreline of the lake. As they passed the spot where they had found the old man's body, she noticed the camera case and equipment lying on the ground near the spruce tree. She collected it and took it back to camp.

The intense solitude of a day alone in the wilderness had been restful and rewarding. She had contemplated the course her career was taking—thanks to a sizable trust fund left her by her maternal grandmother, she was financially independent and able to select only those subjects that most interested her, making her work all the more enjoyable. Her anfractuous projections for possible stories to be investigated, and the anticipation of the chase, gave her an optimistic outlook filled with a sense of purpose. An afternoon of self-analysis served to reinforce her prior assessments of her life and work. She was fundamentally contented with things as they were: successful in a tough, competitive profession, secure in the knowledge of her abilities, and free of fettering responsibilities and emotional ties—a recent love affair that had abraded itself, through demands and strictures, to a rancorous end had left her wary of deep emotional commitments and given her a firm resolve to avoid them in the future.

The reddish glow rimming the mountains after the sun had settled behind them provided no warmth, and the temperature dropped rapidly. Paula put on a thick wool sweater and sat in front of the campfire she had tended to a cheery blaze. Boomer lay a few yards behind her, away from the heat, enjoying the cold night air. She huddled closer to the fire and admitted to a loneliness the depths of which she had never experienced.

Callahan groaned softly, rolled onto his back, and opened his eyes. In the gathering dusk the blurred and hazy branches above him slowly came into focus. A sharp throbbing pain at the base of his skull caused him to wince and groan even louder. He lay quietly for a few moments, organizing the rush of thoughts, and realized what had happened—someone had gotten him from behind. Old skills and extra senses left fallow, he lamented, as though apologizing to a bruised ego. There was a time, not too long ago, when that wouldn't have happened.

He propped himself up on one knee, and the piercing, stunning pain in the lower reaches of his body that accompanied the monumental effort brought with it the realization that someone had done more than knock him unconscious. He remained kneeling until the dizziness passed and the pain subsided, and then slowly, agonizingly made his way around the cabin to the edge of the stream, collapsing as he reached it. Aware of the time of day, and remembering Paula, he fought the promised comfort of a descending curtain of unconsciousness and repeatedly submerged his head in the icy water, washing away the matted blood and leaves from the side of his face and regaining more immediate control of thought and determination.

He walked across the meadow to the jeep on wobbly legs, willing himself to remain upright. He noticed the depressions in the grass where the helicopter had been, and reviewed the details he could recall, to report the incident later. After a brief rest he started up the mountain. A full moon in a cloudless sky illuminated the way, making the flashlight he had taken from the jeep unnecessary and freeing his other hand to aid in the demanding hand-over-hand scramble on the steeper sections. Through dogged perseverance he refused to surrender his command to the pain and fatigue.

Paula sat watching the reflection of the full moon on the quiet lake; a chill, errant breeze caused a gentle, flickering undulation on the smooth surface as it gusted over the water, crossed the grassy meadow, lightly brushed her face, and rattled the aspen leaves behind her. She tried to force the rising anxiety from her mind. She was angry and frustrated by the uncertainty of the situation. It was nearly midnight. Where was he? What had happened? How long should she wait? She decided to try to get some sleep, and make her decision in the morning.

As she got up from in front of the fire and started toward the tent, Boomer emitted a low, mean growl that grew in volume and intensity. Looking in the direction the dog had alerted, she saw nothing. He was standing now, moving slowly, intrepidly, toward the shadows at the edge of the forest. A paralyzing fear gripped her, vanishing instantly when she heard him whining, puppylike, and saw him bound gleefully out of sight. It was Jack, she assured herself. It had to be!

All of the anger and frustration left her when she saw him staggering toward her; Boomer whining and twirling in front of him.

"My God, Callahan! What happened?" she asked, seeing his bloodstained, pallid face. She noticed him tottering and, placing her arm around his waist, she guided him to the tent.

He was cold, exhausted, and barely lucid. She lowered him to the floor of the tent, rolling him into his sleeping bag. Filling a canvas bucket from the lake, she returned to find Boomer lying beside him, licking his face and whimpering.

She applied cold compresses to the gash at the back of his head. Callahan groaned wearily and faded into unconsciousness. After cleaning and dressing the wound, Paula slipped into the sleeping bag and snuggled tightly against him; his trembling soon abated.

SIX

Popcorn drummed impatiently on the steering wheel of the battered, primer-splotched Volkswagen Beetle. An attractive brunette in the car in front of him at the bank's drive-in window was chatting casually with the teller about a party they had both attended the previous night. He listened irritably to the amplified side of the drawn-out conversation.

"Hey!" Popcorn bellowed, his patience stretched to its limit. "What the hell you think this is, a goddam park and bullshit? Move it, will ya, lady?"

The thin, freckle-faced girl in the teller's window cast a disdainful glance through thick granny glasses; her attractive friend in the Porsche ignored him, continuing the conversation.

Popcorn eyed the exotic Porsche Turbo she was driving and grinned mischievously. Paid forty big ones for that ride, huh, lady . . . all right. He slapped his rusting, decrepit clunker into gear and moved forward slowly. Feeling his front bumper contact the rear of the Porsche, he floored the accelerator, sending the sleek sports car bolting from the stall and half-way across the street, into the path of an oncoming pickup truck whose alert driver managed to avoid a collision, skidding sideways and stopping only inches from the frightened, screaming face gaping up at him.

The horrified teller stared at Popcorn in disbelief. "I don't believe you did that," she mouthed, forgetting to turn on her microphone. "She could have been killed."

Popcorn cupped his hand over his ear and shrugged. He watched the Porsche back up and park at the curb. The infuriated driver got out, slammed the door, and stomped toward him, her large, unencumbered breasts jostling beneath a snug T-shirt.

"How dare you!" she fumed. "You insane, stupid, arrogant ass!"

Popcorn smiled sweetly. "I really don't want to be all those names, lady. Now get out of my face or I'll smash that son of a bitch so bad you'll have to have it towed to the junkyard."

The girl backed away, more from revulsion than fear. "I'll have you arrested, you grubby lunatic."

Popcorn affected a salacious grin. "You got great tits, ya know, lady? And your nipples get hard when you're mad."

She gave him a disgusted look. "You pig!" she spat out, and turned away and marched back to her car. The Porsche let out a high-pitched whine and catapulted away from the curb with a force that justified its price tag.

Popcorn put his check in the extended metal tray and smiled at the disapproving face glaring at him from the window; her pale-green eyes, magnified by the thick glasses, were out of proportion to the rest of her features. "Cash that and give it to me in small bills," he said, winking.

She glanced at the check and gave Popcorn a quizzical look. "But this is only for two dollars."

"Yeah," Popcorn replied. "Two ones will be fine."

Stuffing the money in his shirt pocket, he gunned the engine and sputtered away, trailing a cloud of blue smoke. He decided to act on an idea that had been tempting him since yesterday morning, when Jack had told him about Dennecker's death. What the hell, he reasoned. It's not really like stealing. He's dead, and he won't miss anything.

He parked the car a block away and reconnoitered the area as he walked toward the house. The street was lined with quaint, meticulously restored old Victorian homes, with an occasional angular redwood-and-glass structure sandwiched between them. Some of the lots had trees and high hedges outlining the boundaries, obscuring the homes from view on all sides—Dennecker's was one of them.

It was almost noon, and there was no one in sight when he came abreast of the wrought-iron gate to Dennecker's property; he placed both hands on the scalloped top and swung nimbly over, moving quickly behind the hedge and darting across the lawn to the cover of a large shrub beneath a window. He wrapped his hand in his jacket and punched out one of the small panes near the lock.

Candellari removed a slender steel pick from a leather case, and in a matter of seconds the kitchen door swung open.

The sound of voices reached Popcorn in the study. He pocketed the camera he had just removed from a shelf and stood motionless for a few moments, collecting his wits and considering his next move.

"I'll start in the kitchen," Candellari told Halek. "You go to the front of the house."

Popcorn ducked inside the hall closet, closing the door just as Halek entered the hallway. He heard drawers being opened and papers shuffled. Realizing what was happening, he shoved himself to the rear of the closet, behind a long overcoat. He inadvertently toppled a ski pole; it rattled against the wall and slid to the floor.

Halek stopped what he was doing and spun around, his eyes darting in the direction of the sound. He glanced around the room, his eyes coming to rest on the closet door just outside the archway. He pulled a .32 revolver from its holster and removed a perforated cylinder from his jacket, screwing it onto the barrel of the snub-nosed pistol.

Standing flat against the wall, to the left of the door, he flung it open and crouched low, cocking the hammer of the pistol. "Come out very slowly, with your hands in sight," he droned, in a minatory tone.

Popcorn remained silent.

"You have five seconds before I start firing," Halek warned, smiling in anticipation.

"All right, man. I'm comin'," Popcorn answered, getting to his feet. He shoved the clothes aside and came out with his hands high.

"Well, well," Halek said, smirking. "We got us a hippie."

"What are you guys, cops or somethin'?" Popcorn asked nervously, shaken from his usual comic-relief facade.

"Or somethin'," Halek replied, his eyes glinting through half-closed lids. "Hey, Phil."

Candellari entered the hall and stared at the thin, bedraggled young man nervously glancing from him to Halek. "Damn!" he said, deploring the complication. "Where did you find him?"

Halek gestured toward the closet. "He *can* identify us, Phil," he said. A broad grin spread across his face.

Candellari lowered his eyes and shook his head. He knew that the last thing Cook wanted was unnecessary violence, but this kid could connect him to Dennecker—a tenuous connection, but an unacceptable one. He had terminated people twice before for Cook—industrial espionage agents—to avoid embarrassing questions if the infiltrations had become known to the Defense Department, jeopardizing his highly classified contracts by doubts about the effectiveness of his security. Candellari intuitively knew that the Dennecker matter was an extremely vulnerable and sensitive area to Cook, who had been keeping tabs on Dennecker as long as Candellari had been with him, and, Candellari had gathered from some of their conversations, for quite a few years before that.

He looked at Halek and nodded. "Take care of it, Charlie," he said, returning to the kitchen, avoiding the gaze of the frightened and confused young man standing against the wall with his hands cupped behind his head.

Popcorn couldn't believe what he had inferred from the tall, slender man's instructions. Jesus Christ! They're going to kill me! He was less afraid of the gun than the thick-necked, flat-nosed, oxlike creature before him. The man's forearms and biceps were nearly the size of Popcorn's thighs.

"Hey, man. I won't say nothin', ya know," he pleaded, maintaining an inner calm as he decided on the most effective way to attack. Popcorn had reserves and courage that few people would have suspected. He decided on the eyes.

Halek laughed softly, superficially, with a slow, menacing rhythm. "Hippie, you really stepped in it this time."

"Hey, look, man." He gestured, lowering his hands to his sides. "I mean, what the hell could I say, ya know? I was rippin' the place off myself; it's not like I could turn you in," he pleaded more earnestly, taking a step forward, closing the distance and angling away from the gun.

He stiffened the fingers of his right hand and jabbed at his captor's eyes. It was a clumsy, ineffectual attempt.

Halek was waiting. He blocked the blow with his left forearm, clamped a viselike grip on Popcorn's bicep, and spun him around with one hand, slamming him forcefully, face first, into the wall.

"You telegraph your moves, hippie," he said mockingly, dropping the gun to the floor, having no intention of using it.

Positioning his arms expertly around Popcorn's neck, he snapped it easily with a quick, trenchant, jerking motion. His victim never made a sound; his head flopped to the side and his body fell limp in the huge, hairy arms.

John Cook sat behind a large, ornately carved mahogany desk in his tastefully furnished office at the plant. Candellari was seated in a leather wingback to his right, reporting on what he had learned. Halek stood near the door—a silent, malicious sentinel propped against the wall, his arms folded across his chest.

Candellari's matter-of-fact delivery and calm detached expression didn't change when he told Cook of the "complication" at Dennecker's house. As with the two other terminations, he told him none of the details, simply that they had dealt with the matter, knowing that Cook preferred euphemisms to outright declarations of actions of which he disapproved, but reasoned to be necessary and of sound judgment. And, Candellari realized, Cook could deny knowledge of it if it ever came to that.

No one had ever had the ability to gauge John Cook's inner reactions or emotions accurately; his narrow, delicately handsome face and soft gray eyes could, at will, be made totally expressionless, regardless of the degree of provocation or the depth of his feelings. So even the sagacious, intuitive Candellari, and his psychopathic acolyte, had no way of knowing the gut-wrenching disgust he felt at the allusion to the murder of the young man. Yes, the bottom line was that it had been a prudent and necessary action, but so were the other two. They hadn't been thoughtless, heavy-handed decisions implemented without consideration for their consequences and drastic nature. There had been no alternative short of exposing himself to financial ruin if the infiltrations were discovered and resulted in the cancellation of his Defense Department contracts—the life's blood of his corporation. Dennecker's threat was even more sinister and potentially devastating; it could mean the destruction of everything he valued: his business, the respect of his friends and peers, and possibly, though not likely after all these years, his freedom.

Now that the end was in sight, Cook was grimly determined to finish the matter, finally, decisively. He reread the article on Dennecker's death in the Aspen newspaper that

Candellari had brought him. The mention of the ski instructor who had found the body peaked his interest.

"This man . . . Callahan," he said, to Candellari, "may be worth checking out."

"I thought you might consider that, Mr. Cook," Candellari replied. "I collected some equipment from my office on the way here. We can return to Aspen tonight and place his house under electronic surveillance, and stay there until we're certain he's of no consequence."

Cook looked at Candellari and smiled; he appreciated his professionalism and faultless efficiency. He had come to consider him indispensable. "Fine. But you can leave Thursday; I want you here for the next two days while General Talbot is inspecting our security for the new laser project."

"Yes, sir," Candellari said. "We'll leave Thursday morning."

SEVEN

After two days of rest, staying off his feet for the first day at Paula's insistence, the lump on the back of Callahan's head was sensitive to the touch, but otherwise he was feeling no ill effects. He was angry. Angry that echoes of his past had sought him out and disturbed the peace he had found in Aspen. The incident at the cabin had made no sense, but as Paula had pointed out, in these days of mindless violence, sense and purpose seemed to have given way to insane and misguided behavior. The two men in the helicopter couldn't have had robbery as a motive, he reasoned—the cost of the fuel alone would have exceeded anything they might have hoped to find. And he had recognized the mien of the men as that of professionals. There was a good reason for what had happened, but it was far from apparent, aside from the probability that he had walked in on something they didn't want known.

The disruption of his well-ordered life had put him in a reflective mood, and as they lay stretched out on the grassy meadow, he talked freely, candidly, feeling none of the usual reticence about discussing his past. Paula listened, fascinated by the glimpse into a world she had only read about, prodding him gently whenever he fell silent.

His quiet, placid days in the mountains were far removed from his life prior to the past five years. He had never felt the need to apologize for what he had done, or to justify himself;

Captain John P. Callahan, U.S. Army Special Forces, had been a believer, and that was sufficient justification.

Three tours in Vietnam—a moron's war, he had decided in the end, from the standpoint of command and consistent, achievable objectives—one tour in Bad Tolz, Germany, and after leaving the service, four years as a mercenary in Rhodesia: a good part of his adult life spent in the ass end of nowhere fighting someone else's wars, interminable, bloody, senseless slaughters.

Rhodesia had proved to be the crucible of his beliefs. Four years as a bush fighter in the guerrilla war along the Mozambique border and the Zambezi River. Ten-man teams, highly skilled professional killers whose only loyalty was to themselves, tracking guerrillas during the day, ambushing infiltration routes at night, going weeks on end without relief, living off rice and, when unavoidable, a barely palatable African cornmeal gruel called sadza. In the high grass and mountain trails, the fleas, ticks, and flies were a constant harassment, and in December and January the summer rains flooded the rivers and turned the red clay roads to an all but impassable mire. The arid winters brought their own problems, drying up the waterholes and leaving stagnant buffalo wallows as the only readily available source of the precious commodity.

But there had been the camaraderie, and the exhilaration of battle—a ten-to-one kill ratio in their favor—and for Callahan, a cause, a deep sense of purpose and the inner rewards of doing what he did best.

Then one day, in a hut at the edge of a smoldering jungle village strewn with dead and mutilated bodies, it all fell apart, dispelling his belief in the nobility of their cause, the righteousness of their actions.

An Australian, a specialist in interrogation, slowly, mercilessly tortured to death a suspected guerrilla while the men looted and raped. Callahan's overexposure and lack of complete inurement to the escalating, uncommon, dehumanizing cruelty made further delusion impossible. He had had enough.

Aspen was his place of refuge; he simply wanted to live and enjoy life before the world came apart at the seams—as he believed it inevitably would. In five years he had worked his way up through the ski school, becoming one of the top instructors, teaching only private lessons. A summer job in Kurt Bierman's bookstore supplemented his inadequate income

49

from teaching, but the combined salaries of a little over twelve thousand dollars were barely enough to live comfortably in Aspen. The twenty-five thousand dollars he had managed to save during his years of soldiering went for the down payment on his house. The ensuing monthly mortgage payments occasionally made a diet of peanut-butter sandwiches a necessity. That was until Francisco Espada presented a solution to his problems, enticing him to take his first and only step to the other side of the law, a venture that assured he would never have to soldier again.

Espada, a wealthy Brazilian industrialist, each year spent the month of February in Aspen, reserving Callahan for private lessons seven days a week for the entire month. Near the end of the second year of this arrangement, Espada, by now familiar with Jack's background and character, made his proposition. Because of the unstable political and economic climate in his country, he was leaving Brazil and moving to New York City. Strict foreign-exchange controls and currency restrictions, unless circumvented, would cost him millions. If Callahan would act as a courier, so to speak, he would receive ten percent of what he managed to get out of the country. Eight suitcases and four million dollars later, Callahan had augmented his assets enough to ensure that, given moderate self-indulgence, his financial worries were over. He had no qualms about what he had done, believing that he had paid his dues years before.

"I'm talking too much," Callahan said, turning on his side and propping his head up with an elbow. "And I'm probably boring you."

"Not at all," Paula assured him. "You've had an interesting and exciting life. I envy you, to a point."

"To a point," Jack repeated reflectively. He glanced up at the late-afternoon sun; the temperature was still near eighty degrees—it had been an Indian-summer day. "How about a swim?"

"You've got to be joking, Callahan. When I washed in that water this morning it was near freezing."

"It should be just right by now, trust me," he said, stripping off his clothes and running to the shore of the lake and partway into the shallows, diving headlong into the water.

Paula followed moments later, wading cautiously at first, then taking the plunge, against her better judgment. Once over the initial shock, she found it tolerable and refreshing.

She swam out to join Callahan, and they raced back; she stayed with him, much to his surprise.

Most people look their best leaving something to the imagination while subtly suggesting; Paula, nude, was magnificent. Standing in knee-deep water, Jack unabashedly held her at arms' length, admiring the near-perfect symmetry of her body. She blushed and smiled softly.

"You're beautiful," he said, with an earnestness that embarrassed her somewhat. "Absolutely beautiful."

He took her in his arms and kissed her; she responded eagerly, her mouth moving sensuously, her tongue probing, stimulating, arousing. A confluence of raw emotions and unrestrained desires slowly, unrelentingly swept them away on an erotic tide, the equal of which Callahan had never experienced in his utilitarian relationships.

Paula caressed and kneaded the hard, prominent muscles of his arms and broad, sloping shoulders, slowly moving downward along the trim, taut sides and narrow hips. She fondled and stroked, rhythmically, eagerly, and then, feeling his readiness, guided him.

Callahan lowered his hands, lifting, inserting, moving slowly, firmly, then thrusting, driving. The coalescence complete, the rapture engrossing, she possessed him, deeply.

"Oh, yes," she murmured softly. "Yes, yes. Oh, God, yes." It had been four months—and never like this. He was a gentle, attentive lover; sensitive and responsive, not what she had expected.

That night, lying outside in their sleeping bags by the fire, enjoying the cool, crisp night air and the sparkling infinity above them, she came to him again, and again, with nothing diminished by the repetitions, and new pleasures experienced in the variations.

Callahan felt vulnerable, but comforted. He began to sense that this woman could complete his life, adding dimensions he had thought were unattainable. But once more, as had happened last winter, he felt a cautious reserve against allowing what he believed he wanted, to become what he needed. She had enjoyed him, relinquished to him, and given of herself. But there was much more to give, and he had detected a profound abeyance reflected from the depths of her haunting blue eyes. He had not conquered; she had not surrendered; they had shared.

Paula watched him, lying on his back, his hands cupped

51

behind his head, deep in thought. He was a private man, and lonely, but the loneliness was of his own choosing, she decided—perhaps he had to deal with things that were best dealt with alone. She studied the face beneath the thick, light-brown hair. She had dated better-looking men, usually more urbane and intellectual, but none so appealing. His features, if isolated, were coarse and unnoteworthy, but the combination was the matrix that made the whole ruggedly handsome. His eyes, intense, piercing, were a dark, rich brown, almost opaque; keeping everyone out.

It was his inner strength that attracted her most. She was drawn to strong men—not the imperious, selfish, inconsiderate types, but assertive, decisive, sensitive men with the courage of their convictions. With Callahan, there was no role-playing or posturing; he seemed to have neither the patience nor the inclination to bother with facades. She wondered if the life he had led was the androgen that made him what he was, or if what he inherently was had dictated the course his life had taken. Whatever, she liked him and felt secure and relaxed in his company. He had been just what she needed after the bitterness and disappointment of Peter. Tomorrow morning they would return to Aspen, and the following day she planned to leave for New York, feeling much better about herself.

Callahan rolled up the sleeping bags and strapped them to the frames of the backpacks. Paula was on the far side of the tent removing the last of the pegs, with Boomer watching over her, occasionally grabbing for the white plastic stakes, trying to get a game going. She noticed the leather camera case, a few yards behind the tent, moved from where she had put it, forgotten. An animal, probably a raccoon, had chewed through one of the outside pockets, which, judging from the crumbs and bits of shredded paper scattered about, had contained something edible, and there were other exploratory holes chewed into the sides. She picked the case up by the strap, unaware that the top flap was unbuckled, and the camera and lenses spilled out on to the ground. As she replaced them in the case, something odd caught her attention.

With the camera resting on what was the bottom of the inside compartment, there remained a few inches of depth to the actual bottom of the case as viewed from the exterior. It would have been undetectable had the animal not chewed a hole below the false bottom, revealing the hidden space.

Paula removed the camera and inspected the inside of the case. The alteration had been expertly done and was not obvious to the naked eye. Turning the case on its side, she placed two fingers in the small hole chewed into the concealed section, tearing the soft leather, enlarging the opening enough to reach inside and remove the contents: a passport, a small, address-size black leather book, and a thin rectangular leather-covered box.

The West German passport had been issued in 1955 to Karl Dennecker. It had one entry stamp, from American Customs and Immigration, dated six weeks after the date of issue and had never been used again. It had expired years ago. The personal information page showed him to be unmarried, born in Munich in 1904, and gave his last residence in Germany as Landsberg. The photograph was of Dennecker, twenty-four years ago, a little more hair and a thinner, more drawn face.

Paula opened the thin rectangular box. Inside was a military decoration of some sort, she assumed. It had the shape of a German cross, and was black with a silver border; there was a swastika in the center, and "1939" engraved at the bottom. It was suspended from a red ribbon bordered with black and white stripes. In the center of the ribbon where it was attached to the cross was a cluster of small silver leaves with tiny silver swords crossed below them. She put it aside and examined the small black leather book.

The cover was worn, and the gold embossed printing faded, but legible. Holding it at an angle to catch the light, she read the inscription:

SS–GRUPPENFUEHRER und GENERALLEUTNANT
der WAFFEN-SS-KARL DENNECKER
SS-WIRTSCHAFTS und VERWALTUNGS-HAUPTAMT
UNTER den EICHEN 126-135 BERLIN-LICHTERFELDE

She recognized it only as an official title of sorts, and probably an address. She opened the book and flipped through the pages. The first four were filled with rows of numbers, and the remainder were blank. The edges of a faded snapshot protruded from between the last page and back cover—it was Dennecker, much younger, resplendent in a military uniform, his arm around the waist of an aristocratic-looking, attractive light-haired woman in her early thirties, Paula estimated. She noticed he was wearing the military decoration she had just put aside. A handwritten inscription on the back of the photograph said simply: "München—Oktober— 1942." She returned to the four pages of numbers, her curiosity aroused.

Callahan came over to where she was sitting to check on her progress with the tent.

Paula looked up from the book. "Do you speak German?" she asked, recalling that he had mentioned being stationed in Germany.

Callahan nodded. He had made an effort to stay proficient in the language after leaving the army—by reading German magazines and conversing with Kurt Bierman at the bookstore.

Paula handed him the small black book. "Translate the inscription on the cover for me."

His eyes widened as he read. "Where did you get this?"

Paula told him. "What does it say?"

" 'Lieutenant General Karl Dennecker of the Waffen SS, SS Economic and Administrative Office,' and the address in Berlin. The 'Gruppenfuehrer' is an SS designation in addition to his rank."

"And what's this?" she asked, handing him the box containing the military decoration.

Callahan looked at the medal and smiled. "That fits," he said. "It was one of Nazi Germany's highest military decorations during World War II—the Knight's Cross with Oak Leaves and Crossed Swords. He must have been one hell of a trooper."

"Weren't the SS responsible for the death camps?" Paula asked, handing him the photograph.

"Among other things," Jack replied. "They were also the finest group of fighting men ever assembled in the history of warfare. An army general who had fought them in World War II told me that we didn't defeat them, we outnumbered them; and he meant it."

Paula stared at him for a moment thoughtfully. "Callahan, I believe we've stumbled onto something. I may be an incurable *intrigant,* but there has to be a good reason for him to have gone to the trouble to conceal these things." She got a distant look in her eyes, then suggested, "Maybe he was a wanted war criminal?"

"I doubt that," Jack said, dismissing the idea. "He would have at least changed his name."

"Perhaps he did. The passport could be a phony."

"And the address book?" he asked. "If he was going to choose a new identity to keep a low profile, I doubt that he would have chosen an SS general."

Paula nodded in agreement. "But there still has to be a reason for the false bottom."

Callahan shrugged. "I think it might be understandable why he wouldn't want his background to become public knowledge; if for no other reason, the one that came into your mind when you thought of the SS. The address book and photograph could conceivably have had sentimental value for him, and there's little doubt in my mind that he would have been proud of his Knight's Cross. So maybe it was his way of holding on to a tangible part of his past and at the same time keeping it away from prying eyes."

"There's more to it than that, Callahan. I can feel it. What about the two men at the cabin?" she said. She added an inspirational note: "And the attack on you?"

Jack gave her a questioning look. "What about them? How are they connected?"

"I don't know. It's just a hunch."

He removed the remaining pegs and began folding the tent. Paula's hunch interested him. "Let's get down to the jeep, then we'll take a detour to Dennecker's cabin before going back to town."

Paula smiled. "I aroused your suspicions, huh, Callahan?"

"It's contagious," he replied.

The inspection of Dennecker's cabin provided no insights into what had happened to Callahan. Everything seemed to be in place, and a quick inventory of the sparse contents revealed only what one might expect to find in a mountain retreat. Paula, undaunted, held to her hunch that the contents of the camera case and the two men at the cabin were related, but with no firm basis for a plausible connection, she dropped the subject and sat silently, perusing the pages of the small book as they drove along the bumpy, dusty trail leading out of the mountains.

Callahan was rounding a sharp bend in a steep, narrow section of the trail near the top of Ajax Mountain when Paula suddenly turned to face him, grabbing his arm, causing him to lose control of the jeep and veer dangerously close to the edge—Boomer splayed his legs to keep from tumbling over the side.

"I've got it, Callahan!" she said excitedly, waving the address book before him. "It's a code. The pages of numbers in here are a code. I'd stake my life on it."

"You damn near did," Jack said, stopping the jeep, unnerved by the close call. "The drop off the side of this trail is about a hundred feet straight down."

Paula looked over the edge and grimaced. "God! Sorry; I got carried away."

"What makes you think it's a code?"

"Another hunch. If these pages of numbers are a code, then they should contain something important to Dennecker, and others—otherwise, why encode it? So the two men in the helicopter could have been looking for this little book."

Jack gave her a skeptical look. "If I give it a little thought, I think I can come up with a few other explanations."

"Probably. But I think I'm right."

"Okay. How do you plan to test your theory?"

"How much do you know about codes?" Paula asked.

"Not much. I have a working knowledge of military codes, but no idea of how to decode them without the key." He paused and added, "But I do know someone who might be able to help us."

EIGHT

Kurt Bierman winced in pain as he sat wearily on a stool, placing the newly arrived books on a shelf. It had been one of his bad days, the pain more persistent and intense than usual—a constant companion for the past thirty-six years, he had learned to deal with it at its worst. The deformed hip, shattered by repeated blows from a rifle butt at Buchenwald, had been left to mend without medical attention, resulting in his short, fragile frame listing to the right, a constant discomfort.

The cruelties and sorrows of his experiences were indelibly etched on his face, fallaciously giving a hard, cynical appearance to a kind and gentle man—but if one took the time to notice, his soft, expressive eyes belied the unvolitional portrayal. He had survived intact; not in body, but in spirit.

Walking haltingly over to the cash register to total the day's receipts, he glanced outside to see the bright-red jeep pull up to the curb, and Jack hop lithely out, instructing Boomer to stay. He diverted his eyes from the dog, trying, to no avail, to stem the surfacing of the unpleasant memory.

When Jack had first come to work for him, he had asked that he never bring the dog into the store, explaining that he was allergic to animal hair—an explanation that Callahan had accepted but that was far from the truth. A horrifying scene he had witnessed in the concentration camp to this day was brought vividly back to him each time he saw the huge black-and-rust dog—two SS guards, bored and in need of perverse entertainment, had commanded a Rottweiler to attack a camp inmate, and had watched in amusement as it tore him to pieces. Their boisterous laughter and the shrill screams of the defenseless man throughout his lingering death still echoed in his mind. He realized the fallacy of attributing the same temperament to Boomer, but for him, the dark savagery of the German soul was embodied behind the animal's impertinent, challenging eyes. Perhaps Boomer didn't deserve such a harsh judgment, but Kurt was disinclined to give him the benefit of the doubt.

He studied the face of the young woman accompanying Jack to the door, admiring her exquisite beauty, and detecting an ambience of composure about her. He also noticed Jack's attentiveness, indicating she was someone special to him.

"Kurt, I'd like you to meet Paula Carlson," he announced. "Paula, this is Kurt Bierman."

Kurt gently took her hand and smiled. "It's so nice to meet you, Miss Carlson. Are you vacationing in Aspen?" he asked, suspecting she wasn't a local.

"Yes," Paula replied, charmed by the warmth of his voice and manner. "We just returned from a camping trip in the most lovely spot."

"Marvelous. Jack is an excellent guide; he knows the mountains well." Turning to Callahan, he commented, "I read about Dennecker's death. How unfortunate."

"He had a long healthy life," Jack said with a shrug. "And there are worse ways to go." He noticed Kurt leaning on the counter, supporting his weight, and suspected he had had a rough day. "I just stopped in to discuss something with you, and to ask if you mind if I take an extra day off."

"Of course not," Kurt replied, believing he understood the reason for the request. "I was saddened to learn about Harry DeStephano; I know he was a close friend. Is the funeral tomorrow?"

Jack stared at him blankly. "Funeral? What are you saying? Popcorn is dead?"

"Forgive me," Kurt apologized, realizing his mistake. "I thought you knew."

"What happened to him?" Jack asked incredulously.

"Some hikers found him at American Lake. The police said he probably broke his neck diving off a rock ledge into the shallow section of the lake."

"What the hell was he doing at American Lake?" Jack asked, recoiling from the shock.

Kurt shook his head sympathetically, not knowing how to respond to the question. "It's what the article in the newspaper said."

Callahan's expression changed to one of bewilderment. "There's something wrong with that," he said calmly, gaining control of his emotions. "There's no way in hell he would have hiked to American lake. Popcorn never left town, and he was deathly afraid of the water; he couldn't swim."

Kurt knew about Popcorn's use of drugs, and thought to offer that as an explanation, but decided against it; Jack was aware of it as well. He had never quite understood Jack's tolerance and indulgence of the rude, erratic young man, but had always been courteous to him when he stopped at the store. "Perhaps if you talk with the police?"

"I think I'll do just that," Jack said. "I'll call you later."

"I'm closing now," Kurt told him. "I'll be home for the evening. Goodbye, Miss Carlson. I hope to see you again."

"Goodbye, Mr. Bierman," Paula answered with a warm smile. His eyes told her he was feeling some of Callahan's pain, along with his own.

As they drove across town to the police station, Jack considered the possibility of drugs being the reason for Popcorn doing the unexpected, but ruled it out—he knew how to handle what he used.

"Who was Popcorn?" Paula asked, breaking the silence.

"A friend," Jack replied solemnly. "One of the thousands of poor bastards who paid their dues with their bodies and minds and got nothing for it."

The same young cop he had talked to at the hospital was the only one in the office, sitting behind a desk, his feet propped up, eating a huge pizza. His eyes moved slowly, offensively over Paula as they entered the room.

"Oh, it's you," he said, recognizing Callahan. "I don't have any more questions for you or I would have looked you up."

"That's not why I'm here," Jack said sharply, irritated by the slovenly arrogance of the man. "I'd like some information on the death of Harry DeStephano."

"What would you like to know?"

"The cause of death," Jack replied.

"The chief said he dove into the water, hit his head on a rock, broke his neck, and drowned."

"Was anyone with him?" Jack asked. "Did he have any camping equipment?"

"Not that I know of," the young cop said, getting up from the desk and opening a file cabinet from which he removed a camera and a few wrinkled and crumpled dollar bills. "This is all we found on him." He placed the things on the desk as he sat down.

Callahan examined the camera, recognizing it as similiar to the one in Dennecker's case—a Leica, the same make, but a vintage model; pre–World War II, discernible by the "Made in Germany" stamp. "Did the coroner's report say anything about drugs in his system?"

The cop let out a short harsh laugh. "I didn't read it, you'll have to ask the chief, but that little creep was a space cadet, half out of his mind most of the time, so I imagine he was stoned on something."

Jack tensed, fighting the urge to punch the sneer from the face before him. "I'd appreciate it if you would keep remarks like that to yourself. He was a friend of mine."

"You were probably the only one he had, then," the cop continued, feeling the weight of his badge and embarrassed by the admonishment in front of Paula. "That dirt bag damn near killed a girl at the bank a few days ago, and he owed half the people in town, although I'll be damned if I can figure out why anyone would loan that degenerate money."

Callahan had heard enough. He reached across the desk and flipped the open box of pizza into the cop's lap. "Shut your goddam stupid mouth!" he snarled, looming threateningly over him.

Paula, alarmed by the menace in his voice and the atavistic change, grabbed his arm. "Callahan, please! Calm down."

The young cop put his hand on his gun.

Callahan grinned. "Go ahead," he taunted. "But if you take it out, you'd better use it—instantly, or I'll stick it so far up your ass it'll take a team of proctologists to remove it."

"That's enough!" Paula yelled, pulling Jack away from the desk. "Please stop it!" she pleaded.

Callahan responded, backing away. The frightened young cop stood up, pieces of pizza clinging to his shirt and trousers.

"You're under arrest!" he fumed, regaining some of his composure.

"For what? Accidentally tripping on the rug," Callahan said, heading out the door. "If you have any further questions, be sure and look me up." He left the angry and frustrated cop standing behind the desk; his mouth open, unsure of his next move.

"That was smart, Callahan," Paula said, as they got into the jeep. "Really smart. Assaulting a police officer in the police station. Jesus!"

"I apologize for subjecting you to that, but not for what I did."

Paula reached out and squeezed his hand. "I'm not questioning what you did, just your choice of time and place."

Not more than a half hour after they had returned to the house, Jack saw the police car, driven by Chief Struther Nelson, pull into the driveway. It came as no surprise.

Callahan liked the tall, lanky southerner; he considered him a competent and fair man—if a little reluctant to enforce the laws he personally disagreed with. The town council had hired him after a small southern city had dismissed him for refusing to strictly enforce their marijuana statutes—a laudable stance by Aspen's standards. The first winter Nelson spent in Aspen, he had joined a skiing clinic Jack had taught at the start of the season; at age forty-five, he was a beginning skier with a great deal of natural ability, and progressed rapidly. He and Callahan were on friendly terms, occasionally having a cup of coffee together when their paths crossed.

Jack opened the door before he had a chance to knock. "Come in, Struther," he said, extending his hand.

Nelson shook hands with him, at the same time shaking his head in the manner in which one might show disappointment in an errant child. "Damn, Jack," he said, in a slow, casual drawl. "You put me between a rock and a hard place." As Callahan closed the door, Nelson noticed Paula sitting on the sofa. "Excuse me, miss," he said, tipping his cowboy hat. "I didn't see you there." Jack introduced them. "Pleasure," Nelson drawled.

Paula smiled and nodded, assessing his intentions, deciding he had come to lecture, not to arrest.

Boomer came out of the bedroom and trotted down the hall, growling and snorting. Jack put him on a down-stay and offered Nelson a seat.

He settled slowly in the chair, in his deceptively lethargic way, removing his hat and placing it carefully on an end table. "You gave Bob Steel a hard time, Jack. He wants you arrested." His long angular face had a serious and troubled look.

"Is that what you came to do?" Jack asked.

"No," Nelson replied, "but we've got to find some middle ground here. I just can't overlook what you did; it would make me look bad to my men."

"Did he tell you why it happened?"

"His side, but I can pretty much imagine the truth of it. Steel's an overzealous young man, and he didn't like your friend. If I recall right," Nelson said, running his fingers through his hair and slowly scratching the back of his head, "DeStephano spit on him a few months back—not exactly something that would endear him to the boy."

"Popcorn got carried away sometimes, but he was basically harmless," Jack said. "Your boy cop made a few disparaging remarks about him, and I asked him nicely to knock it off; he persisted, and I lost my temper. Popcorn wasn't just a worthless bum, you know," Jack added, feeling the need to defend him.

"I know about his war record," Nelson said. "I took that into consideration a number of times when I should have locked him up. But let's get back to the immediate problem. I'd appreciate it if you would apologize to Officer Steel, and it might be nice if you offered to buy him a new shirt—I'm told that tomato stains are near impossible to get out."

Callahan bristled, but understanding Nelson's position, suggested a compromise arrangement. "How about if I give you the money for the shirt and you give him my apologies?"

Nelson smiled. He had guessed before he arrived that, knowing Callahan, that was the most he was going to get. "That sounds like something I can live with," he said, getting up from the chair.

"Before you leave," Jack said, "can you tell me if the autopsy showed any signs of drugs in Popcorn's system when he died?"

"None. He was clean."

"Was there water in his lungs?"

"No," Nelson replied, holding Callahan's gaze. "Why do you ask?"

"Popcorn couldn't swim."

"I didn't know that, but I did find it strange that a man found in a lake had no water in his lungs. That was until I took a close look at the area where his body was found. The rock ledge I assume he jumped or dove from has another ledge about twenty feet below it that sticks out a little farther. If DeStephano didn't push off with enough force, he could have struck his head and broken his neck, killing him before he hit the water. Which would explain the absence of water in his lungs."

"How do you explain a man who is afraid of the water and can't swim diving into a lake?"

"We both know that DeStephano had a drug problem," Nelson replied.

"It doesn't wash, Struther. If the lake was in the middle of town I might give it some credence, but I assure you that Popcorn didn't hike into the wilderness; I knew him better than that."

"There's nothing to indicate otherwise, Jack. But if I find anything to the contrary I'll let you know."

Callahan considered telling him about the incident at the cabin, and the camera that they had found on Popcorn being the same as Denneckers', but he wasn't certain they were related, and decided to do some investigating on his own first. "When's the funeral?" Jack asked.

"His body was shipped back to his family in New Jersey. They want him buried in Arlington National Cemetery."

"I hope he's not screwed out of that, too," he said, walking Nelson to his car.

"I'm truly sorry about your friend, Jack."

Callahan thanked him, knowing he meant it.

Before going back inside, Jack took a short walk through the woods behind the house. Standing at the edge of a small stream that ran through a grove of aspens, he said goodbye to Popcorn.

Kurt Bierman told Callahan to come by anytime after eight o'clock. They left an hour early for the ten-minute drive—there was a stop Jack wanted to make.

He turned out his headlights as he entered the alley behind Dennecker's house, driving the short distance to the gate at the rear of the property in darkness. The surrounding homes were concealed from view by high hedges, and his presence went unnoticed. He sat quietly, watching the house for signs of movement.

Paula gave him a curious glance, raising an eyebrow. "I don't think we're going to surprise him, Callahan," she said lightly, uncertain of what he was doing. "He's expecting us."

"This isn't Kurt's house," Jack said. "It's Dennecker's."

Paula looked at the darkened house through the break in the hedge at the gate. "What do you have in mind?"

"The camera the police found on Popcorn was the same make as the one in Dennecker's case," he told her. "A Leica. To my knowledge, Popcorn didn't own a camera; he had long ago hocked anything he had of value. I think he got it here."

Paula chilled at the implication. "Jesus, Callahan! If the same two men you saw at the cabin were here—which makes sense if they were searching through Dennecker's possessions— and Popcorn got in their way; *they* could have killed him." She shuddered at the thought. "When you were questioning the young cop and Nelson about the coroner's report, I knew you were suggesting he was murdered, but I thought over some drug-related incident."

"That was the first thing that entered my mind, until I saw the camera, and remembered telling Popcorn about Dennecker's death. He wasn't above stealing when he was in a bind. And something else—I noticed that his car is parked in the next block. I not only think he was here, I think he was killed here."

Paula fell silent. The excitement and intellectual challenge of a possible code, the reason behind it, and the prospect of a good story diminished somewhat with the chilling sobriety of its becoming a deadly game.

Jack removed the flashlight from the glove compartment. "Wait for me here; I shouldn't be long."

"Not on your life!" she protested. "I coming with you."

Jack doubted that he could dissuade her. "All right, but follow closely, and if there's any trouble, do *what* I tell you to do *when* I tell you to do it."

Silhouetted in the moonlight, they moved quickly across the lawn and ducked into the deep shadows on the back porch. Callahan carded the door with ease.

Turning on the flashlight, keeping the beam angled low and away from the windows, he inspected the rooms, with Paula at his side. As in the cabin, everything was orderly and seemed undisturbed; but the house had been unlived in for the summer months, and the thick dust that had settled on the furniture revealed the meticulous care with which someone had searched the house.

A stack of papers on the desk in the study had been moved and replaced a few inches to the right of the old dust mark, leaving a clear outline of their original position, and there were smudges on the leather top where someone had placed a hand.

Jack shined the light along the wall of bookshelves, stopping at a section containing a row of cameras. There were six of them, all Leicas, pre–World War II models. To the immediate right of the first camera in the row was a dust-free space approximately the size of the space taken up by the others.

"He *was* here!" Paula whispered, feeling a tightening in her stomach.

Callahan stared, unseeing, his eyes hard, ominously fixed on some distant point.

Kurt Bierman's home was an extension of the warm, gracious greeting Paula and Jack received. The living room was cozy and inviting, attributable to the carefully selected and painstakingly acquired appointments. The patina of old wood, the texture and subtle aroma of volumes of rare leatherbound books, and the delicate colors and intricate designs of oriental rugs and Chinese porcelains gave the room an atmosphere of grace and character. The overstuffed, down-filled cushions on the sofa and chairs, each with an ottoman, were thoughtfully chosen to comfort guests and stimulate casual, relaxed conversations.

The pleasing strains of Mozart's *Jupiter* symphony filled the room at a volume that soothed without distracting. Kurt opened a bottle of wine—"A special year for special friends."

During the four years that Jack had known him, he had been to his house twice each year, for Christmas and Thanksgiving dinners. Each time, he was poignantly aware of Kurt's loneliness and solitude; and yet he felt that this sensitive and intelligent man was somehow content, fulfilled by his memories and mementos—not living in the past, but comforted and sustained by vestiges of his halcyon days before his life was eviscerated by a nation gone mad.

Paula moved slowly about the room admiring the collection of fine porcelains, stopping to look at a grouping of photographs on the mantel of the marble fireplace: faded images in sepia tones, of Kurt, his wife, and their children, taken forty years ago.

For years Kurt had kept them packed away, unable to look at them, but as time passed and the pain numbed and he needed to remember, he found that the old photographs stirred other memories, pleasing vignettes of Ida, her gentle ways, her shy smile, and on very special days, faint, ethereal echoes of the children's soft laughter.

"Your family, Mr. Bierman?" Paula asked.

"Yes. My wife and daughters."

"What lovely girls," she said, studying the two dark-haired smiling children clinging to their father's side in an attractive, well-landscaped garden. "How old are they now?"

"Rebecca would have been forty-five, and Anna forty-three," Kurt answered, without hesitation.

"I'm sorry, Mr. Bierman," Paula said, in response to his use of the past tense. "An accident?"

"A madness," Kurt replied. "They died in Auschwitz in 1943 . . . or '44, I'm not certain."

With all that had happened, Jack had forgotten to brief Paula on Kurt's background. He gave her an apologetic look.

"Well, Jack," Kurt said, breaking the awkward silence. "What is it you wish to discuss?"

Callahan detailed what had happened, what they had found, and what they suspected.

"Dennecker's background doesn't surprise me," Kurt said. "Quite a few German soldiers settled in Aspen in the late forties and early fifties, mostly from the Alpine Corps. There was a time when speaking without a German accent was a detriment to working for the ski school. When Dennecker came here in 1955, skiing was in its infancy, and the permanent population was only a fraction of what it is today, and we all knew each other, at least by sight. I remember that Dennecker began as a lift operator, but it wasn't long before he was promoted to a managerial position. I'm told he was the most efficient mountain manager they ever had."

"Did you know him personally?" Paula asked.

"No. He came into the shop only once a year, in the fall, usually, to buy a book for his annual trip. We made idle conversation about the weather, and once he told me he was going fishing in Canada, but he always seemed uncomfortable and never stayed to chat. Until now I never understood why, although something that happened a few years after he

66

came here should have given me some indication." Kurt unbuttoned the cuff of his shirt and rolled up his sleeve, revealing a faded five-digit number crudely tattooed on his forearm. "My identification number from Buchenwald," he explained to Paula; Jack had seen it before.

Paula cringed at the thought of all that it implied.

"Dennecker came into the shop for his annual visit on a day when I was cleaning shelves," Kurt continued, rolling down his sleeve. "When I rang up his purchase, he saw the tattoo and stepped back as though he had been struck. He seemed shocked and offended and left without another word. I ascribed his reaction to the collective German guilt about the death camps, but it may well have been due to a personal involvement, considering his rank and assignment to SS Headquarters."

"Do you agree that the pages of numbers in his address book could be a code?" Paula asked.

"It's not an unreasonable speculation," Kurt replied.

"Do you have any experience with codes or decoding methods?" Jack asked, with the knowledge that Kurt, before the war, had been a professor of mathematics at the University of Heidelberg—finding it impossible to return to academic life after the debilitating, dehumanizing experience of Buchenwald, and the emotionally desiccating loss of his family.

"Some. But with my outdated methods and the possible permutations, it could take me months. However, I have a friend with the Aspen Institute, a former history professor at Princeton, who was with Army Intelligence during the war; I'm certain he will be able to help you. He has written a number of books on World War II, and one on the history of codes; it's considered to be the definitive work on the subject. I'll see him tomorrow and give him the address book." He excused himself and left the room, returning with a tray of pastries.

Jack smiled when he saw them. "You've been to Delice," he said, referring to a local bakery renowned for its excellent pastries.

"But of course," Kurt replied, grinning broadly, placing the tray on the coffee table within everyone's reach. "If you are among the uninitiated," he said to Paula, "you have a delightful surprise in store."

*   *   *

Boomer's ears twitched as he grumbled from a deep sleep disturbed by the rustling noises and hushed voices coming from outside, behind the house. He raised his head, still lying on his side on the bed, and listened. The unfamiliar voices reached him again; this time they were closer to the front door. Flipping quickly over onto all fours, he crouched low, cocked his head, and stared intently in the direction of the voices.

Candellari expertly picked the lock and stepped into the pitch-black house; Halek followed, holding the silenced pistol at his side.

Boomer crept quietly off the bed and stalked slowly down the hallway. Seeing the two men, he lunged at them in a snarling rage.

Candellari reacted instantly, sidestepping and dropping to a crouch as Boomer leaped forward, dove past him, and slammed into Halek's side, chest-high. Biting deeply into his upper arm, the dog caused him to drop the gun, and with a powerful twist of his massive neck tore away a chunk of flesh. Halek screamed in pain and dropped to his knees, instinctively reaching for the gun.

Boomer quickly clamped down on the extended arm, and with a toss of his head, flipped Halek onto his side. Releasing his grip on the arm, he sank his teeth into the inside of the desperate man's thigh, eliciting another piercing scream.

Candellari scrambled over to the gun, unnoticed by the enraged animal, took careful aim, and fired, hitting him in the head.

Boomer collapsed on the floor, shuddering briefly before his eyes rolled back in his head and his tongue flopped limply from the side of his muzzle.

Halek struggled painfully to his feet. "Son of a bitch! What the fuck was that?"

Candellari cast the light over Boomer. "A Rottweiler," he said, moving the beam to Halek. "Are you all right?"

"I hurt like hell," Halek replied, "but I can function."

"I've seen one of them in action before; consider yourself lucky."

Halek limped over to the fireplace, groaning with each step, and picked up the poker. Returning to where Boomer lay, he brought the iron bar down on the dog's head, across his front legs, and into his ribcage, uttering vile curses with each blow.

"Knock it off, Charlie; he's dead," Candellari commanded. "We have work to do."

"Rotten bastard dog," Halek muttered, dropping the poker.

Candellari stared thoughtfully at the huge animal lying at his feet. "He's a complication we didn't count on." He moved the light around the living room, bringing it to rest on a gun cabinet in a corner near the fireplace. It contained Callahan's set of skeet guns. "We can't pull this off now without Callahan knowing someone was here; we'll have to make it look like a robbery. Take the shotguns," he instructed Halek, "and anything else that might be easily fenced by a sneak thief."

In less than half an hour Candellari had finished concealing the tiny transmitters—one in each room, and one in the telephone.

Halek had found two pairs of skis to add to the shotguns, and was sitting in the living room reattaching the tape he had used to secure a piece of toweling on the gaping wound on his upper arm, while Candellari made certain that the transmitters were operating properly. The glow from the flashlight illuminated two framed photographs on the wall across from where Halek sat; he got up to inspect them closer.

The larger of the two was of Callahan, in camouflage fatigues, kneeling in a field of tall grass, grease streaked across his face, holding an automatic weapon, with ammo pouches slung around his neck; he was flanked by two mean-looking black Rhodesians dressed and equipped in the same manner. The other photograph was of Callahan alone, standing near a thatched-roof hut, dressed in the combat uniform of a Green Beret.

"Hey, Phil," Halek said. "Come and have a look at this."

Candellari replaced the telephone on the hook and came over to where Halek was standing.

"This is the same guy I smacked on the head up in the mountains."

Candellari examined the photographs, making a mental note to handle the man accordingly if a confrontation became necessary.

* * *

At first Callahan thought that Boomer was dead, but then he detected the faint, shallow breathing. Lifting him from the floor, he cradled him in his arms and carried him to the jeep.

Paula ran from the house and got behind the wheel. "Dr. Elkins said he'd meet us at the office," she said, her voice strained and high-pitched. She sped out of the driveway, spraying gravel behind her. The jeep leaned precariously on the curves as she raced toward town, her vision blurred by the welling tears.

"Goddammit!" Jack muttered repeatedly, holding a handkerchief over the wound in Boomer's head.

Dr. Elkins was standing in the doorway as Paula pulled in and screeched to a halt. He rushed to the jeep, taking Boomer as Jack got out. "What happened to him?"

"I don't know," Jack said, following him as he hurriedly carried Boomer inside. "I found him lying on the kitchen floor in a pool of blood."

Elkins frowned and shook his head as he began his examination. "I want you and the young lady to stay in the waiting room while I work on him," he said, stretching Boomer out on the operating table. "This is going to take a while."

"What are his chances?" Callahan asked, fearing the worst.

"Not good, Jack," Elkins said dolefully. "I'll do what I can, but he's in bad shape."

It was two o'clock in the morning when Elkins entered the waiting room, flopped wearily in a chair, and propped his long, thin legs on the coffee table; his soft, gentle face was drawn and haggard. "He's going to make it," he said to the two anxious faces across from him. "But I'll be damned if I can understand why someone would do something like that."

"Like what?" Paula asked, her eyes red from crying.

"The X-rays show that he's been struck on the head, *hard,* and I removed a bullet from his skull. Either one would have knocked him out instantly. Someone did one or the other after he was unconscious." Elkins grimaced with disgust. "He also has three broken ribs, and his right front leg has a compound fracture. My guess is that he was beaten while unconscious."

"Will he recover completely?" Jack asked.

"I think so. The blow on the head did little damage, and the bullet entered at an angle and didn't penetrate deep enough to do anything more than give him a bad concussion. Rott-

70

weilers have bone as dense as ivory; a less sturdy breed could never have absorbed the punishment. It also didn't hurt that the bullet was a small caliber—a .32, I think."

"May I see him?" Jack asked.

"He was still out when I put him in the recovery pen," Elkins said, stifling a yawn. "It'll be a few hours before he's fully awake."

"Mind if I wait here?"

Elkins smiled. He had been treating Boomer since he was a puppy, and knew how much he meant to Jack. "No. I don't mind. Lock the door when you leave; I'm going home and get some sleep."

"Thanks, Sam," Jack said, grasping his hand. "I appreciate what you did."

"I wouldn't have it any other way. Boomer is one of my favorites." As he opened the door, he stopped and turned to Callahan. "By the way, I found bits of flesh and skin between Boomer's teeth. He got a piece of whoever worked him over."

Callahan nodded, his expression hardened. "With a little luck maybe I'll get the rest."

"I'm not a man of violence, Jack, but if you do, give him one for me," Elkins said, closing the door behind him.

Now that the trauma of Boomer's life hanging in the balance was over, Paula could see the rage mounting in Callahan. She saw the wheels turning, his eyes flicking about the room.

"Do you think this is tied in with Popcorn and the incident at the cabin?" she asked, having decided for herself that it was.

"There are too many coincidences," Jack replied. "It has to be."

"Are you going to call the police?"

"I'll report the theft of the shotguns, and what happened to Boomer, but I'll look into the other aspects of it myself. I know Struther will chalk it up to just another off-season break-in; there's no sense in telling him anything else. I know damn well that it wasn't done by any of the local down-and-outers; carrying guns isn't their style."

"This may not be the end of it," Paula said uneasily. "Not if we have what they're looking for."

"I can deal with that," Callahan said with a grim determination, "now that I know how the game is to be played."

Paula followed him through the door to the kennel area; he wanted to be with Boomer when he came to.

They sat cross-legged on the concrete floor of the recovery pen. Boomer was lying on a bedboard in the corner, breathing deeply and evenly, occasionally quivering as the effects of the anesthetic wore off. Half of his head was shaved and painted with an antiseptic solution, and a small patch covered the spot where the bullet had been imbedded; his ribcage was tightly wrapped, and his right front leg was encased in a plaster cast.

It was early morning when Boomer opened his eyes. Paula and Jack had dozed off and were awakened by a pitiful whimpering—Boomer was struggling to get to his feet, trying to reach them; it was a valiant effort, but he collapsed, crying in pain.

"No, Boomer. Stay!" Jack said, going to the side of the suffering animal. He placed his head in his lap, slowly massaged his neck, and talked soothingly to him. Boomer emitted an elongated high-pitched whine; he had a frightened look in his eyes; he was confused and unable to grasp his limitations.

Jack stayed with him for an hour, until he drifted back to sleep, then left, certain that the worst was over.

Paula had nothing pressing her to return to New York; she had thirty days before her deadline for an article due *Esquire,* and only a week's work, at the outside, to complete it. She decided to extend her stay in Aspen for a few days, until Boomer came home, and, with luck, some word from Kurt Bierman on his friend's progress with the code.

Jack had no luck with the local doctors and pharmacists; they hadn't seen anyone seeking treatment for a dog bite. His inquiries among friends were just as unproductive. Either Boomer hadn't inflicted much damage, or the person he attacked had taken care of it himself. Jack suspected it was the latter.

A flight-line attendant at the Aspen airport remembered the helicopter Callahan described; he had refueled it, but upon checking the log, found that they had paid in cash, leaving no record of the purchase other than the amount of fuel and the cost. The FAA could trace the helicopter to its owner for him if he knew the identification number, but he had never put it to memory.

By the morning of the second day, Boomer was feeling well enough to wolf down the two cheeseburgers Paula had brought him. Dr. Elkins said that he could go home in another day, but it would be six to eight weeks before the cast could be removed and the ribs knitted, and he must be kept quiet—a prescription of Valium given when he was most restless would help.

Jack and Paula had spent the afternoon at the hot-springs pool in Glenwood, and the evening at home, making love. Paula had just gotten out of the shower, bundled in Jack's terry-cloth robe, when the telephone rang. Jack was propped up in bed, watching the evening news.

"I'll get it," Paula called. "I'm halfway there."

Moments later, she stood in the doorway of the bedroom, her eyes wide with excitement.

"Something wrong?" Jack asked.

"Not this time, Callahan," she said, sitting on the edge of the bed. "Something is right. That was Kurt Bierman; we're to be at his house at nine o'clock tonight. Professor Girard will be there. It *is* a code."

Professor Colin Girard, his black horn-rimmed glasses resting on the tip of his aquiline nose, removed a stack of papers from an attaché case and spread them out on the coffee table. He peered over the top of his glasses at Paula and Jack, looking for all the world as though he were about to begin a lecture, brushing a perpetually uncooperative lock of grayish-brown hair from his forehead, only to have it flop back seconds later. He had an open, friendly face with alert perceptive eyes that occasionally twinkled, suggesting a detached amusement tempered with a benevolent tolerance for lesser intellects. The narrow lapels on his rumpled tweed sportcoat were of another era, and his worn, baggy gray slacks had seen better days—one got the impression that he neither cared nor noticed.

"Allow me to begin by defining terms," he said, his authoritative manner of speech confirming his appearance, "to enable you to better understand how the code was broken. Dennecker's code falls into the cryptography category which does not conceal the message, but rather makes it unintelligible by arranging it in an unrecognizable form. There are two forms of cryptography: transposition and substitution. When using transposition," he said, pointing to Paula, "your name, Paula, would become Aluap, or any variation of arrangements of the five letters. They would simply be rear-ranged, but unchanged. With the substitution method, the letters would be replaced with numbers, symbols, or other letters; Paula could become 6-13-9-3-8, or NZAQE. In trans-position, the letters keep their identities, but lose their position; in substitution, the letters keep their position, but lose their identities. On the surface, this seems relatively uncomplicated, but bear in mind that there are any number of variants that can addle the process; homophones, nulls, monalphabetic codes, polyalphabetic codes—all of which are unrelated to the matter at hand and would bore you if I went into detail.

"To get to the point. The morning that Kurt gave me the address book, I called a friend who heads the Cryptologic Research Department at the Institute for Defense Analysis at Princeton. He was extremely helpful with the research for my book on the history of codes. His first reaction was that the four pages of numbers I read to him were insufficient to work with; he usually has thousands of pages of transmitted codes, collected over a period of months. But he said he'd try. If it had been a modern code with such a small message, and no previous transmissions for comparison, the chances of breaking it would have been one in ten million. Fortunately, Dennecker's code was a simplistic one, unlike those used by the Germans during the war. However, that was not obvious from the outset. He fed the information to a computer capable of over two hundred thousand additions per second, pro-grammed to recognize a message by storing letter frequen-cies and grammatical redundancies in its memory banks. Frequency analysis is the most effective way of breaking a code. The computer can sort out the message by counting the frequencies, finding the repetitions, and noting the intervals between them. After this is accomplished, a probable solution can be tested by mathematical analysis extended forward and backward."

Professor Girard sensed he was beginning to lose his audi-ence. He smiled apologetically. "Sorry, I have a habit of transporting myself back to the classroom. I assure you there won't be a test on this material."

Paula laughed. "Please continue, professor. It's fascinating."

"I'll spare you the details of how he found out what it

wasn't," Girard continued, "and tell you how he discovered what it is."

He shuffled through the notes, located the page he was looking for, and placed it on top of the pile. "The frequency analysis I mentioned didn't apply, due to the text of the code. Actually, it was pure speculation and intuition that led him to the system that Dennecker used. The method of encoding is an ancient and rather uncomplicated one devised over two thousand years ago by a Greek writer, Polybius.

"The letters of the alphabet are arranged in a five-by-five square and the rows and columns are numbered one through five. The letters I and J are placed in one square so everything fits properly. Each letter of the alphabet is designated by two numbers; one from its row and one from its column. The principle is to change letters into numbers, and it is known as a Polybius square, or more commonly, a checkerboard."

Girard placed one of the note papers in the center of the table, turning it toward Jack and Paula. "Now to the heart of the matter. The reason the frequency analysis didn't work is that the text of the code is not a message, but a list of names."

Jack and Paula leaned forward and read the names:

John Wilson Cook
2130 Maryland Avenue
Phoenix, Arizona

Edward Tyler White
5850 Wayside Avenue
Cincinnati, Ohio

Thomas Martin Hill
1400 Brinton's Bridge Road
Chadds Ford, Pennsylvania

Frederich Bauer
Center Island, Oyster Bay,
Long Island, New York

The second name on the list caught Paula's attention; she had been born and raised in Cincinnati, and after graduating from Vassar, had worked for a year for the *Cincinnati Post*. She turned to Callahan with an expression of incredulity.

"Edward Tyler White is the chief justice of the Ohio state supreme court! I met him years ago at one of my grandmother's dinner parties."

"I can help you with another of the names," Girard said. "Thomas Martin Hill is a United States Senator from Pennsylvania."

"My God!" Paula said, her mind racing back over the events of the past few days, evaluating the tangential but highly suspicious incidents.

Professor Girard pulled another of his note papers from the stack. "There were two sets of numbers at the bottom of the last page that made no sense when decoded in the same manner: 25-22-33-35-13-32 and 038-193862. In my judgment, there are two possibilities: It is a separate code, in which case there is not enough text to decode it, or it is as it appears to be, a series of unrelated numbers, not part of the code. I think it's the latter. The numbers were on a line separated from the coded list of names. That being the case, I feel it's safe to assume that they are not related to the list."

He picked up another paper and read from it. "The first set of numbers if decoded using the same key as the list of names would read 'Jochen,' or 'Iochen,' remembering that I and J are designated by the same number."

"Jochen," Kurt interrupted, "is a German given name for a man."

"That's a possibility," Girard acknowledged, "but the second set of numbers doesn't give us a last name, and are erratic in relation to the decoding procedure. Any number above five or below one cannot be used in a code from the Polybius square. Therefore, from 038-193862, the only usable numbers would be 3-132, or any combination of them. For example, 31-32 would decode to XN. I feel that they are not related to the code and are probably just a list of numbers with some personal significance to Dennecker."

Girard handed the paper to Paula, along with the list of names and the address book. "One last bit of information," he said. "While I was at the Colorado University library yesterday, doing some research, I gave the address book to a friend of mine in the chemistry department. He submitted the ink and the pages containing the code to a radio-carbon test and other chemical tests. The paper is at least thirty-five to forty years old and the ink is approximately twenty-five years old, so the coded names and addresses were most likely written in

76

the book in the early 1950s. The sets of numbers we could not decode were written with a different pen and ink, and the tests suggest that they were entered in the book a few years after the list of names, which reinforces the probability that they are unrelated to the code."

"I can't thank you enough, Professor Girard . . . and you, Mr. Bierman," Paula said. "You've been a tremendous help."

"You're more than welcome, my dear," Girard said, taking the glass of wine Kurt offered him. "I imagine you'll be researching the names on the list; just let me know if you tie it all together. I'll be interested in hearing what the common denominator is—if, in fact, there is one."

"I'll do that," Paula replied.

"Just remember," Girard cautioned, with that charming twinkle in his eye, "that all you have at this point is a list of names an ex-Nazi general wrote in his address book; interesting possibilities, but among those possibilities is a reason that may prove to be perfectly harmless, unconspiratorial, and inane."

"Agreed," Paula said, "but why encode them?"

Girard shrugged. "Ah, there's the rub," he said, suspecting that the young lady's physical attributes weren't her only assets.

"And the things that have happened in the last week," she added.

"Not proved, but grist for the mill."

"I *will* keep you informed," Paula said, smiling.

Girard raised his wineglass to her. "I'll look forward to it."

On the drive home, Paula broke the silence that had lasted most of the way. "If the men on this list are responsible for what has happened here, we're taking on some heavyweights." She paused, shaking her head. "Why would this list be so important to them? Important enough to murder someone?"

"If that's what they were after, and if they're the ones responsible," Jack said, remembering Girard's point.

"It is, Callahan. I can feel it. I'm going back to New York tomorrow and finish some work, and in three or four days I'll be able to devote full time to this."

Jack reacted inwardly to her leaving, but said nothing. "I'll see what I can do on this end. You'll keep in touch?"

"Of course," Paula said, surprised by the question. "I'll call you the moment I have anything."

* * *

Paula's imagination was in full swing, and they stayed awake into the small hours, projecting theories and discussing the merits of each.

The next morning, after Paula made reservations on a noon flight to Denver, connecting to New York, Jack placed three telephone calls. Paula listened as he tried his ploy for the third time, having guessed wrong with Senator Hill and Judge White.

"May I speak to Mr. Cook?" he asked the woman with the Spanish accent.

"Mr. Cook is not at home; he can be reached at his office."

"Which office is that?" Jack asked.

"His office at Allied Electronics, of course," the housekeeper replied, matter-of-factly.

"Of course," Jack said.

The switchboard at Allied Electronics rang him through to Cook's office. The secretary informed him that Mr. Cook was in a meeting and couldn't be disturbed.

"This is rather important," Jack told her, "and I haven't much time."

"If you can tell me what it concerns, I'll have Mr. Cook call you just as soon as he returns."

"It concerns his helicopter, but I'm afraid I won't be able to wait for his call, and it is a pressing matter."

"Perhaps Mr. Johnson at our hangar at the airport might be of some assistance," she offered. "He's in charge of the aircraft."

"Yes, perhaps he could," Jack said, writing down the number she gave him.

"Bill Johnson here." The voice was nearly drowned out by background noise.

"This is Tom Howard of Monarch Aviation in Aspen, Colorado, Mr. Johnson," Jack said.

"Just a minute," he shouted above the roar.

Callahan heard the noise increase in pitch and volume, then trail off.

"Sorry," Johnson said. "A plane was taking off; couldn't hear a thing you said."

Jack repeated it. "I'm calling about Mr. Cook's helicopter."

"Which one?"

Jack hesitated, caught off guard and unsure of the make and model. "The black-and-silver one," he tried.

"Oh, yeah. The Bell Jet Ranger. What about it?"

"I was told it was for sale."

"Not to my knowledge," Johnson said. "Hell, we've only had it six months."

"Are you sure? I was led to believe it was."

"Sorry. I don't know anything about it. May be Phil Candellari can help you."

"Phil who?" Jack asked, not hearing the last name clearly.

"Candellari," Johnson repeated. "He's Mr. Cook's chief pilot; flies his Lear and both helicopters."

"Where can I reach him?"

"Don't know. I haven't seen much of him for the last week. Mr. Cook's office might know."

"I think I know this Candellari," Jack said. "A tall, wiry man with dark hair?"

"That's him."

"I talked to him and another man; a heavy-set, strong-looking fellow. He's the one who said the helicopter was for sale. His name is on the tip of my tongue . . ."

"Charlie Halek," Johnson said, in a tone that suggested he wasn't fond of the man. "He's always with Phil."

"Yes, that was it, Halek. Thank you, Mr. Johnson. You've been a big help."

"Sure. Give the office a call; they'll put you in touch with him."

Paula understood the significance of the conversation from the side she had heard. "You've found the two men you saw at the cabin?"

Callahan nodded. "I'm sure of it."

"What are you going to do?"

"Nothing . . . for the moment. They're just soldiers; I can get them anytime. I want the generals, and it looks like this Cook is one. Let's see what your research on the other names turns up."

John Cook, already upset by the message his secretary had given him and his conversation with Johnson, was prepared for Candellari's report, having reasoned for himself the crux of what he was being told.

"The list of names was encoded in some sort of book Dennecker kept," Candellari said, consulting the notes he had made from the recordings. "Professor Girard, a friend of Kurt Bierman's—Callahan's employer at the bookstore—

79

decoded them. They don't know the significance of the list, and the girl has returned to New York and is going to look into it."

"Anything else?" Cook asked, knowing that Candellari had to know about Callahan's calls to Phoenix.

"A complication," Candellari said hesitantly. "Callahan knows our names and has connected us to you. He remembered us from Dennecker's cabin; he's the man we knocked unconscious. He called—"

"I know," Cook interrupted, satisfied that Candellari wasn't holding back to save face. "I talked to Bill Johnson, and called Monarch Aviation in Aspen; there's no Tom Howard there."

"I'm sorry, sir. I didn't know he had seen us in the mountains. If you say the word, I'll take care of it immediately."

"No!" Cook said harshly. "All they have is coincidences and suspicions. And now there are other people involved who would ask questions if anything happened to either one of them. I want to see how far this is going to go before deciding on a definite course of action. Just maintain surveillance on Callahan, and keep me informed."

"I'd like to send Charlie to New York to wire the girl's apartment."

"Fine. But give him implicit instructions to take no action unless he checks with you first; and you check with me before issuing any orders to that effect."

"Yes, sir," Candellari said, embarrassed by the veiled admonishment.

Cook pressed the intercom, grasping his wrist tightly to stop the tremor in his hand. "No more calls this afternoon," he told his secretary.

The dryness in his mouth and the knot in his stomach persisted despite the Scotch and his efforts to relax.

Thirty-three years ago it had all seemed so uncomplicated; the perfect crime, victimless for all intent and purposes—if one accepted the premise that justice, however convoluted, was served. Then came the retribution; unpleasant, but tolerable; and now, after all these years, having to face the possibility of being destroyed by it.

He could handle the pressure once he accepted what was happening and resigned himself to what he knew must be done if the situation worsened, but this fence-walking, hoping it would go away like a bad dream, was not conducive to insightful, effective decision-making. This time it must be eradicated completely, but not through impulsive, careless actions. His adversaries were manageable—a ski instructor and a young free-lance journalist. Any clumsy, ineffectual measures to eliminate them could bring in more formidable opponents. It was best to wait; let it run its course, stepping in only when there were no alternatives.

NINE

For Paula, Aspen had been a pleasant diversion, Callahan a reassuring, lingering interlude, and the Dennecker business a transfusion—far more promising than anything since her exposé on the corruption in the state construction projects.

Halfway through the first day she was back in step with New York. The supercharged atmosphere was her life's blood, injecting her with a vitality and alertness she had never experienced in staid, conservative Cincinnati.

The messages left with the answering service reminded her of what she had neglected to reschedule before leaving for Aspen—a missed dental appointment being the most crucial. A message to call Al Verity made her smile; now they were even. He had forgotten a luncheon date last month. A senior editor at *Time*, he was a trusted and valued friend. She had met him when she had sold the magazine an article; they had dated, found they made better friends than lovers, and set-, tled into an open, honest relationship. She made a note to call him in the morning for lunch that day, feeling certain that he would be intrigued with the Dennecker story.

Her best friend's message was enticing: two tickets to the ballet she was willing to share if Paula got home in time. Despite her vow to finish the *Esquire* article, for which her enthusiasm was fast fading in light of Dennecker's code, she called Marsha and arranged to meet her for an early dinner.

* * *

Charlie Halek surveyed the one-bedroom apartment, deciding that transmitters in the living-room and bedroom telephones would suffice, allowing him to monitor all calls and to activate them at will when the phone wasn't in use.

That completed, he studied the array of snapshots in clear plastic frames on the bedroom dresser. One in particular struck his fancy—a picture of Paula and Marsha, bikini-clad, in an island setting. Placing it aside, he opened the top drawer of the dresser, removed his gloves, and selected a pair of panties.

"You're mine, little lady," he whispered, fondling the panties. "Sooner or later you're *mine*."

Taking the snapshot and panties into the bathroom, he placed them on a shelf above the toilet. His eyes glazed, riveted on the image of Paula; his breathing changed to a deeper, heavier cadence. He unzipped his trousers, a broad grin fixed firmly in place.

Paula was already seated at a cozy corner table, an acknowledgment of her steady patronage, when Al Verity entered the restaurant.

He stood head and shoulders above those waiting to be seated; he had a look of casual ambivalence and was indelibly stamped New England prep school, Ivy League. Waving to Paula, he angled his way to the table, gently parting the chatting throngs while denying their existence.

"Welcome home," he said, pecking her lightly on the cheek. "You look renewed; Aspen must agree with you."

"I had a marvelous time, and an interesting one."

Verity feigned disbelief. "What could possibly have happened in such a primitive, uncultured, nouveau-riche carnival that would hold my interest through lunch?" he said, referring to her phone call that morning.

"Would a murder to conceal the identity of people involved with an ex-Nazi general get your attention?"

"It depends on who the people are and the extent of their involvement."

"In all probability a United States Senator, a state supreme court justice, and a wealthy businessman."

Verity raised an eyebrow. "You have my undivided attention."

Paula told him the story, leaving out none of the details.

Verity listened attentively, pecking intermittently at his chef's salad.

"The story is *Time*'s for an eight-thousand-dollar advance, to cover expenses, with the balance to be discussed later," Paula said, expecting the size of the advance to be argued.

Verity considered the proposition thoughtfully. "How do you plan to approach it?"

"I've decided to go to Washington and try the National Archives for background on Dennecker. It seems like the most logical place to start. Are you interested?"

"It has potential, but to get the advance approved I may have to assign one of our staff reporters to work with you."

Paula balked. "No deal! You're not going to saddle me with a wet nurse; I've argued that priapic principle before. I have a proven track record with your people; that has to count for something. If not, I'll try *Newsweek*—they may be more accommodating."

"That's not cricket, my dear. Shame on you," Verity said, smiling sheepishly. "Perhaps a five-thousand-dollar advance and a free hand would be more acceptable."

Paula laughed softly. "Acceptable, Alfred dear, but if this proves to be as big a story as my instincts tell me it is, your tightwad magazine will pay until it hurts."

"That doesn't take much these days," he said, leaning back in his chair and folding his hands over his flat stomach. "Now with that onerous business out of the way, I'll offer you some assistance, for old time's sake. Some of the World War II records at the archives are still classified. If you find that to be the case with Dennecker or any of the names on the list, I have a source at the National Records Center in Suitland, Maryland; it's a sort of national trivia bank. His name is Harvey Martinson—a bit of a lech, so wear something suggestive. I'll call and tell him who you are just in case. He may not be receptive, but at least my call will open the door wide enough for you to get a foot in and work your charms."

"Thanks, Al. That would be nice."

"Call me periodically so I can assure the powers that be that you haven't gone south on me; you know how paranoid we all are since the Howard Hughes hoax."

"Promise," Paula said.

That evening, after packing for Washington, she took a halfhearted stab at completing the *Esquire* article, but fell short; her concentration was gone, the Dennecker code looming overpoweringly in the background.

A call to Callahan brought gales of laughter at Jack's description of Boomer's first day home, stomping around the house like a peglegged sea captain. She told him about her conversation with Verity and her trip to Washington, and much to her surprise when the words came out, she said that she missed him terribly.

"All inquiries regarding World War II," Paula was instructed, "should be made in the Modern Military Branch of the Military Archives Division."

She first had to go to room 201 and apply for a card of admission to the research rooms. That processed in a matter of minutes, she was directed to room 13-W, the office of the Modern Military Branch.

"I believe we have a rather extensive file on Karl Dennecker," the middle-aged, tweedy-looking man with the neatly trimmed beard told her. "If I'm not mistaken, he was one of the defendants in the Pohl case, which was tried at Nuremberg by the United States government subsequent to the International Military Tribunal."

"Karl Dennecker was a war criminal?" Paula asked in surprise.

"Yes, I believe so," the man replied, "but let's have a look at the information we have available."

Paula spent the next six hours in the microfilm reading room. The Pohl case had thirty-eight rolls of microfilm, containing the twenty-one volumes of transcript of the trial, over eight thousand pages. Fortunately it did not all pertain to Karl Dennecker, allowing it to be scanned for the main points of interest to Paula. The trial had begun on January 13, 1947, and ended August 11, 1947.

The Pohl case concerned one Oswald Pohl, *Obergruppenfuehrer* (general) in the SS, and chief of the Wirtschafts und Verwaltungs Hauptamt (WVHA), the SS Economics and Administration Main Office. He was tried along with seventeen other defendants, all principal officers of the WVHA, and all charged with a number of crimes stemming from the administration and control of the concentration camps. The charges were torture, brutal utilization of labor, illegal medical experiments, and euthanasia.

85

The WVHA was divided into five sections (*Amtsgruppen*), each having various areas of responsibility. Amtsgruppe A handled the administration and finances of the SS. Amtsgruppe B controlled the billeting, food, and supplies for the SS and the concentration camps. Amtsgruppe C was responsible for the maintenance of grounds and construction of buildings, including the concentration camps. Amtsgruppe W administered the business enterprises of the SS. Amtsgruppe D was responsible for administering the concentration camps and was headed by General Richard Gluecks, who had disappeared at the end of the war and had never been captured. His second in command had been *Lieutenant General Karl Dennecker*.

Of the eighteen defendants in the Pohl case, three were acquitted, two were sentenced to death, and thirteen were given prison sentences ranging from ten years to life. Dennecker was originally sentenced to hang, but his sentence had been commuted to ten years. He was released in 1955, after serving seven years.

Paula carefully read the biographical information contained in Dennecker's indictment. Dennecker, as a comparatively young major general, was commander of a Waffen SS Panzer division, seeing action in the invasion of Poland, Holland, Yugoslavia, Greece, and Russia. He was awarded the Knight's Cross for his services in Holland. The Oak Leaves were added for his achievements in Yugoslavia, and the Crossed Swords for individual heroism on the Russian Front in 1941. The Russian counteroffensive near Rostov nearly decimated his division, and he was forced into his first defensive action of the war.

His badly mauled division was withdrawn from Russia for reforming in June of 1942. While on leave in Berlin, he was asked to give up his combat command by General Oswald Pohl, an old family friend and head of the newly formed WVHA. Pohl needed his administrative and organizing abilities. According to Pohl's diary, Dennecker wasn't eager to leave his division, but had the foresight to see the handwriting on the wall after his recent Russian defeat. Pohl convinced Reichsfuehrer Himmler to transfer Dennecker to the WVHA and promote him to lieutenant general.

At the end of the war Dennecker went into hiding, not far from the town of Waging, in southern Germany, near the

Austrian border. Eleven months later he was captured by the Americans and sent to the Nuremberg detention center to await trial.

Paula poured over the transcripts of the trial. By the end of the day, her eyes burning, neck stiff, and legs beginning to cramp, she had found nothing to give her a clue to the names on the list. The research rooms would be closing in fifteen minutes. By rote, more than anything else, she started over again, threading the first roll of microfilm into the machine and slowly turning the handle.

At first what she saw didn't fully register. She kept staring at the section of film. She reread it, eyes widening, and thumped the table loudly, drawing glances from others in the room. There it was! On the very first roll! How the hell had she missed it? Scanning too quickly, probably.

PRESIDING JUDGE, EDWARD T. WHITE	Judge of the Superior Court for the 4th Judicial District of Ohio
CHIEF COUNCIL FOR THE PROSECUTION, THOMAS M. HILL	Attorney, United States Department of Justice

Paula sat in her hotel room, nibbling on a room-service meal, going over her notes. There had been no mention of John Wilson Cook or Frederich Bauer in the transcripts; perhaps there would be something at the National Records Center. She decided to discuss what she had found with Al Verity, and called him at his apartment.

Verity settled in a chair, sipped his drink, and listened to Paula's report. Lighting a cigar, he sent a cloud of blue smoke rising to the ceiling—Paula had once told him that he was one of the few people capable of carrying off a cigar with style.

"I suspected that the war-crimes trials were the tie-in to Dennecker," he said when Paula had finished. "My curiosity got the best of me this morning, so I did some research in our files. Senator Hill received considerable press coverage from the trials, and when he got home he put it to good use as a springboard for his political career. He ran for Congress before his name faded from public memory."

"Did you come across anything on Cook or Bauer?"

"Sketchy stuff," Verity said, brushing away a clump of ashes that had dropped in his lap. "An old friend, an associate editor at *Fortune*, had some stock material on them. Cook is the president of an electronics firm in Phoenix that does top-secret government work; not one of *Fortune*'s 500, but a comer. He has Washington connections, as might be expected. So far nothing to connect him to Dennecker."

Verity reached for the notes he had made. "You might want to copy this information on Bauer."

Paula got her pad and pencil. "Ready." She scribbled rapidly as Verity read.

"Frederich Bauer III, great-grandson of founder of Bauer Toy Company, Hamburg, Germany. Now president and sole owner. Took over as head of company at twenty-four, in 1935. Company manufactured famous mechanical toys for over one hundred and twenty-five years. Left Germany 1938, supposedly because of anti-Nazi beliefs, taking family to Argentina. Ran his factories in Argentina and Brazil for the duration. During the war, Nazis took over factories in Hamburg and Hannover and converted them to manufacturing land mines and hand grenades. German factories returned to Bauer at end of war. Also built a new factory and general offices on Long Island in 1952. Spends most of his time in the U.S. at home in Oyster Bay. Runs his business from his American office, with periodic trips to Hamburg and Buenos Aires for business conferences."

"Any affiliation with Dennecker?" Paula asked.

"Nothing documented, but I have a theory why his name is on the list, and possibly the reason for the others, too."

"Let's hear it."

"You're not going to like it."

"Try me."

"The SS used slave labor from the concentration camps in some of their war-production plants," Verity told her, "and I imagine Bauer's converted toy factories were among them. Bauer probably gave testimony at Dennecker's trial concerning the use of his factories."

"Scratch that," Paula said. "Bauer didn't testify at Dennecker's trial; his name wasn't listed among the prosecution or defense witnesses . . . and how would that apply to the other names?"

"Revenge," Verity said. "God only knows who that man considered an enemy, and for what reason. But Hill and

White would have been on the top of the list, one having prosecuted him and the other having sentenced him. It's not uncommon for a man in prison to brood and plot revenge for a real or imagined injustice. However, once released from prison and no longer faced with the boring regimentation and lack of mental stimulus, most revenge plots are soon forgotten. You must admit it's not an unreasonable explanation. An intelligent man, as Karl Dennecker's rank and accomplishments suggest he was, would have soon realized how unproductive and self-defeating it would have been to pursue the idea; he probably gave it up within the first few weeks of his release, after he began feeling and functioning like a normal human being again."

"I can't subscribe to that," Paula said. "I'd consider it if it wasn't for the murder and the other skulduggery in Aspen; those two men who work for Cook were after something, and it wasn't anything as innocuous as a revenge list."

"That's the reason I didn't hold up your check for the advance today, dear."

"Such abiding faith."

"Business," Verity said dryly.

Paula laughed. "I'm going to tap your source tomorrow, and concentrate on Cook; something tells me that Bauer is ancillary to this and will fall into place later. I'll keep in touch."

"A word of caution," Verity said, smiling to himself. "Harvey Martinson is hell on women."

"Not to worry. I'll be on my best, or worst behavior, whichever it takes. And thank you, Al, you're a dear."

"Anytime; you know that."

"Mr. Martinson?" Paula asked, standing in the doorway, uncertain that she was at the right office—the heavyset man behind the desk didn't fit Verity's characterization.

"Yes. Please come in," he said, rising and offering her a chair next to his desk, never taking his eyes off her. He sat down and continued staring. "Excuse me, Miss . . ."

"Carlson," Paula said. "Paula Carlson."

"Oh, yes," Martinson acknowledged. "We have a mutual acquaintance." He continued studying Paula's face. "I realize this is going to sound like a worn-out opening line from a singles bar," he said, nervously fumbling for a pack of cigarettes inside his suit coat, "but haven't we met somewhere before?"

"I don't believe so," Paula replied, searching her memory. "I'm certain I would have remembered," she lied, unconvincingly, judging from the embarrassed look on Martinson's face. He was not the type one would remember easily: short, grossly overweight, and with so much nervous energy that if it were applied commercially it would provide Washington with an alternate source of electricity.

Martinson flicked away at an uncooperative cigarette lighter, finally succeeding. The cigarette stuck to his lips, and as he tried to remove it, his hand slid down to the tip, burning the inside of his fingers. A reflex action knocked the cigarette from his mouth into his lap, causing him to leap up, swatting away the hot ashes. He briefly examined the small hole burned in his trouser leg.

That was all Paula needed to jolt her memory. Harvey Martinson ... or, as he was more affectionately known, Fumbles. At his best he had been an amorphous chub; he must have gained thirty pounds. He usually came up to Vassar on weekends with a group of boys from Trinity College. He was responsible for spilling more glasses, dropping more forks, and burning more tablecloths than any other dinner guest in the history of Jewett House. Paula had all she could do to keep from laughing aloud as one incident in particular flashed in her mind; Fumbles had damn near burned the dress off his conscripted date one evening at dinner, dumping an ashtray with three lighted cigarettes in it into her lap.

She recalled the frantic search on Saturdays to find Harvey a date, the bribery and coercion on the part of her roommate, who dated Harvey's best friend. Harvey had become notorious, and by their senior year, getting him a date was an impossible feat.

The telephone rang on Harvey's desk; reaching for it, he knocked the receiver to the floor. He shook his head in disgust, beads of perspiration forming on his forehead. Finishing the call, he turned his attention to Paula.

"Vassar," Harvey said, trying to regain his composure. "That's where." He smiled proudly, pointing a finger at Paula. "Your roommate, Beth Miller, dated my best friend, Tom Atkinson. I dated quite a few girls from Jewett; sorry to say I never got around to you."

Paula smiled politely, recalling the time she had lost when they drew straws—it had come to that—to see who had to date him; it had cost her one of her best sweaters, given to Pat Thomas for taking her place. "Of course," Paula said cheerfully. "How could I have forgotten?"

"Out of sight, out of mind," Harvey offered. "It's not as though we really *knew* each other, and looking at you now, I realize what I missed. But I now have a second chance, right?" His still-burning cigarette dropped from the edge of the ashtray onto the desk blotter. leaving a smoldering black smudge when he picked it up.

Paula smiled inwardly. *"Plus ça change . . ."* she mumbled under her breath.

Harvey cocked his head, reminiscent of Boomer. "Mmm?"

"Nothing," Paula replied, smiling pleasantly. She decided to concentrate on the information she wanted.

Harvey sat back in his chair, eyeing Paula lecherously. "How can I help you?" he smiled broadly and winked. "My time is your time."

Paula decided to keep her explanation uncomplicated, no outright lies, just a little embellishment here, a little omission there. "I'm working on a feature story about an ex-Nazi general who was tried as a war criminal at Nuremberg at the end of the war. I found most of what I needed in the transcripts of the trial at the National Archives, but I'm having difficulty finding any information on a man by the name of John Wilson Cook, who, according to some of the footnotes in the research material I've read, was involved in the trial. It's possible he was connected in some way with the prosecution staff, but I've been unable to verify that."

"Do you have anything other than his name?" Harvey asked.

"Nothing," Paula said, giving him her most helpless, Arcadian look. "Just that he was in some way connected with the trial of SS General Karl Dennecker."

Harvey frowned, drumming his fingers on the arm of the chair. "We can begin by cross-referencing his name with the general's trial, and seeing what we come up with." He squinted across the room, focusing on a distant point over Paula's shoulder. "I believe that many of the men on the prosecutors' staffs were military officers. We can check and see if his name crops up under any of the military units."

"It's very nice of you to help, Harvey. If I can ever return the favor . . ." Paula could have bitten her tongue, realizing too late it was just the wrong thing to say.

Harvey picked up on it immediately. "Oh, I'll think of something," he promised. "We can start with lunch. I was just about to leave when you arrived. I'll put someone to work on this immediately, and by the time we return we should have some answers." He reached in his coat pocket for his pen. He had left the ball point extracted and removed it point first, getting ink on his fingers. He licked his fingers and rubbed them on his trousers. Paula rolled her eyes up and sighed quietly. Harvey picked up the phone and dialed someone in another section of the building, giving them the details and necessary instructions.

Over lunch, Harvey spent quite some time earnestly telling Paula how great it was to live in Washington. "Prime hunting grounds for a bachelor with savvy."

Paula smiled politely. He hadn't changed much, other than the weight he had gained since she'd last seen him.

"Are you staying in town long?" Harvey asked hopefully.

"No. As a matter of fact, I have to get back this evening. I have a great deal of work to finish before the weekend."

"Oh, that's too bad," Harvey said, frowning. "I thought I might show you the town. We could really have a great time; I know all the in spots."

"Sounds wonderful, Harvey," she lied, "but I really must get back. Perhaps another time."

Harvey nodded, sensing a nonexistent spark of encouragement. "You could come down for a weekend—then we could really spend some time together and get to know each other. I'll check my social calendar," he added, "and see when I can fit you in. Call you next week, okay? They really keep me busy down here," he said, smiling. "Just like the old days; variety is the spice of life."

Paula didn't reply, but interpreted that to mean he was still having the same old problem; he couldn't get anyone to go out with him twice.

He reached across the table to clasp Paula's hand, spilling his glass of water in the process. He completely ignored it, and she supposed these things happened so frequently they no longer registered.

"It's really great seeing you, Paula," he said, apparently

overcome by some unexplainable emotion. "Small world, isn't it?"

"Very small!" Paula agreed.

When they returned to Harvey's office there was a note on his desk asking him to call a Mr. Thompson in the security section. After completing the call, he turned to Paula with a disappointed look. "I'm really sorry, Paula. We do have some information on John Cook, but I'm afraid it's classified."

"Classified!" Paula said in disbelief. "That doesn't make any sense! The information I'm looking for is over thirty years old."

Harvey raised his hands in a gesture of helplessness. "That's not unusual. We have some classified files older than that."

"Why are they classified?" Paula asked. "National security?"

"That's generally the reason. In Cook's case, Thompson tells me the only file we have on him is military."

"Surely thirty-year-old military information can't affect our national security," Paula argued.

"I don't know, but if you think this country is bad about declassifying information, you should try the British archives. A friend of mine told me that they still have a classified label on the amount of toilet paper shipped to their troops in Europe in World War I."

"Oh, Harvey," Paula pleaded. "Al Verity said I could depend on you," she exaggerated. "Isn't there anything you can do?" Harvey's eyes were averted for a moment, and Paula quickly undid another button on her blouse, deciding a little more cleavage was in order. Harvey homed in on it seconds later. "Perhaps you could just check and see if there's any connection between Cook and the trial; that's all I really need to know. You could do that, couldn't you, Harvey? I mean, a man in your position would surely have the authority to look at the file. Wouldn't he? Harvey?"

"Yes, well, uh, I do of course have a clearance that allows me to examine *any* of the files," Harvey said officiously. "But it's highly irregular."

"Can't you make an exception, just this once?" Paula sighed.

Harvey stood up and placed his hand on Paula's shoulder, massaging it awkwardly. "I'll see what I can do."

Harvey was gone for a little more than thirty minutes before he reappeared with a thick file folder in his hands. Placing it on the desk, he said to Paula, "I have to go down the hall to see a friend. I shouldn't be gone more than ten minutes or so." He winked at Paula and patted her shoulder. "Keep an eye on that file for me, will you? I really shouldn't allow it out of my sight."

The moment Harvey left the office, Paula fell to reading the file. It soon became evident why the file was classified secret; most of John Cook's military career was with the OSS—the Office of Strategic Services—in Europe during World War II. Paula skimmed quickly through the information covering his assignments prior to 1945—parachute drops behind enemy lines, an assassination of a double agent in the Polish underground, and an assortment of covert assignments in Sweden and Switzerland—and concentrated on the years immediately following the war. She soon found what she was looking for.

John Cook, at age twenty-six, was attached to the Research and Analysis Branch of the Office of Strategic Services. Because he spoke fluent German, he was assigned to work with the preparatory staff of the war-crimes trials, helping to interrogate prisoners and prepare briefs against the Nazi war criminals, among whom was Waffen SS Lieutenant General Karl Dennecker. When President Truman disbanded the OSS in September 1945, Cook stayed on with the preparatory staff to help with the subsequent trials, and later worked briefly with the High Commissioner's Office. He returned to the United Sates in 1948 and went into private business in Phoenix, Arizona.

Paula was back in her chair at the side of the desk no more than a few seconds when Harvey returned to the office. "Well," he said, fondling the back of Paula's neck, "I hope you found something to keep you occupied while I was gone."

"Oh, yes," Paula replied, removing his hand and slapping it lightly as one would a naughty child's. "It was most enlightening."

Harvey sat at his desk, leaning forward and smirking at her. "Anything else I can help you with?"

"No thank you, Harvey. You've been most helpful. Well . . ." She got up and held out her hand. "If I'm going to get back to New York at a decent hour, I'd better get started."

Ignoring her outstretched hand, Harvey put his arm around

her, squeezing her clumsily. "I'll call you next week and we can set something up."

Paula extracted herself from his grip, causing him to lose his balance. He kept himself from falling by placing his hand on the desk top, a move which scattered the blotter, ashtray, calendar, and telephone. He turned to Paula as though nothing had happened. "It has certainly been nice seeing you again, Paula, and I look forward to our next meeting."

"Yes, it certainly has, Harvey," Paula replied, managing not to laugh, "and thanks again for all your coordination . . . I mean cooperation!"

That evening, through a prodigious effort born of guilt, Paula managed to complete the article for *Esquire;* it was now or never, she had reasoned. Al Verity was enthusiastic about her progress with the Dennecker investigation—meaning he had no negative comments—and agreed with the logic of her next angle of attack. "Pour it on," he told her.

It took four calls to reach Callahan, or to get him to answer the phone, she wasn't sure which.

"Germany!" he said, after she told him what she had learned and decided. "Why Germany?"

"I'll tell you when you get here. Can you manage it?"

Callahan hesitated for a moment. "I can board Boomer with Sam Elkins," he said, thinking aloud, "and Kurt doesn't need me this time of year. How long?"

"A week, maybe two," Paula said. "How soon can you get here?"

"How soon do you plan to leave?"

"As soon as possible."

"Give me three days."

Paula had ulterior motives for wanting Callahan along: it would be a convenient, synergistic alliance, he spoke fluent German, and if things got rough he could handle it—that's what she told herself, while admitting that being with him again would be pleasant.

Callahan had been fighting the urge to go to Phoenix and confront John Cook and his men. The invitation from Paula was the nudge he needed to direct him away from a move he knew would be ill-advised at this point. He wasn't interested in the enigma of Dennecker's code, only in the people responsible for the intrusion into his life and in honoring his commitment to Popcorn.

For him there were no more inviolate childish beliefs; the secret garden had long been discovered and littered with protest placards, hazarded by terrorist bombs, and invaded by indolent hordes celebrating the age of undeserved entitlement. He cared only on an individual basis; he was seasoned and wisened by exposure, past caring and believing in a brain-damaged world beyond redemption, a world of anomie where the abnormal and perverse were given credence and accepted as normal. It was a descending spiral, perhaps brought on by Dennecker and his ilk. Perhaps the Nazis were the beginning of, and justification for, this age of terror and violence, making everything seem permissible by the sheer brutality of their acts—what could be more obscene than the systematic annihilation of millions simply because of race or religion?

He decided to join Paula only because he wanted to spend more time with her. Like most Aspen locals, he vacationed twice each year, in May and November. He had a diving trip to Cozumel planned for the middle of November, returning in time for the opening of the lifts, but he had done that the past three years, and he hadn't been to Europe since he was stationed in Germany. He had no qualms about boarding Boomer with Elkins. Sam always took him home for the duration; his wife loved Boomer.

He called Kurt and ~~brought him up~~ to date on Dennecker, and the following day dropped Boomer off at Elkins's.

"Why Germany?" Callahan asked Paula on the drive from the airport to the city. "The people involved are all in this country."

"I agree that the logical approach would be to question the men on the list," Paula said, "but if they are behind what happened in Aspen—and Cook's men make a strong case for that—we certainly aren't going to do ourselves any good by letting them know what we're up to. And," she added, raising a finger to make a point, "considering how we came into possession of Dennecker's little book, there's a definite possibility that no one knows we have it."

Callahan grunted in tentative agreement. "The only name not connected with Dennecker's trial is Frederich Bauer. Maybe we should concentrate on him."

"I don't think so," Paula said. "I think Dennecker should be the target. If we find out all there is to know about him, Bauer's involvement will eventually fall into place."

"If you're considering Germany as a source of information for Dennecker's past, you couldn't choose a worse place," Jack replied. "Anyone old enough to have been involved in the war isn't going to be very eager to talk about it, and with good reason."

"I'm aware of that, Callahan," Paula conceded, "but there *are* official agencies in the German government that keep extensive records of that period. Our National Archives have information on Dennecker's trial only because that's the only direct contact our government ever had with him. The German records will be far more complete, starting with the day he was born, and knowing them, probably how often he changed his socks."

"But how willing are they to open up their files to outsiders?"

"Believe me," Paula said, "they are most cooperative. They can't risk being accused of covering up the past."

Jack reflected on Kurt Bierman's recent experience with the Germans' openness and contriteness about the past; their idea of atonement was to deny culpability.

Kurt had returned to Germany, to Dusseldorf, in 1977 to testify at the trial of former concentration camp guards and officials of the Maidanek camp where he had been before being transferred to Buchenwald. He was grilled and bullied and warned of giving false testimony at the risk of being tried himself for perjury.

The accused, guilty to varying degrees of gassing, beating, hanging, burning, or starving to death hundreds of thousands of inmates, were, by the defense attorneys, made to seem the victims. The denials and attempts to discredit the witnesses were shocking to those who had suffered at the hands of the Nazis—the diary of Anne Frank was a well-known forgery, the assertion that six million Jews had died in the camps was preposterous, the alleged war crimes of the Nazi era were absurd and at best grossly exaggerated beyond the point of credibility. The charges against the deputy commander of the Maidanek death camp were dismissed as being prejudiced and unsubstantiated.

The onlookers in the courtroom had laughed at Kurt when, during cross-examination, the defense attorney ridiculed him and claimed that his entire testimony should be stricken as ridiculous and inaccurate. Kurt, in a tearful, angry outburst, raged that the deaths of his wife and daughters were not exaggerations or absurd abstractions. He was told that any further disruptions on his part would result in a contempt charge.

The experience had had a devastating effect on him, and Jack recalled that it was months before Kurt was himself again.

"I don't know," Callahan said, still unconvinced. "I understand that there are quite a few ex-Nazis in positions of authority in the West German government today, and they've had ample opportunity over the past thirty-four years to rearrange history to suit their purposes. They have a lot to lose if the truth were known. It doesn't add up to a very promising trip."

"It's worth a try," Paula said, after a few moments of silence. "And something else occurred to me. It might be a good idea to look up Dennecker's lawyer. Who would know more about what was going through Dennecker's mind at the time of his trial, and during his prison term?"

Callahan's admiration was genuine. "That's an excellent idea."

"I think so, too. He could give us a wealth of information about the precise time period Senator Hill, Judge White, and John Cook came into Dennecker's life," Paula said, filled with enthusiasm.

"He might . . . if he's willing to talk to us."

"We'll never know if we don't try," Paula said. "And I think approaching him cold will be the best way."

"What do you know about him?" Jack asked.

"Only his name and address, which were listed in the archives files. Ernst Froeschmann from Fürstenfeldbruck. Where the hell is Fürstenfeldbruck?"

Callahan knew the area well; it wasn't far from where he had been stationed in Bad Tolz. "It's a town on the Amper River, about ten miles west of Munich."

"You do know Germany," she said, duly impressed. "I couldn't find it on the map."

"I know that section," Jack said. "We played war games with the West German army all throughout that area."

"Well?" Paula asked.

"Well what?" Jack said playfully.

"You're still going with me then? You haven't changed your mind?"

Callahan nodded.

"Good," Paula said, kissing him on the cheek. "We can get a flight out tomorrow night."

"That kiss had better not be an indication of how this trip is going to go," he said jokingly, taking her in his arms and kissing her properly.

"Not on your life, Callahan," she said, responding warmly.

TEN

"Why are they going to Germany?" Cook asked.

"To dig into Dennecker's past and to interview the lawyer who represented him at Nuremberg," Candellari replied. "The girl made reservations on Lufthansa for an open-ended ticket to Munich, and booked a room at the Munich Hilton for tomorrow."

Cook smiled as Ernst Froeschmann's face flashed before him; that base was well covered. "Where are you?" he asked Candellari.

"New York City. I followed Callahan here. Do you want us to continue surveillance in Germany?"

"Yes, but again, no personal contact. Give them a wide berth; I don't want them spooked."

"Sir," Candellari said, making his question as inoffensive as possible, "don't you think it's time you filled me in on this so I know what I'm dealing with? It's impossible for me to anticipate their moves and plan ahead without knowing precisely what we don't want them to find."

"No," Cook replied curtly. "Just keep me informed on what they are doing."

"Yes, sir," Candellari said, recognizing the finality in his tone. "I'll report in as soon as I have anything."

Cook was disturbed by the involvement of the *Time* editor; the last thing he needed was that pack of relentless bloodhounds getting the scent. He would have to evaluate the information the girl uncovered carefully and make certain that any hard evidence, if any existed, was destroyed before it could be used. He smiled inwardly, aware that the tension and nervousness in his stomach were no longer present—he was conditioned now to see this thing through to a final burial.

His thoughts drifted back to an interrogation room in the prison behind the Palace of Justice in Nuremberg, thirty-three years ago; his first meeting with Dennecker.

Dennecker was stripped of his personal belongings and clothed in an ill-fitting, inexpensive suit; his army-issue shoes flopped as he walked and he had to hold up his trousers when standing—shoelaces and belts were confiscated after two of the prisoners had hanged themselves.

But from the moment the MP removed the handcuffs and Dennecker entered the room, Cook knew that this was not a man who would take his own life. His suit was rumpled and dirty, his hair shaggy, and his pale face was covered with a stubbly beard, but despite the purposely degrading conditions, he emanated a strong sense of pride and self-assurance. Standing tall and erect, his eyes calm and hard, he was composed, defiant, unbroken by the probability of his being sentenced to death.

During the third day of interrogation, he attempted to strike his bargain. Initially, the arrangement he suggested offended Cook, making him wonder what innate weakness this arrogant man had detected in him that made him believe he was susceptible to the venality of his proposal. Only days later, after sleepless nights and preoccupation with its possibilities, did it begin to work its insidious way into the very fiber of his being. The intervening sessions brought no further mention of the subject from Dennecker, but when Cook finally told him, after much anguish and soul-searching, that he would pursue it to the extent of attempting to enlist the aid of the others required, Dennecker had smiled knowingly, as though there had never been any doubt about the outcome.

Cook reflected on the scheme eventually decided upon to deal with him; it had seemed foolproof, given the situation and the mood of the times, but Dennecker was an extraordinary man and had managed to elude their grasp despite their best efforts. When he had sought them out after his release from prison, Hill, in a moment of panic, had argued for killing him, but Cook's logic had prevailed; they didn't know what arrangements he had made for just such an eventuality, and if they failed in their attempt, he would be an awesome foe to deal with—they had learned to live with his demands.

Cook fixed a drink and walked across the terrace to the gardens. Sitting on a specially placed meditation bench, he watched the desert sunset and felt the cool evening air descend. In light of the recent developments, he decided it was time for a meeting. He would call Tom Hill tomorrow.

Senator Hill paused for a moment between the stone gateposts framing the entrance to his driveway. The view from this vantage point always filled him with a feeling of accomplishment, of having arrived where he had always wanted to be. From here he could see most of his fifty acres of the magnificent, gently rolling countryside of Chester County, Pennsylvania. When he had purchased the property thirty years before, it was a simple farm with an eighteenth-century farmhouse, badly in need of repair, a dilapidated barn, and a few collapsed outbuildings; now, after countless man-hours and a few hundred thousand dollars, it was one of the most beautiful estates in the area. There had been additions to the house, in keeping with the basic architecture of the period; renovations included new wiring and plumbing, central air conditioning, and all the modern conveniences. The horse barn had been completely rebuilt, using steel beam supports where needed, assuring another two hundred years of service. He had forgotten how many tens of thousands of dollars had been spent on landscaping, ponds, and finishing touches such as placing all the wiring underground and stowing the television antennas in a crawl space in the attic. The latest addition, and the last—at least that's what he told himself this year—was an Olympic-size swimming pool situated on a hill behind the house overlooking the grounds.

He often reflected that it had not always been this way. He'd not been "born to the purple," as he liked to say. He had vivid memories of the crowded, noisy, squalid four-room apartment above his father's neighborhood bar where he had spent the first sixteen years of his life. He was a far cry from that now, and reveled in it.

He started down the steep hill at the top of the drive, and was doing at least fifty when he reached the bottom and roared across the stone bridge spanning one of the smaller ponds, pressing the accelerator to the floor as he rounded a bend and headed toward the house. There was only one word to describe Tom Hill's driving habits: insane. His wife constantly pleaded with him to at least restrain himself from speeding in the narrow driveway. That habit had already taken its toll. Over the years the Senator had run down three dogs, two of his son's pet ducks, and five kittens, and had damn near killed one of the groundskeepers when he crashed into his tractor, sending him flying through the air, fortunately into a haystack. In a fit of anger one summer, after the Senator had narrowly avoided hitting one of her friends, Janet Hill had decided to take some positive action. While the Senator was away on a fact-finding tour of Vietnam, she'd had the driveway resurfaced, with raised strips in the macadam spaced at intervals from the bridge to the house, giving the driveway a washboard effect. However, when the Senator had returned to Washington and called to tell her he would be home that evening, she had neglected to mention what she had done. Hill had sped across the bridge in his usual abandoned manner and started the mad dash to the house. He was airborne before he knew what happened, landing full force on another of the bumps, nearly separating the car from its frame and slamming his head against the steering wheel. The drive to the Chester County hospital, for the fourteen stitches required to close the gash, was a silent one. Three days later, the driveway was resurfaced to a smooth finish.

Senator Hill parked in the cobblestoned area in front of the house and slammed the door violently as he got out of the car. He was annoyed by a conversation he had just had with a township official over lunch—their new zoning laws were interfering with the progress of a housing developement he had invested heavily in. His aide, Harry Talbot, was sitting on the patio that overlooked the largest of the ponds. Talbot was spending the weekend in the guest house, working on a bill the Senator was taking to committee the following week. He got up and sauntered over to greet the Senator.

"Have a nice lunch, Senator?" Talbot asked.

"I've had better," Tom Hill growled.

"John Cook called while you were gone."

"Call him back," he said, brushing aside the English sheepdog, Janet's pet, that jumped up to greet him, soiling his beige linen suit. "Goddam brainless beast. I'm going for a swim," he grumbled, wiping away some of the dirt with his hankerchief. "Bring the extension phone to the pool and plug it in," he yelled.

"Mrs. Hill said to tell you she would be home around five," Talbot called after him. "She went to the Hunt Club with some of her friends."

The soiled suit put him in an even blacker mood. The Senator was a natty dresser, proud of his custom-tailored, extensive wardrobe, conservative, but obviously expensive. All part of the image he strove to project. His speech and mannerisms when before the public were calculated to give the impression of breeding, Ivy League education and all, but when angered, or after a few drinks with people he didn't feel the need to impress, the foulmouthed, beerhall braggart surfaced. In private he was a crude, vulgar man. Professionally, he was a charmer who could smooth ruffled feathers with a disarming smile and an eloquent line.

The last of a vanishing breed—the solidly entrenched, power-wielding, backslapping, pure Washington animal—he had few friends in the Senate, but even fewer enemies who had the courage to challenge him; his power was acknowledged and feared. He had told many of his fellow Senators he didn't give a damn about their respect, just as long as they recognized his clout and his expertise in applying it. His effectiveness in manipulating his colleagues was further extended to the proper representation of his constituents, making certain they got a healthy slice of the federal pie.

Knowing that attention to the voters back home was the key to reelection, he had made an art of the practice: a weekly television show taped for the local stations, touting his accomplishments; street festival and parade appearances; job-creating federal projects, recreational dams, parks, and anything else he could manage to steer their way with his considerable influence. His simple credo was: Give them what you promised . . . or a reasonable facsimile. And if judged by what he achieved, measured against his stated objectives and promises, he was an effective legislator.

Not an intellectual lightweight, he had graduated at the top of his class in college and law school. He had a brilliant if misdirected mind, and channeled a great deal of his efforts in a profitable direction. He had used his publicity from the war-crimes trials to capture a seat in the Senate, vacated by an untimely death, after only one term in the House of

Representatives. It didn't take him long to learn the rudiments of abusing his office and the privileges that went with it, polishing those tactics in the years that followed. Corporations with vested interests in bills before the committees he sat on beat a path to his door, fat wallets and fringe benefits in hand. Government payroll funds were put to unauthorized, self-serving use, and campaign contributions were used for a variety of miscellaneous personal matters.

His press relations and public image were excellent; he was known as a hardworking, diligent, uncompromising champion of the People, no small feat, considering the aggressiveness of the investigative reporters and his worsening attendance record in the Senate—exceeded only by that of an ancient and senile member who had great difficulty each morning remembering who he was, let alone where he was supposed to be or why.

There were rumors about some of his shadier dealings, but there was no hard evidence; he covered his tracks well. Those of his fellow Senators who knew some of the facts kept the time-honored tradition of keeping it within the Club. His occasional well-prepared, grandiloquent appearances on the Senate floor were perfectly timed and limited to the most popular and controversial issues of the day, assuring him of maximum press coverage. He even looked the part he was playing, a large, broad-shouldered man, classic profile, silver-gray hair; a bit fleshy, but for sixty-four years old, a still-arresting, even dashing figure.

The Senator stripped off his clothes as he proceeded up the flagstone path to the pool. He changed to his swim suit in one of the dressing rooms in the pool house. Glancing at the shrubs just planted along the edge of the deck, he made a mental note to have the hideous golden arborvitae removed. "Goddam junk," he mumbled. "One step above a plastic plant."

He was holding on to the side of the pool, catching his breath, after completing six full laps, when Talbot arrived with the extension phone, plugging it into an outlet at the pool house.

"Mr. Cook's secretary said he was in conference," Talbot reported. "She'll have him call as soon as he's available."

"Conference," the Senator grunted. "He's probably having a quickie on his goddam desk."

Talbot chuckled dutifully. "Another call came in, just before

I came up," he said, anticipating the Senator's reaction. "Congresswoman Delgotto. She wants you to call her immediately. I told her I wasn't sure you were here, but I'd try to locate you. She told me to cut the crap and to tell you it was urgent."

Tom Hill did not take kindly to liberals, and Congresswoman Delgotto was his *bête noire*. "Do you know what that slutty idiot wants?" he asked rhetorically. "She wants me to muster support from my connections in the House for another one of her giveaway bills for the welfare slugs and human defectives she represents. I won't give her the time of day."

"May I remind the Senator," Talbot said gingerly, "that she has hinted at returning the favor with some help on the Cottman issue."

The Senator roared with laughter. "If God loved cheerful liars, he'd hug her to death. I can't think of a single pertinent issue on which we agree. She'd stab me in the back and twist the knife if she could. Fuck her!"

"You wouldn't want to do that, Senator," Talbot said, straight-faced.

"You bet I wouldn't," Hill said, breaking into another raucous laugh. "My career couldn't stand an indictment for bestiality; might cause people to have grave misgivings about my sterling character and good taste."

"If she calls back," Talbot offered, "I'll tell her you are aware of her situation and are taking the matter under advisement."

"You do that, Harry," the Senator said, swiping his hair away from his eyes. "And you can further advise her I am a man who fully appreciates the value of discussion and disagreement, but at the moment I am not up to listening to any of her pseudo-intellectual, dumb-assed convolutions."

Talbot hesitated before bringing the next matter to the Senator's attention, but with Mrs. Hill out for the afternoon and no one else around, he decided the possibility of being overheard was virtually nonexistent. "Just before I left the office in Washington, Senator," he said, lowering his voice, "one of the secretaries gave me a message for you to call the guest staying at your Georgetown house. She said the young lady who called seemed troubled. Or drunk. Or both."

The Senator let out an elongated groan. "Damn her! I told her to use my private line when she calls the office. Goddam stupid bitch. Every time I leave her alone she smokes that goddam weed and sops up every ounce of booze in the house, then gets a case of the mad staggers and goes out shopping. She's getting a reputation, Harry, and people are beginning to tie her to me. We're going to have to send her packing; she's getting to be a distinct liability."

Talbot was well aware of Kathy's potential liabilities. He had lunch with her a few times a week, at the Senator's request, to occupy some of her time and keep her under control. She had been living at the Senator's fashionable Georgetown home for the past ten months, serving as a hostess for some of his more lavish parties and sharing his bed whenever he was in the mood. She was an outrageously sexy girl, but also the stupidest human being Harry Talbot had ever encountered. The Senator never unleashed her for any of Washington's official functions, keeping her well out of sight of his critics and colleagues. However, in the last month, she had become increasingly hard to handle, on the brink of becoming an embarrassment and a burden. It was only a matter of time before she did some irreparable damage.

"When I had lunch with her on Wednesday," Talbot said, "she was adamant about not wanting to stay locked up in the house anymore."

"What the hell *does* she want?"

"To work in your office," Talbot replied, bracing himself.

The Senator pulled himself out of the water and settled on the edge of the pool.

"That's not even funny, Harry. My once powerful and highly esteemed friend from Ohio pushed a self-destruct button on his life by having his dimwitted concubine on the payroll when she couldn't type, and I'm not about to suffer the same fate over a giant set of tits. I don't believe Kathy can even *read*, for Christ's sake! You'd have to prepare a whole brochure to explain her to the rest of the staff! It wouldn't take the jackals long to pick my bones clean once they caught sight of that dunderhead." He motioned to Talbot to hand him the towel on one of the lounge chairs. "She's got to go. Give her a few thou with the stipulation that she leave town." He stared thoughtfully at Talbot for a moment, then said, "Call Tony Matolla in Las Vegas. He owes me a few favors. Tell him to get her a job in one of his girlie shows."

"I'll take care of it as soon as I get back to Washington," Talbot said. "Would you care for a drink, Senator?"

"Yes, I would. Scotch and water." His voice was muffled by the towel as he dried his hair.

The telephone rang as Talbot came out of the pool house with the Scotch. "It's Mr. Cook, Senator," he said, bringing the phone to the side of the pool.

"Sorry to keep you waiting, Tom," Cook said. "I was in the middle of a board meeting."

"Have you sewed up that new Defense contract?"

"We've run into a few snags," Cook said. "Those Pentagon pencil pushers are getting sticky about cost-overrun clauses, and General Baker isn't pulling his weight when it's needed. I told you when you asked me to put him on the board that he wasn't worth a tinker's damn, and he's proven me right ever since."

"Don't be too hard on the general," the Senator rumbled. "We owe him. He's responsible for sending one hell of a lot of fat contracts your way in the last twenty-five years."

"That was then, Tom," Cook said sarcastically. "He's excess baggage now."

"Live with it," Hill snapped. "If nothing else, he's good window dressing." At times, Hill resented Cook's superior attitude. Still, he admired his intelligence and strong-mindedness. When he had first met him in Nuremberg, after the war, he had recognized in Cook what he considered to be the three most important ingredients for success: singleness of purpose, dedication, and total indifference. He had purchased a large block of stock in the electronics company Cook started in 1950, and with Cook's business expertise, and his own seat on the Armed Services committee and connections in the Pentagon, the company had grown to be one of the country's largest defense contractors, specializing in highly sophisticated, top-secret electronic gadgetry used in satellites and missile defense systems. Cook was shrewd, opportunistic, tough, and methodical—a survivor. When he had first come to Hill in Nuremberg, with his plan concerning Dennecker, the Senator never had had a single doubt about their ability to pull the deal off. However, the recent developments Cook had been keeping him abreast of were beginning to give him an uneasy feeling in the pit of his stomach.

"What was it you called about?" the Senator asked, changing the subject.

"Some further developments on the Dennecker business," Cook replied. "I think it would be best if we all get together and discuss the whole matter at length. Things have taken a turn for the worse since I last talked to you; nothing terminal, but the opposition has caught the scent and are closing in."

"Shit!" Hill said. "Where do you want to meet?"

"Your place in Pennsylvania would be best, I think."

The Senator gulped the remaining Scotch, and indicated to Talbot to refill his glass. "I don't have anything on for tomorrow I can't cancel," Hill said.

"Tomorrow will be fine," Cook agreed. "I'll call Ed White in Cincinnati and pick him up on the way in."

"How much have you told Ed about what's going on?" Hill asked, remembering what a nervous little twit the judge was, like a rabbit, always on the alert for impending disaster. He was the one weak link in the chain. Unfortunately, it had been necessary at the outset to include him in the scheme. The Senator hadn't seen him in twenty years, and at that time, twelve full years after the trial, he was still looking over his shoulder. He never did understand why the judge had agreed to go along with them; it was completely out of character.

"I only told him somebody was digging into the past," Cook replied. "I was reluctant to go into any details. You know the judge—he might panic and get diarrhea of the soul and go whimpering to the Justice Department and blurt out the whole story."

"Did he seem upset when you told him?" Hill asked.

"I couldn't really tell. There were some long silences on his part. My guess is he hasn't slept much since." He glanced at a flight chart on his desk. "I don't want to fly into Philadelphia International; the service there for private planes is miserable. I see on my chart that there's an airport near Avondale: New Garden. They have four thousand feet of runway, a tight squeeze for a Lear jet, but it'll have to do."

"That's only ten minutes from here," Hill said. "Call me when you leave Cincinnati and I'll meet you when you land."

"We'll leave Phoenix at nine o'clock sharp your time. If we have a decent tail wind, and a quick stop in Cincinnati," Cook said, making a few quick mental calculations, "we should get to New Garden between one and one-thirty. If it's going to be any later, I'll call."

* * *

The Senator hung up and handed the phone to Talbot. "I'm going to have some guests tomorrow, Harry, and no offense, but I'd like you to make yourself scarce."

"I understand, Senator," Talbot said. "I was hoping for a chance to see the new exhibit at the Brandywine Museum. Tomorrow would be a good time."

Judge White scraped the mud from his shoes before entering the kitchen. He was tired, and his back ached a little from the afternoon's work in his vegetable garden, but it was a good feeling. He spent most of his spare time in the garden, and received more than a little criticism about it from his wife, who couldn't appreciate the pleasure he got from making things grow. Their marriage had deteriorated in the past ten years to a point beyond reconciliation, and the garden had become a retreat to which he could escape from Carla's constant nagging. Any objective observer who knew them could have told from the start that the marriage was doomed; the judge was a quiet, private, inward man, with an intellect far superior to his wife's, and Carla was a boorish, shallow social butterfly with a country-club mentality. They had discussed the possibility of divorce and decided against it, each for his own reasons. The judge thought it best to stay together for the children's sake, and Carla simply enjoyed being Mrs. Edward T. White, wife of the supreme court justice. The judge couldn't recall one full day of happiness or contentment with her since they were married. God knows he had tried. It was because of her he had gotten involved in this Dennecker mess. During the first few years of their marriage, he thought they had had enough money and luxuries to overcome her basic insecurities and make her happy, but for Carla there had never been enough. The small estate on a hill overlooking the city, far beyond the means of a newly appointed judge, had been only the beginning. There flowed a constant stream of outrageous bills every month, for clothing, jewelry, and floral arrangements. The ones from her beauty salon staggered the imagination. Not a year went by without at least three or four rooms in the house being redecorated with the costliest fabrics and overpriced antiques and oriental rugs. Carla's latest status symbol had been delivered the previous day: a new, limited-production Mercedes 6.9, capable of cruising at 130 mph; a striking contrast to the

Judge's 1971 Buick sedan, and a tacit comment on the difference in their personalities.

The only worthwhile things that ever materialized from their marriage were their two daughters, Lisa and Emmy, both beautiful girls, getting their looks from their mother and (thank God, the judge often thought) their character from him.

Carla White had just finished changing after her tennis match at the country club and was sitting in the kitchen, having a cup of yogurt, when the judge entered.

"My Lord, Ed," she said, giving him a disdainful glance, "you look like a vagrant! Be sure you change before our dinner guests arrive. I'd hate for them to see you like that."

"Who's coming?" he asked. "It's getting so I can't keep track of the players without a scorecard. We haven't had one peaceful evening in the past two weeks."

"It's better for you than burying your head in some damn book," she said scornfully.

"I'd recommend you try a book, dear," he said softly, "but I suppose it's better to keep your illusions."

"Roger Davis and his wife are coming for dinner," she said, ignoring his last remark. "He's the new attorney who just joined Jack Milroy's firm. I met his wife at the club; she's absolutely charming. He's most eager to meet you, so try and be a bit more sociable than usual."

The judge was familiar with Milroy's law firm, an unscrupulous pack of ambulance-chasing whiplash specialists, with one of the worst reputations in the city. It was too much to expect Carla to invite anyone worth talking to. Her crowd's idea of raising the level of conversation was by decibels, with the volume increasing in direct proportion to the amount of alcohol consumed. He poured himself a glass of orange juice and started to leave the kitchen.

"By the way, Ed," Carla said, "please don't talk about your damn vegetable garden tonight. The last time you did that, you gave everyone a case of the early yawns. Believe me, dear, no one cares a hoot about the growth rate of your frigging melons and beans."

The judge smiled grimly. "Any other last-minute instructions?"

"Just one," she said, gritting her teeth. "Get out of my sight, you sanctimonious sorry son of a bitch!"

Judge White straightened his tie, put on his sport coat, and went downstairs to the library to read until the dinner guests arrived. He selected a recently acquired leather-bound volume of W.H. Auden's poems and settled down in his favorite chair next to the window. He hadn't finished the first poem when the telephone rang.

"We're all going to meet at the Senator's tomorrow in Pennsylvania," Cook told him. "There have been further developments concerning the matter we discussed last week."

"What developments?" the judge asked nervously.

"It's not anything I care to discuss over the phone," Cook said firmly. "But the sky isn't falling, so just relax. I'll pick you up at Lunken airport around noon tomorrow. I'll be in a red-and-white Lear jet; the last three identification numbers are 097. Please be prompt, Ed," he said, hanging up abruptly.

The judge sat back in his chair, feeling weak and dizzy. "Damn! Damn! Damn!" he swore softly. "After all these years!"

There was a light knock on the library door, and his daughter Lisa entered. She went over to where he was sitting, gave him an affectionate hug and an understanding look.

"I gather from Mom's mood that you two have had another . . . uh . . . discussion," she said sympathetically.

The judge patted the arm of the chair, motioning for her to sit there, and as she perched there he put his arm around her waist. "I'm sorry, honey," he said apologetically, "but it isn't going to get any better."

"I know, Daddy." She kissed his cheek tenderly. "I love you very much."

"I love you, too," he said, rubbing the spot on the small of her back that was always sore after a day of riding. "I wish it could be different between your mother and me, but I'm afraid we're long past that. How did Big John perform today? Did he miss any jumps?"

"Not a single one," she said proudly. "He was magnificent. He's primed and ready for the Louisville show."

"And how did Emmy do?"

"Not too well," Lisa replied, sharing some of her older sister's disappointment. They were very close, and as the judge recalled, had never had the usual childhood problems of sibling rivalry. "Thunder is still having trouble with his leg, and Emmy is thinking of passing up the Louisville show to prepare him for Indianapolis. It's a shame. He's a great horse, with a lot of heart, but he's so prone to muscle pulls."

"I'll talk with her when she gets home," he said reassuringly. "Perhaps we should put Thunder out to pasture and get her a younger mount."

"Oh, Daddy," Lisa said enthusiastically, "that would just make her day. She feels so bad about Thunder, even guilty about riding him at all."

"I'm certain we can work something out," he said. "Are you enjoying your first year of college?"

"Oh, yes," she said, smiling broadly. "With Emmy there, it's a snap learning the ropes, and I especially like being able to come home almost every weekend to ride."

The judge looked into his daughter's eyes for a long moment and squeezed her hand gently. "I love you very much, Lisa," he said emotionally. "I want you to remember that always, no matter what."

Lisa looked at him, puzzled. "Well, sure," she said.

Carla appeared in the doorway and announced that the Davises had arrived, turning on her heel after an approving glance at the way the judge was dressed.

"Mom must be really angry," Lisa said. "She's wearing her highest heels."

The judge smiled. He was five feet seven inches tall, and Carla was an inch and a half taller in stocking feet; in heels she towered over him and so usually wore flats, knowing he preferred her to. "The curse of the Welsh," the judge said with a wink. "Have you ever seen a St. David's Day parade? It's four miles long and five feet high."

"Oh, Daddy! I like you just the way you are . . . tiny." She let out her infectious laugh, and the judge joined in.

"Are you ready for another evening of sparkling conversation and brilliant wit?" he asked.

"Maybe it won't be so bad," she said.

"Would you like to place a small wager on that?"

Lisa shook her head.

The Judge put his arm around her shoulder and escorted her to the living room, where Carla was already handing around drinks.

Lisa whispered in her father's ear as they entered the room, "Tell them how well your tomatoes are doing, Daddy. That always sends them stampeding for the door."

The judge broke into a hearty laugh, the kind only Lisa could get from him. Carla cast an angry glance in their direction.

John Cook sat comfortably stretched out in the passenger section of his private plane, carefully reading a feasibility study given him the previous day by the head of his engineering department, on a projected modification for a revolutionary miniaturized power source for lasers now in the early production stages. If the engineers' assessments were correct, and they usually were, the nagging problems they were having with the highly sophisticated unit should be over, but the cost overruns on the government-supplied equipment, design changes, and inflation still had to be brought under control. His concentration was interrupted by the co-pilot's voice as he reported his position to Lunken tower.

"Report at the outer marker," the tower directed.

Cook heard two clicks, the co-pilot acknowledging receipt of the instructions by pressing the microphone button twice—accepted procedure, but not the way Candellari would have done it; he went by the book. The pilot Cook had hired temporarily in Candellari's absence was good, but not as smooth and efficient.

Judge White watched the sleek, fighter like jet scream down the runway, roar momentarily when the pilot reversed thrust, and taxi to the ramp in front of the terminal. A small door just behind the cockpit opened and the co-pilot got out, followed by the pilot, and then Cook emerged.

The judge hadn't seen him in ten years, and he looked much the same; perhaps a little more gray and a few more facial lines, but the same trim, cold, emotionless predator. He walked out to where Cook was standing, giving instructions to the pilot.

"Have the tanks only half filled," he said. "I'd prefer taking off from that four-thousand-foot strip in Pennsylvania with a light load." He turned away from the two men and greeted the judge with a smile that wasn't a smile. "We'll leave in a few minutes, Ed, after the boys check the weather."

The judge had never liked Cook. From the moment they had first met in Nuremberg, Cook had struck him as a man not to be trusted. There was something frightening about him, an aura of evil that made the most secure and self-confident of men uneasy in his presence. His air of authority was out of proportion to his physical size; he was of medium height, small-boned and wiry, with catlike reflexes. His was a mind trained to spot any sign of weakness and exploit it to his advantage. He was, in Judge White's opinion, the quintessential Machiavellian type.

"What are the recent developments you mentioned yesterday?" the judge asked. He had slept fitfully, several times waking drenched with perspiration, anticipating the worst.

"Nothing that can't wait until we get to the Senator's," Cook said, taking a sadistic pleasure in the judge's obvious anxiety. "Get on board," he commanded, seeing the pilot and co-pilot coming out of the terminal.

Cook rudely ignored two attempts by the judge at idle conversation on the flight to Pennsylvania, staring out the window, in a bitter mood after reading a letter received that morning from his son; the third such letter, begging him to help get him out of the Mexican prison.

"Stupid, irresponsible son of a bitch," he muttered under his breath. He had no intention of lifting a finger to help this time. He had given the boy every opportunity to straighten out his life; this time he would have to pay the piper. Ever since they had taken his wife away in a straitjacket, he had overindulged his son, providing him with the best of everything: boarding schools, clothes, cars, and an allowance exceeding the salaries of some of his executives. There was a limit to what he could be expected to do, and he had reached it. As far as he was concerned, he no longer had a son.

The judge sat quietly, watching the scenery stream by below, reflecting on Nuremberg, Dennecker, and his involvement in a scheme that contrasted so drastically with everything he believed in. He recalled the mixed emotions he felt when learning of Dennecker's commutation of sentence and subsequent release from prison—relief at not being responsible for an unjustifiable execution, and fear. The fear had decreased in intensity over the years, once the unknown quantities became known, but had never left him completely. He had never in his life, before or since the Dennecker incident, done anything of which he felt ashamed, or which compromised his principles. But that was no consolation now; he would pay—was paying—for his one moment of weakness, his only betrayal of his own values. It seemed to him inevitable that Dennecker would reach from the grave to have his final revenge.

"Mr. Cook," the pilot announced over the intercom, "I suggest you cinch your seatbelt snug. This four-thousand-foot strip isn't exactly going to leave us a hell of a lot of margin for error. I might have to stand on the brakes some."

The pilot hadn't understated the situation; he had to use every inch of the runway and apply the brakes most of the way. The judge, knuckles white from his grip on the armrest, felt certain they were going to run off the end and cut a path through the woods. Cook looked at him and laughed.

The ride from the airport, with the Senator driving, was an even more harrowing experience for the judge. After turning off the main highway onto a secondary road leading to his home, Hill sped recklessly through the S turns and hairpin curves on the dangerously narrow road. The suspension on the overweight and underengineered Lincoln was not intended for high-speed maneuvering, and the clumsy car swayed precariously with each violent turn. Judge White braced himself in the back seat to avoid being tossed about like a rag doll.

"If you insist on driving like a maniac, Tom," Cook said coldly, "it might be wise to invest in a Mercedes or a Ferrari, something to compensate for your lack of skill."

"I wouldn't buy any of that foreign crap," the Senator replied, straying out to the middle of the road halfway through another turn. "It wouldn't look right for a United States Senator to be driving a Nazi staff car, or a Wop hotrod."

Cook laughed. "You're consistent, Tom," he said. "I can't remember when you weren't a narrow-minded, image-conscious bigot." The Senator glanced at him and winked.

Judge White got out of the car, happy to have survived the ride, and followed Cook and the Senator across the lawn to a narrow footbridge leading to a small island on the largest of the ponds. They sat in lounge chairs surrounding a table beneath a huge old weeping willow.

"Will one of you be kind enough to bring me up to date?" the judge asked, at the end of his patience. "I didn't come here to listen to you two discuss the relative merits of your respective mistresses," he said, referring to the past fifteen minutes of small talk.

"I suppose we'd better get down to business," the Senator said, "before Ed here has a stroke."

"The two people I told you about," Cook said to the judge, "have gotten to the point where they have something to work with—our names and the fact that we were involved with Dennecker's trial—"

"That's a matter of public record," the judge interrupted. "Why should that concern us?"

"It's what they found when Dennecker died, and what they suspect, that concerns us," Cook said brusquely. "They found an address book in which Dennecker had written our names and the name of Frederich Bauer of Long Island. Our names encoded and kept hidden by Dennecker aroused the curiosity of the girl."

"Who are these people doing the investigating?" Judge White asked.

"The girl is Paula Carlson, a free-lance journalist from New York City, and a friend of hers, Jack Callahan, a ski instructor from Aspen who may be more than he seems."

"Much more," the Senator added. "I had his military record pulled and ran a check on him after you told me about the photographs in his house. He's an ex–Green Beret, awarded the DSC in Vietnam, and was a mercenary in Rhodesia. There is also a possibility he had CIA connections, although I couldn't verify that. The Special Forces unit he was attached to when he was stationed in Germany was occasionally loaned to the Agency for special operations; that might be the extent of his involvement with them. I'm certain he's not affiliated with them now."

"Who is Frederich Bauer?" the Judge asked.

"He's a bit enigmatic," Cook said. "At least to the extent of why his name was included on the list with ours. He's a German expatriate businessman who spent the war years in South America; there seems to be no connection between him and Dennecker that I can find. I think it's a reasonable assumption that he may have had an arrangement with Dennecker similar to our own for the past twenty-four years, although for a totally unrelated reason."

Judge White stared suspiciously at Cook and asked, "What is this free-lance journalist and her friend doing now?"

"They've left for Germany to dig into Dennecker's past and interview the lawyer who represented him at Nuremberg."

Senator Hill raised an eyebrow. "What are their prospects

with him?" he asked, hearing this new wrinkle for the first time.

"They'll get nothing from him," Cook said confidently. "I made certain he understood the rules of the game before I left Germany."

"That was thirty years ago," the Senator said.

"Granted, but with his past he still has a lot to lose. Believe me, he's not a problem."

"There's something you're not telling us about this," the judge said. "It just doesn't make sense that these people would continue this investigation on the strength of our connection with Dennecker's trial. Our names on that list could be rationally explained and accepted as the revenge list of a bitter man. Any investigator, no matter how wet behind the ears, would immediately suspect that as the reason. They must have cause for further suspicions."

Realizing that the judge wouldn't be quieted without an explanation, Cook decided on a half-truth. "I'm afraid it was a slip-up on the part of my men. I sent them to Aspen to see if Dennecker left anything behind that might compromise us, and the ski instructor, Callahan, saw them going through Dennecker's cabin. They had used one of my helicopters to get there, and he traced it back to me."

"Damn!" the judge swore. "If they dig deep enough," he quavered, one hand massaging the other, "they'll find what they're looking for and we'll all be exposed."

"Stop sniveling," Cook said disgustedly.

The judge's face flushed with anger. "I'll not sit here and be insulted by the likes of you," he snapped. "It's your fault we all got involved in this mess."

"I didn't hear you complaining in Nuremberg," Cook observed. "You were more than willing to get involved then."

"Gentlemen," the Senator interrupted, "this is getting us nowhere!" He leaned forward in his chair and spoke directly to the judge. "Ed, the possibility is remote, at best, that any investigation could uncover evidence, after thirty-three years, leaving us open to criminal prosecution, or any legal action whatsoever, for that matter. However, we should worry about the press getting enough information to create a scandal and ruin our lives. As far as I know, the only living witnesses to what took place in Nuremberg in 1947 are seated here at this table, and that doesn't leave them much."

"You're forgetting the photographs," the judge said.

"Those photographs are not conclusive evidence in and of themselves," Cook interjected, "even with the negatives."

"If there is enough circumstantial evidence to support them, they are," the judge argued.

"Dammit, Ed," Cook shouted. "If *we* couldn't get our hands on the photographs, what makes you think anyone else will?"

"They do exist," the judge said intractably. "And so does the person—still unknown to us—who took them,"

"Yes," Cook said. "And if they surface we'll know about it in ample time to do something about them."

"What do you mean, do something?" he asked shrilly. "I won't be a party to any more criminal activities."

"If it comes down to it, *your honor*"—Cook spoke the title disparagingly—"you'll have no choice. But let's not get ahead of ourselves," he added, softening his tone, not wanting to alarm the judge to the point of doing something rash. "The only measures I've taken are personal and electronic surveillance, and if the bugging devices are discovered they can't be traced to us."

"How trustworthy are the men you have on this?" the Senator asked.

"Unquestionably so," Cook replied.

"Aren't you also forgetting our dealings with Dennecker since his release from prison?" the judge asked. "If any of that becomes known it would open up another area of investigation where the trail is far from cold, and provide corroborative evidence of the strongest kind."

"As John said, let's take it one step at a time," the Senator soothed. "There's no reason to suppose that they'll get that far, but even if they do, we've covered our tracks extremely well in our dealings with Dennecker."

"Just to set the record straight, Ed," Cook interposed, "all they've discovered up to now is our connection to Dennecker. They know nothing of the conspiracy itself, or more important, the *reason* for the conspiracy. They have a long road ahead of them, and not much to work with."

The judge sat brooding wearily. It was a convincing argument, and the time factor was certainly in their favor, but he was far from feeling reassured.

The Senator got up and put his hand on the judge's shoulder. "I know this hasn't been easy for you, Ed," he said, "but try not to worry yourself into an early grave. We have things under control, and I'll keep you informed on any further developments. Now if you'll excuse us for a few minutes, John and I have some business to discuss, unrelated to all this. We'll be back shortly."

Senator Hill and Cook walked across the footbridge and around to the far side of the pond. The judge sat staring out across the water, moodily watching a pair of ducks bobbing for food. He envied them.

"Are your men following the girl and Callahan to Germany?" the Senator asked Cook.

"Yes. I've given them instructions to bug their hotel room, and keep them under surveillance, but to stay out of sight. I'm convinced that the proper response at this time is no response at all—give them room and see what they uncover. If we try to retrace our steps at this late date and attempt to cover up any mistakes we made, and they catch wind of our interest, we'll just be encouraging them. Our best bet is to monitor them and step in only when it's absolutely necessary—let them do the work, and if they come up dry, it's over for good. The other alternative is to deal with them now."

"I'd ask you what the hell you mean by that," the Senator said, "but I'm afraid you'd tell me."

"That's right, keep your head buried in the sand; I won't burden you with details. Just understand, though, that if it comes to that, it's counterproductive to treat a cancer like a head cold. You don't fool around with mild remedies, you cut it out. Halfway measures only lead to future complications."

"Don't misunderstand me," the Senator said. "If it's them or us, I'm with you."

"One more thing," Cook said, "the girl, Carlson, has a friend at *Time* with whom she's discussed this, and he has *his* antenna up."

"Christ," the Senator said. "They'd love to do a job on me." He stopped walking and turned to Cook. "Look at it this way, John," he said with gallows humor. "The worst that can happen is that we'll spend our declining years sunning ourselves on a beach in Costa Rica, turning over most of our ill-gotten gains to some Beaner dictator to keep him from throwing us to the wolves."

Cook was not amused. "As you damn well know, Tom," he said coldly, "that's not the worst that could happen."

The Senator nodded grimly.

Cook insisted on driving the Senator's car back to the airport, in the interest of self-preservation. Hill stayed to watch the plane take off, curious to see if they would make it. His interest was shared by the airport employees, many of whom joined him in front of the hangar to watch. Cook's precautions had not only been prudent, but necessary; with a full load of fuel, it would have been impossible. As it was, the small jet, screaming at full throttle, used all of the runway and was only a hair above stall speed as it barely cleared the trees at the far end of the field.

ELEVEN

The taxi driver pointed out Olympic Park; memories of the newsclips Paula had seen of the tragedy that had occurred there unreeled in her mind. The driver explained, in passable English, the significance of a large grassy mound on their left: the rubble from all over the city, caused by Allied bombings during the war, had been brought there, graded, covered with topsoil, and seeded. It was a war memorial for the people of Munich. Jack remembered photographs he had seen, taken the year the war had ended; the city had been almost totally destroyed. It was ten years since his last visit, and new buildings and thruways, signs of the ever-expanding West German economy, were in evidence throughout. In the process of rebuilding, however, they had managed to recapture much of the city's former Old World charm.

The Munich Hilton was an exception—a modern highrise of concrete and tinted glass, an excrescence on the banks of the Isar River, near the English Garden. The suite with living room, kitchenette, and bar which Paula had reserved against her conservative instincts, but in consideration of Jack's dislike for small rooms, was on the top floor, with a magnificent view.

Callahan unpacked, satisfying a compulsion he had to get settled quickly in hotel rooms, and joined Paula on the balcony off the living room. They decided to spend a lazy day to ward off some of the effects of jet lag, go to bed early, and start fresh in the morning. Below them the city spread out in all directions. On the horizon to the south, the late-morning sun illuminated the distant peaks of the Bavarian Alps; in front of the hotel the Isar flowed rapidly by and cascaded down a small waterfall; off to the right, the wooded area of the English Garden bordered the hotel grounds. The splendid scene partially justified the architectural monstrosity that made it possible.

After a steaming bath in an oversized tub, they spent a few hours browsing in the shopping arcade off the hotel lobby. Paula picked up a few articles she had forgotten to pack. Jack stopped by the concierge's desk and asked him to have a rented car arranged for the following morning. They napped away the remainder of the afternoon, waking in time to take an early-evening walk before dinner.

They walked the short distance to the English Garden, following a narrow footpath through the woods, strolling in silence and enjoying the cool evening air.

Callahan stopped suddenly and cocked his head. "Do you hear music?" he asked.

Paula listened for a moment. "Yes, I do. It sounds like a marching band."

As they continued, the path branched off in myriad directions, and they chose the one that led them closer to the music. As they drew nearer, they heard crowd noises—loud talking, laughter, singing. A few moments later they discovered the source of the sounds, a huge outdoor beer garden in the heart of the park, a favorite haunt for natives and tourists alike. Picnic tables and benches were scattered everywhere among the trees, in an expansive open area, and surrounding a building resembling a pagoda. Open on all sides, this housed a large bar, a food counter, and a German brass band playing Bavarian folk music and traditional drinking songs. The atmosphere was festive and boisterous.

Paula laughed with delight, took Callahan by the hand, and waded into the thick of it. The crowd was enormous and seemed to be having a wonderful time. The band leader raised his hand to begin another number, and after a few short bars there was instant recognition from the audience. A thunderous pounding grew in intensity as beer steins banged on table tops, and the crowd sang as one the words to an apparently well-known song:

> "Du, du liegst mir im herzen
> Du, du liegst mir im sinn
> Du, du machst mir viel schmerzen
> Weisst nicht wie gut ich der bin."

Callahan noticed to his surprise that Paula was singing along at the top of her lungs. When the song ended and the tumult had died, he said quizzically, "I didn't know you spoke German."

"I don't," she replied with a smile, enjoying his bewilderment. "I learned the song from one of the girls at college, a German exchange student. She taught a group of us to sing it one afternoon when we were drinking beer in her room. It's an old German song from World War I. She never translated it for us, though."

Callahan smiled and recited the words:

> "You, you live in my heart
> You, you live in my soul
> You, you cause me great sorrow
> You don't know how good I am for you."

Paula wrinkled up her nose. "I think I preferred not knowing." She looked around at the crowd, deciding they were all locals. It was early October, and by now all the tourists had gone home. She suggested they join the party. Jack was reluctant, but gave in to her enthusiasm and bought a large pitcher of foaming beer. Casting her diet to the winds, Paula bought two oversized, fat, doughy pretzels. They weaved their way through the crowded tables to a recently vacated spot under the trees.

Paula sipped her beer and people-watched, feeling a small twinge of guilt each time she bit into her pretzel. Unnoticed, she studied a group of young German couples at a nearby table, fixing her gaze on one young man in particular, a tall, lean fellow with strong, handsome features, almost white-blond hair, and light-blue eyes. Paula thought that Karl Dennecker had probably looked much like that young man when he was the same age. No doubt he had frequented beer gardens much like this one, if not this very one, and had sung the same songs, drunk warm beer, and pounded his stein on the table. How far removed was this young man from the German of Dennecker's day?

Paula's thoughts were interrupted when Jack began tapping his hand on the table as the band started another rousing tune. She smiled at him affectionately and then turned her attention back to the young Germans. What was it that made her distrust and dislike them as much as she did? Arrogance? Belligerence? Yes, that was it! If she had to describe the German character in two words, they would be arrogant and belligerent. Arrogant and belligerent to the point of self-destruction. She shook her head slightly, in a gesture of self-disgust for what she was thinking. From the German history she had studied in college, and books she had read, she was familiar with some of the brutality the Germans had demonstrated in World War II, and she had on occasion heard discussions about what had gone on in the concentrations camps, but it had never been made so realistic until she had read the transcripts of Dennecker's trial, and the lurid details of what these people had done. Since then, she had been unable to rid herself of an increasing dislike for them. She knew it was not intelligent or rational to make a sweeping generalization about an entire nation, but somehow what the Nazis had done seemed to justify it in this case. It was hard to conceive of the atrocities these people had committed in the name of patriotism.

Callahan nudged her gently. "What are you thinking about? You're in another world."

"Sorry. Some of what I've learned about these people is beginning to effect my objectivity."

Jack put his arm around her shoulder and shook her gently. "Let's get smashed and then stagger back to the hotel like good little ugly Americans and sleep it off."

Paula laughed. "I've never seen you drunk."

" 'Tis an experience you'll not soon forget," he said, affecting the accent of his paternal grandfather. Taking the empty pitcher, he stood up. "Time for a refill if we're going to do this properly." As he was about to leave the table, he froze in position.

"What is it, Callahan?" Paula teased. "Can't handle the German beer? You're a disgrace to the Irish."

Jack handed her the pitcher. "Stay right here until I get back," he told her sternly.

Alarmed by his tone, she now noticed the hard look in his eyes. She watched him move through the crowd toward the pagoda, fascinated by his quickness and agility—like a stalk-

125

ing cat closing in for the kill. She stood to see where he was going, but soon lost him in the jostling, exuberant crowd.

Callahan stopped behind a particularly rowdy group of Germans, standing, arms linked, and swaying to the music. Using them as a shield, he observed the man at the pagoda bar, his back now turned to him. It was one of the men he had seen at Dennecker's cabin; he was certain of it! Halek. He had only had a brief, distant glance at the man's face that day, but it was he; the blank, glowering stare and the short, thick neck, so short that his head appeared to be affixed directly to his shoulders. He had caught a glimpse of him watching Paula at the table, and it wasn't the idle gaze of a crowd-watcher. His expression had changed and he had turned quickly away when Callahan had looked in his direction.

Jack moved more cautiously now, approaching at an angle to keep out of Halek's view should he turn toward the table where Paula was sitting. When he was within ten yards of him, Halek turned back to watch the table. Jack saw him tense and move laterally for a clearer view; upon confirming Callahan's absence, he jerked his head in a slow sweeping arc, scanning the crowd, then spun quickly around, looking behind him.

Callahan decided to close the distance before Halek spooked and disappeared into the crowd. Amid angry shouts and curses, he broke through a tightly clustered group of singing, swaying Germans, sending beer steins flying, knocking one man to the ground as he charged toward Halek.

Hearing the disturbance, Halek turned and caught the movement out of the corner of his eye; reacting instantly, he plowed into the crowd in the direction of the woods, his powerful arms shoving people violently to either side.

Callahan saw him bolt, and angled in the same direction, bulling his way through the seemingly endless mass of humanity. Losing sight of Halek, he redoubled his efforts, now at a flat-out run, scattering people, beer, and tables in all directions.

As he reached the edge of the woods he caught a brief flash of Halek's tan jacket rounding a sharp bend in the narrow footpath a short distance ahead. Upon reaching the bend, the path branched off in three directions, all winding through the dense woods. Halek was nowhere in sight. Callahan paused and listened for heavy footsteps—nothing! The evening light was failing and the woods were full of deep shadows, making it impossible to detect anything until you were upon it. He had lost him.

"Who was it, Callahan?" Paula asked.

"Halek," Jack replied. "I lost him in the woods."

"He followed us here? Christ!"

"And no doubt they'll continue to follow us—which means I'll get another chance at him soon."

"They?" Paula said.

"His sidekick, Candellari, is probably with him."

"You seem pleased," Paula said, noticing a smile of satisfaction. "Doesn't it bother you that they're here . . . watching us?"

Callahan shook his head. "I prefer knowing where they are; it makes things that much simpler." He picked up the pitcher and started for the pagoda. "Time for some serious drinking."

"What would you have done had you caught him?" Paula asked, genuinely concerned.

Callahan turned and stared down at her, his expression cold, ruthless. "Broken his *goddam* neck."

The next morning Jack was amazed to find he wasn't suffering from a hangover. How many pitchers of beer had they had? At least six. He hadn't consumed that much beer in one sitting even in his army days. Paula, too, was feeling no pain and was eager to get started for Fürstenfeldbruck. They ate a hurried breakfast in the hotel restaurant and stopped at the concierge's desk for the keys to their car. After signing the necessary papers, the concierge told him their Mercedes was parked under the portico outside the main entrance. He assured them that the sporty little convertible would best suit their needs and satisfy their obvious good taste. Jack tipped him generously, telling Paula, "For that polished line of bullshit, he deserves it."

Once outside the confines of the city, the gently rolling Bavarian countryside was picturesque, and the Mercedes was a pleasure to drive on the narrow winding roads. Callahan couldn't resist the urge to put the throttle to the floor on some of the less harrowing stretches, and the little automotive masterpiece handled better at 120 than most cars did at 50.

"German engineering," Callahan shouted above the rush

of the wind. "It's no overstatement when they say it's the finest in the world."

"They can accomplish anything they put their minds to," Paula replied, her hair flying in all directions. "Everything from sports cars to gas chambers."

Jack shook his head. "Let's not start *that* again."

As they crested a hill, Fürstenfeldbruck appeared before them. Callahan stopped at a small grocery store near the center of the town and asked directions to the home of Ernst Froeschmann. The short, rotund cherub behind the counter instructed him to go back to the bridge at the town's entrance and take the first right turn after crossing the bridge. That was the driveway to the Froeschmann's; the house was approximately one kilometer from where they had entered the road. The cherub spoke almost perfect English, and as Jack and Paula were leaving, he said, "Frau Froeschmann is at home now."

"I'm looking for her husband, Herr Froeschmann," Jack said.

The cherub stared at him blankly for a moment, then turned his back on them and busied himself arranging his shelves. *"Guten Tag,"* he muttered.

"Good day to you," Callahan replied, smiling, remembering that the provincial Bavarian was a closed-mouthed, distrustful type, giving strangers only the information he decided they should have.

The dirt road was bordered on both sides by dense woods and was deeply rutted and potholed. After a kilometer, as the cherub had told them, the road turned sharply to the right, revealing a few acres of landscaped grounds with a massive stucco-and-stone mansion in the center. The grounds must have been magnificent in their day, but were now desperately in need of attention. The house, in a bad state of disrepair, hadn't fared much better: Sections of the stucco walls had large cracks, the paint on the shutters, windows, and trim was chipping and peeling, and the overabundance of ivy growing up the sides had totally covered some of the windows on the second and third stories. The driveway ended in front of the house, alongside a large algae-choked pond.

Callahan applied the huge wrought-iron knocker to the carved oak door, and after waiting a few minutes with no response, knocked again.

"Someone's coming," Paula whispered, peeking through the narrow leaded windows next to the door.

Callahan couldn't believe that the woman standing before them had actually managed to open the huge door. Frau Froeschmann was a tiny, frail woman, well into her eighties, Jack imagined, but remarkably well preserved. She had a distracting affliction that caused her head to bob up and down, and Jack had to restrain himself from following it like a bouncing ball.

"Mrs. Froeschmann?" Paula asked.

"Yes," she replied with a warm, somewhat vague smile.

What a darling little woman, Paula thought. "My name is Paula Carlson," she said, "and this is Jack Callahan."

"Oh, yes. How nice to see you," she said cheerfully. "Have you been well?"

"Ah . . . yes," Paula replied, realizing that the poor woman was probably a bit senile. She acted as though she knew them. "We've been quite well, thank you."

"What a handsome young man," she said, glancing at Jack and still smiling. "You remind me of my Dieter . . . but he was not quite so tall . . . I do not think. You are Americans?"

"Yes," Paula said. "We've come to see Mr. Froeschmann."

"Ernst?" the old woman asked, the smile slowly fading from her face.

Paula nodded, sensing something was wrong.

"I am sorry, Fraulein Carlson," Frau Froeschmann said. "Ernst has been dead these seven years."

Paula looked helplessly at Jack, knowing he was thinking the same thoughts. How could they have been so damn careless and impulsive? They should have checked before they came.

Mrs. Froeschmann noticed their disappointment. "Please come in," she said, smiling again. "As friends of Ernst's you must accept my hospitality and visit with me. Perhaps I can help you."

Paula got the impression it was a plea rather than an invitation.

"We weren't really . . ." Jack began, stopping when Paula elbowed his ribs.

"Thank you, Mrs. Froeschmann," Paula said. "Perhaps you can."

"I must apologize for my English," she said to Paula. "It

has been years since I have had the opportunity to practice it." Paula assured her that her English was excellent.

She led them through the drawing room, library, and dining room to a glassed-in sun room at the back of the house. In all the rooms except this one the furniture was covered with sheets, and the dust on the window sills, Paula noted, appeared thick enough to require tilling as opposed to being wiped away. The old woman obviously lived in this one room, bright and sunny and crowded with plants. The furniture was old and worn and faded but comfortable. Mrs. Froeschmann motioned Paula and Jack to a sofa, taking a chair across from them. She seemed to enjoy having visitors. And Paula guessed that she had very few.

"Ernst liked Americans," Mrs. Froeschmann said, looking from Paula to Jack, her head bobbing. "When the war ended, and there was so much . . ." She hesitated, searching for the proper words. ". . . desolation and despair, he told me the Americans would help us restore our pride and dignity, and he was correct." She lowered her eyes for a moment, slowly shaking her head. "I shudder to think of our fate had the Russians occupied all of Germany." She ended her brief reverie abruptly and asked Paula, "How did you come to know my Ernst?"

"I didn't really know him," Paula said. "I know of him."

"What a shame," Frau Froeschmann said with a sad smile. "He was such a fine man; you would have liked him."

"I'm sure that I would have," Paula said.

"Why have you come to see him?" the old woman asked.

"I'm a journalist," Paula told her, "and I'm doing research for an article on the war-crimes trials. I came across your husband's name as the attorney for one of the defendants and thought he might have been able to give me an informed viewpoint."

Callahan watched Paula out of the corner of his eye, amused and impressed by her skillful handling of the interview.

"Those trials," Mrs. Froeschmann said, lowering her eyes again, "a terrible, terrible thing. Ernst did not believe in them, you know. No man should be made to answer for what he did in times of war. You cannot expect a person to act sanely in an insane situation. That is what Ernst believed. But the victors dictate the terms, as he said, not the vanquished."

Paula felt the urge to argue the point, but held it in check to pursue her objective. "Were you familiar with any of the details of the trial in which your husband was involved," she asked carefully.

"Oh, yes!" Mrs. Froeschmann replied emphatically. "Ernst and I discussed the trials many times. He was involved with two trials. The first was the International Military Tribunal, when the principal leaders of the Third Reich were tried. Ernst," she said proudly, "was one of the attorneys defending Foreign Minister von Ribbentrop." She stopped for a moment, looking directly at Paula. "They hanged the poor man!" she said, leaning forward and speaking in a confidential tone. "Shameful business! Ernst was *very* upset about that. He said it was totally uncalled for."

"What about the second trial?" Paula asked gently.

"General Dennecker of the SS," she said, looking away from her and concentrating on a large fern hanging from the ceiling at the other end of the room, as though trying to recall something that had slipped her memory. "There was something about that trial that bothered Ernst until the day he died, although he never told me what it was. General Dennecker came to see him when he was released from prison, and after that Ernst seemed to feel a little better about it, but I could tell he was still troubled."

Paula, her interest piqued, continued her questioning in a low, patient tone of voice. "Are you familiar with any of the details of your husband's preparations for the trial? Or do you know if he had any contact with General Dennecker while he was in prison?"

"No," Mrs. Froeschmann said, "he was very . . . uncommunicative"—she pronounced the word slowly and smiled when Paula nodded, confirming her pronunciation—"about his dealings with the general."

"I imagine he kept complete records of all his correspondence and conversations with his clients," Paula said, gingerly.

"Oh, my yes. Ernst was a most thorough man."

"And I imagine General Dennecker was no exception," Paula said, trying to prompt an offer granting them access to the files.

"I would think so," Mrs. Froeschmann replied, "but I have never read Ernst's files. He was a man who demanded his privacy in certain matters, and I always respected that.

Somehow, even though he is no longer here, I feel it is still a matter of respect to honor his wishes."

Paula's hopes were dashed for an easy victory. With no alternative, she decided on a direct approach. "Is there any possibility that we could see Mr. Froeschmann's files on General Dennecker's trial?" she asked, anticipating the reply.

"Oh. No. I could not allow that," the old woman said firmly. "No. No. Ernst would never forgive me."

"Perhaps he would," Paula offered. "If it prevented his good name from being ruined."

Mrs. Froeschmann's pale, cloudy eyes widened and her head bobbed faster. "I don't understand," she said, her voice taking on a sharp edge. "My Ernst was a good, decent man."

Callahan glanced at Paula, puzzled by her change of tactics, uncertain of the direction she was taking.

Paula sat on the edge of the sofa to reach Mrs. Froeschmann's hand, touching it lightly. "I don't mean to upset you, Mrs. Froeschmann; I believe that your husband was a good man, but there are those who don't. I came here to prove to them that what we believe is true, and to prevent them from printing lies about him. But I can't do that without your help."

"What are they saying about my Ernst?" she asked, responding to Paula's false sincerity. "And who is saying it?"

"Certain people in the publishing field in the United States," Paula answered vaguely. "You know how *they* are; suggesting, insinuating, always dragging up the past, claiming all Germans are responsible for what happened to their people during the war."

The old woman's eyes narrowed. "Yes. Yes. Will they never stop with their vile accusations; blaming an entire nation for the actions of a few, if indeed it *ever* happened the way they say it did. The Fuehrer was right about those . . ." She stopped abruptly in midsentence, looking away for a moment. "You must not let them print filthy lies about my Ernst, Fraulein Carlson," she said with a helpless, pleading look. "You must not!"

"I won't, Mrs. Froeschmann," Paula said earnestly, sensing that the bond was complete, "but you *must* help me!"

Callahan looked at Paula and rolled his eyes upward, a hint of a smile showing at the corners of his mouth.

Mrs. Froeschmann didn't answer immediately, but seemed

to be comforted by Paula's assurance. Then: "Does either of you understand the German language?"

"I have a good working knowledge of your language," Jack answered in faultless German.

"Excellent, Herr Callahan," the old woman said, smiling again.

Jack watched as she drummed her fingers lightly on the arm of the chair, painstakingly marshaling her thoughts.

"If you will go to the library," she instructed him, "you will find that one of the wall panels to the right of the fireplace is actually a small sliding door. The pewter sconce attached to the panel activates the latch. If you turn it to the left, the door will slide open." She looked at Paula and smiled. "I used to call it 'Ernst's hideaway.' He always went in there to work when he didn't want to be disturbed. All his records are there." She made a sweeping gesture with her arm to Callahan. "You go along now, Herr Callahan, and Fraulein Carlson and I will have a nice visit."

Jack excused himself and left the room. Paula smiled warmly at Mrs. Froeschmann, feeling a bit guilty about her coercive methods, but immensely pleased with their results. There wouldn't be any slandering of Ernst Froeschmann's name, she rationalized, so her promises would be kept. Paula sensed that the old woman was lonely, and desperate for human companionship. "Have you any children?" she asked.

"We lost our only child in the war," Frau Froeschmann said sadly. "Dieter was killed during the bombings in Dresden." She reached for a large framed photograph on the table next to her chair and handed it to Paula.

Paula stared at the darkly handsome brooding face. The young man, in his early twenties, was dressed in a military uniform. Her eyes riveted on the twin lightning bolts on the collar of his tunic—the insignia of the SS. "What a handsome man," Paula said, handing back the photograph.

The voices from the sun room faded as Jack entered the library. He followed Mrs. Froeschmann's instructions and the wall panel slid open easily, revealing a tiny cubicle with a desk on one wall and file cabinets lining the other. The wall space above the desk was filled with a gallery of photographs of, he presumed, Ernst Froeschmann with a wide assortment of the Nazi hierarchy: Himmler, Goering, Hess, and others he recognized from photographs in books he had read but whose names he couldn't remember. He glanced down at a large leather-framed portrait on the corner of the desk and picked it up for a closer look. It was of Ernst and Mrs. Froeschmann, splendidly dressed, at what looked like a rather gala affair. Standing in the center of the photograph, only two people away from Ernst, were Adolf Hitler and Eva Braun. A well-connected man, Jack thought to himself, placing the photograph back on the desk. Most of the surfaces in the room were thick with dust, and Jack decided that the room hadn't been entered since Ernst had died. He read the tags inserted in the slots on the file-cabinet drawers, all in alphabetical order. The D's were in the bottom drawer of the first cabinet. Opening the drawer, he sorted through the folders until he found the one he was looking for: DENNECKER, KARL—GENERALLEUTNANT der WAFFEN SS.

He sat at the desk, after wiping some of the dust away with his handkerchief, and slowly, carefully read the contents of the file. He soon realized that his German vocabulary was lacking; he returned to the library and found a German-English dictionary. The account of Dennecker's military career was more detailed than what Paula had read in the transcripts at the National Archives, but it revealed nothing new. The following fifty pages were outlines for the presentation of evidence and defense witnesses, briefly describing their testimony; notes for the summation, closing remarks, and final plea. Callahan was impressed by Froeschmann's thoroughness and expertise; it was a valiant effort for a cause that was doomed from the outset.

The next twelve or so pages were stapled together; letters from Dennecker to Froeschmann while Dennecker was in Landsberg prison. Each letter was followed by a copy of Froeschmann's reply. In the first, Dennecker asked why Froeschmann had not come to the prison to see him in the month since the trial ended. Froeschmann's answer explained that the "red-coated" prisoners (Jack had read somewhere that the condemned men wore red coats to distinguish them from the other prisoners) were not permitted visitors under any circumstances and were allowed to correspond only with their attorneys, a procedure adopted after some of the top Nazis had committed suicide with poison smuggled to them by visiting relatives. The American army didn't want any more of them cheating the hangman.

The remainder of the letters were urgent requests by

Dennecker for information concerning the status of the clemency petitions and appeals for commutation of sentence, and Froeschmann's answers were assurances that the petitions had been filed, telling him to keep his spirits up and that he would inform him the moment he received word. The last three letters from Dennecker, two with answers from Froeschmann, the third unanswered, contained a number of paragraphs that puzzled Jack. They referred to some sort of agreement Dennecker had made with someone. Callahan reread the paragraphs, starting with Dennecker's first mention of the agreement.

My execution date is drawing near. I can no longer allow myself to believe my sentence will be commuted. It is imperative you contact the people involved and remind them of our agreement.

Froeschmann's reply was just as cryptic, shedding no light on the "agreement":

I spoke with the men concerned. They refuse to acknowledge the existence of such an agreement as you related to me during your trial. I am sorry, Karl. Considering my position in relation to these men, there is nothing more I can do.

The final letter from Dennecker, unanswered by Froeschmann, was another agitated plea for Froeschmann to appeal to the people with whom he made the "agreement."

The last document in the file was a letter to Froeschmann from the office of the High Commissioner—the man chosen by President Roosevelt to govern the American sector of Germany—reprimanding him for failure to represent his client properly. They had received no clemency petitions or appeals on behalf of Dennecker and could not understand Froeschmann's negligence in the matter. The letter went on to explain that had it not been for the priest at Landsberg prison delivering Dennecker's handwritten appeal on prison stationery, he would surely have been hanged. The letter concluded with the statement that after consideration of all the evidence against him, the death sentence should not have been imposed. All the Nazis sentenced to death were either directly responsible for policy-making or war crimes that resulted in the death of others; Dennecker had not been instrumental in setting policy, nor directly involved in carrying it out. His primary duties were organizational and administrative in nature, solely concerning internal matters within his own department and not directly related to the administration of the concentration camps. Therefore, his sentence was commuted to ten years imprisonment.

Callahan could not believe that an attorney as competent as Froeschmann would not have filed appeals on behalf of his client. He went back to the letter in which Froeschmann had assured Dennecker the appeals had been made, and reread it. But there were no copies of the appeals in the file! He began going through the file cabinets, checking for files labeled "Appeals," "Clemency," "Petitions." Nothing. He decided to go through every file in every cabinet.

A thorough search turned up nothing whatsoever. Jack sat slumped at the desk. He had an ache in the small of his back. Why hadn't Froeschmann filed any appeals? It made no sense, considering the fact that he had ample grounds for a commutation of sentence ... he *must* have known that! Callahan glanced at his watch; two hours had passed since he'd left the sun room. He was about to join Paula and Mrs. Froeschmann when it occurred to him he hadn't looked in the desk drawers. The center drawer was cluttered with an assortment of note pads, pens, pencils, a stapler, a tobacco pouch, and two pipes. The others were empty.

Jack got up, stretched, picked up the German-English dictionary, and returned it to its proper shelf. A series of leather-bound books next to the dictionary caught his eye. They all had labels pasted on them, and years typed on the labels. Removing the first book, labeled 1933–1935, he opened it out of curiosity; his eyes widened as he read the first page. He quickly put it back on the shelf and scanned the rest of the labels until he found the one he wanted: 1947–1949. They were diaries of Ernst Froeschmann's personal life, from 1933 until his death in 1972. Each page, in some cases two or three pages, depending on his schedule, contained a weekly summation of events, and his comments concerning them.

Callahan removed the covering from one of the library chairs and sat down, rapidly turning the pages of the diary to the time of Dennecker's trial. The trial had lasted nineteen months, and the entries for most of those weeks described Froeschmann's impressions of how the case was progressing and his difficulty in finding witnesses with untainted pasts to testify on Dennecker's behalf. A page titled "Week of August 11, 1947" contained what Jack was looking for: The trial had ended on August 11, and after a brief entry commenting on his anguish over Dennecker's sentence of death, there was this paragraph:

> The visit from the American intelligence officer, Cook, made brutally realistic how totally defeated Germany is. It is not that I did not anticipate the possibility of revelations concerning my work with the Reichsfuehrer SS and his legal staff, but to have it used against me in this way is vile and contemptible. I have no choice but to abandon my efforts to have General Dennecker's sentence commuted to one more lenient and in appropriate accord with his alleged crimes. The threatened indictment for war crimes would be more than I could bear. I must cast General Dennecker to the wolves. There is nowhere to turn. Who would listen? Who would care? The Fatherland is truly defeated. We have been emasculated.

Callahan scanned the entries in the diary for the remainder of 1947. There were two more visits from Cook, reemphasizing the threats of prosecution for war crimes if any efforts were made to keep Dennecker from the hangman. In January of 1948, there was an entry commenting on the letter from the High Commissioner commuting Dennecker's sentence to ten years imprisonment. Froeschmann was relieved and elated. Out of curiosity, Jack looked at the diary for 1955, the year of Dennecker's release from Landsberg prison. Froeschmann had made an entry concerning a visit from Dennecker when he had explained the threats that were made against him. Dennecker understood and forgave him. The remainder of the diaries contained purely unrelated personal matters. Jack went back and reread the period covering the actual trial, looking for any mention of, or allusion to, the elusive "agreement." He found nothing and decided that Froeschmann had either forgotten to enter it or for some reason had decided against recording it in the diary. He replaced the book on the shelf, recovered the chair, and returned to the sun room.

Frau Froeschmann's expression changed the moment she

saw Callahan. "Were my Ernst's files helpful?" she asked hopefully.

"Yes, they were," Jack replied. "I can promise you," he added, glancing at Paula, "that Herr Froeschmann's reputation will not be ruined. His records show that he was a careful and thoughtful man."

"Oh, I'm so pleased," the old woman beamed. "Ernst was a good German."

"Yes, he was," Callahan said, straight-faced. "In all that the term has come to mean."

Mrs. Froeschmann smiled proudly. "I do hope you will forgive me for the dreadful condition of the library. Somehow I have been unable to bring myself to spend time there since Ernst died. It was his favorite room. It is full of his memory."

"No apology necessary," Jack said. "I understand."

"Would you like some pastries?" Mrs. Froeschmann asked, indicating a tray on a small table next to her chair. "Or perhaps a sandwich? Fraulein Carlson and I had lunch while you worked."

"The pastry will be fine," Jack said, choosing a chocolate-covered, cream-filled something-or-other that he imagined capable of dissolving the enamel of his teeth with the first bite.

Mrs. Froeschmann excused herself and went to the kitchen to refill the coffee pot. Paula nudged Jack and whispered excitedly, "Mrs. Froeschmann has given me a fantastic piece of information. The woman ..." But the old woman was returning with the coffee. Jack had a second and third cup while Paula and Mrs. Froeschmann discussed the Wagner festival at Bayreuth and the prewar grandeur of Nuremberg's architecture. Callahan observed that the old woman was most anxious to discuss every conceivable topic, jumping headlong into another whenever one had exhausted its possibilities. She was afraid that her guests would leave her to her loneliness, he concluded.

Two hours later, they managed to get to the front door, amid a profusion of thank-you's and invitations for future visits that everyone understood would never materialize.

Mrs. Froeschmann took Paula by the arm and said gratefully, "I will rest easier knowing that *they* won't be attacking my Ernst."

Paula patted her hand. "I assure you that won't happen."

Frau Froeschmann stood in the doorway and waved as the

car started down the drive. Her situation was not quite so sad or depressing as it had first appeared, Paula thought, reflecting on their conversation. She had many cherished memories from happier times that were a great comfort to her. Paula knew more than a few people who would trade what they had for that.

"What were you trying to tell me when Mrs. Froeschmann left the room?" Callahan asked.

Paula's thoughts returned to the present. "I gathered from the look on your face that you had a successful afternoon?"

Jack nodded complacently.

"Well," Paula continued, "that talkative little woman gave us an added bonus. On the off chance that it might stimulate her memory, I showed her the photograph of Dennecker that I found in the back of his address book."

"I'd completely forgotten about that," Callahan said. "Taken in Munich in 1942, and Dennecker was in his uniform with his arm around an attractive woman."

"Yes, Callahan," Paula said, pleased with herself, "and Mrs. Froeschmann *knew* the woman—Inge Bauer. Inge is Frederich Bauer's *sister!* Which gives us a connection between Bauer and Dennecker! Mrs. Froeschmann told me that Inge Bauer had come to see Ernst shortly after the trial ended, asking him to make arrangements for her to visit Dennecker at Landsberg prison. Ernst told her it was impossible and under no circumstances would it be allowed. She was only there a short time, but her visit impressed Mrs. Froeschmann, primarily because Inge was from an old-guard, socially prominent family." Paula turned in her seat to face Jack, resting her back against the car door. "Now, fill me in on what you found."

Paula listened intently, occasionally punctuating his sentences with "My God, Callahan!" as he told her about the "agreement," the letter from the High Commissioner, and the visits from John Cook.

When he finished, Paula sat quietly, arranging her thoughts, and arrived at what seemed to her to be an undeniable solution to the enigma of Dennecker's coded list of names.

"John Cook interrogated Dennecker prior to his trial, Senator Hill prosecuted him, and Judge White presided on a panel of three judges who handed down a sentence apparently far in excess of what it should have been. When you add that to the threats Cook made to Ernst Froeschmann after the trial, you would have to believe that they all conspired to make certain Dennecker hanged."

"That takes us back to the revenge theory for Dennecker's list," Jack said.

"Yes," Paula agreed, "but there are different kinds of revenge. We only considered the possibility of Dennecker's plotting to murder them for sending him to prison. But there's also the possibility that Dennecker *has* been avenging himself all these years for their conspiring to hang him! That might shed some light on the reason Popcorn was murdered when he discovered someone in Dennecker's house. In all probability, they were making certain Dennecker hadn't left any evidence of what he'd been doing all along, and Popcorn got in the way."

"Are you suggesting Dennecker was blackmailing them?"

Paula nodded emphatically.

"No," Callahan said, shaking his head impatiently. "There's something wrong with that. What possible reason could a judge, a lawyer, and an intelligence agent have for conspiring to hang a Nazi general? There's no evidence that any of these men knew each other before or during the war, or that any of them knew Dennecker until his trial. Given the extreme anti-Nazi feelings at the end of the war, I could accept the idea of an overzealous judge's imposing unnecessarily harsh sentences on high-ranking Nazi officers, but to have an OSS agent threaten the defendant's lawyer, to prevent him from keeping his client from the gallows, is going too far. It just doesn't wash. There's got to be more to it. As for the blackmail theory, Dennecker would have had little or no leverage. I can't imagine Hill, Cook, and White losing any sleep over the fact that it might become known they went to extraordinary measures to have an SS general hanged. No, there's something else."

"Callahan!" Paula half screamed, causing him to swerve the car to the shoulder of the road in an attempt to avoid some unseen, impending collision. He jerked the car to a jolting stop. "Damn! I wish you wouldn't do that. What the hell is wrong with you?"

"I'm sorry," she said, "but you know how impulsive I am at times."

"So?"

"I think I know what we've missed," she said calmly,

containing her enthusiasm. "The 'agreement.' You said both Dennecker and Ernst Froeschmann referred to some 'agreement' Dennecker had made with someone. Perhaps he made an agreement, or deal, with Cook, Hill, and White, to assure a lenient sentence . . ."

". . . and they didn't keep their end of the bargain," Jack said, finishing her thought. "That's a fascinating idea, but the only reason I can think of for a prosecutor to make a deal with a defendant is to get something he wants or needs from him. Did Dennecker testify as a witness for the prosecution in any other trial?"

"Yes, briefly," Paula answered. "I noticed on the information sheet at the National Archives that prior to his own trial he was called as a witness for the prosecution before the International Military Tribunal to give testimony concerning certain SS activities. But there was a notation after the entry stating that he was most uncooperative and contributed nothing at all to the prosecutor's case. That's hardly the behavior of someone who had been promised a lenient sentence *if* he cooperated."

Callahan remembered something he had read in the letter the High Commissioner had written to Ernst Froeschmann. "There are a lot of possibilities that could keep us going around in circles forever, but I think I know someone who might have some worthwhile information. Dennecker's handwritten appeal that finally got his sentence commuted was delivered to the High Commissioner's Office by the priest from Landsberg prison. Landsberg isn't far from Munich. We could drive there tomorrow and talk to the priest."

"If he's still alive," Paula said ominously, bearing in mind their mistake in not checking out the possibility of Ernst Froeschmann's death.

Callahan gave her a thumbs-up sign. "Maybe we'll luck out this time. By the way," he said with a grin, "I forgot to congratulate you on your interview today. You're one hell of a con artist."

Paula winked and smiled broadly. "All in a day's work, Callahan. All in a day's work."

Jack and Paula were having dinner that evening in the hotel restaurant when she was paged for the call she had put through to Al Verity. The man at the desk directed her to a booth in the lobby.

"You do realize that it's two in the morning here," Verity said, his voice heavy with sleep.

"Would I disturb you if it wasn't absolutely necessary?" Paula quipped. "Would I? Al? Dear? Don't fall back to sleep on me."

"What is it?" he groaned, propping his head up with a pillow.

"I need some help from *Time*'s bureau in Munich. Will you intercede for me?"

"Depends . . . we don't have a bureau in Munich; we have a stringer there. But go ahead."

"Ask your stringer to get me anything he can on Inge Bauer, sister of Frederich Bauer. I'll be at the Munich Hilton until checkout time the day after tomorrow."

"How considerate of you," Verity said dryly. "I'll see what I can do. Anything I should know?"

"Nothing that can't wait. See you in a few days; you're a dear."

Verity switched on the lamp next to the bed and reached for a cigar, knowing it would be futile to try and get back to sleep. He lit the cigar and asked for the overseas operator—the Berlin bureau would have the Munich stringer's name and telephone number.

After dinner, Paula cajoled Callahan into an evening at the opera; the Bavarian State Opera Company—highly recommended by Mrs. Froeschmann—was performing Wagner's *Tannhauser*.

The drive to Landsberg was on the easy side of an hour, through more of the charming Bavarian countryside. Callahan watched the rearview mirror for any sign of someone following, but spotted no one. Since his run-in with Halek, he had made a point of making periodic checks, without alarming Paula. They had either cleaned up their act or terminated surveillance; Jack guessed it was the former.

Paula studied a guide book during most of the drive, pointing out the magnificent Gothic gate as they entered the old medieval town. The Bavarian Gate of Landsberg had been built in 1425, and was one of the finest in Germany. The central square of the town, with its cobblestone streets, baroque and rococo adornments, and eighteenth-century fountain, had a fairytale atmosphere. In response to Paula's request, Jack parked the car and they played tourist, strolling through the square and visiting the shops. Two beer steins and a cuckoo clock later, they drove to the outskirts of town to Landsberg prison.

The old fortress-prison, with its high stone walls, was an imposing structure. Callahan remembered reading that Hitler had been imprisoned here for nine months in 1924 and had dictated the first part of *Mein Kampf* to his faithful sycophant Rudolf Hess during that time. He also recalled photographs he had seen of a massive Nazi rally in the town square, ending in a torchlight parade to the prison to commemorate Hitler's imprisonment and the writing of the gospel.

Paula and Jack waited in front of the huge oak door at the entrance to the prison. A small wooden porthole opened, revealing a nose and one gimlet eye. Callahan asked if he could see the prison priest. The eye and nose told him to wait. A few minutes passed, then the eye and nose reappeared, telling them he would take them to the priest's office. The imposing doors swung open and the eye and nose became the largest man Callahan had ever encountered—at least six feet eleven and a solid three hundred pounds, he estimated; his broad, flat features gave him a frightening appearance. Created by a flash of lightning in a swamp, Jack mused. All that was missing was a bolt through his head.

Stepping inside, Jack noticed a small, cramped guard room to his right; another hulking creature sat on a stool, his lips moving as he read a magazine. The hulk looked up, devouring Paula with his eyes.

"You're being admired, Esmeralda," Callahan said, nudging Paula.

The arch over the entranceway opened onto a colonnaded courtyard, separating the outside wall from the prison buildings. The huge lumbering man led them along a stone path to the end of the courtyard and a cozy, paneled office at the rear of the chapel.

The man who greeted them, dressed in a priest's frock, left no doubt in their minds that the trip to Landsberg had been in vain: he was no more than thirty years old, hardly the priest who had been there when Dennecker was an inmate. Callahan explained their mission—more or less.

"Father Lindner died two years ago," the young priest told them, "but I am familiar with some of the details of General

Dennecker's reprieve. It was one of the most rewarding moments of Father Lindner's time here at the prison. I assisted him here for the last three years of his life, and he often spoke of the period immediately following the war, very frustrating days for a man of God. So much senseless, unnecessary, brutal retribution."

"Hardly comparable to what they did to put themselves in that position," Paula muttered.

"Excuse me," the priest said. "I did not quite hear what you said."

"It wasn't important," Paula replied. "Just thinking out loud." Jack glared at her. "Have you any knowledge of the events that led to Father Lindner's intervention on Dennecker's behalf?" she asked.

"It's been a long time and I can't with any certainty recall anything," the young priest said, "but I believe there are file copies of a number of letters here from Father Lindner to the High Commissioner's Office concerning an appointment to discuss a commutation of sentence for General Dennecker." He flipped through the folders in a drawer in the file cabinet behind him, removing one and shuffling through the papers, sorting out anything of significance. Paula read the series of letters the priest handed her, but they revealed nothing Jack hadn't already learned from Ernst Froeschmann's diary. The priest returned the letters to the file and placed the file back in the cabinet.

"Do you remember Father Lindner ever mentioning anything about an agreement Dennecker had made with anyone concerning his sentence?" Jack asked.

The priest thought for a few moments, reaching for his pipe and filling it with a tobacco that, when lighted, had a very pleasant aroma. Callahan watched the smoke swirl and rise in the slanting rays of the late-morning sun that filtered through the office window.

"Yes, there *was* something about an arrangement," the priest said after a prolonged silence. He removed the pipe from his mouth and jabbed the stem at Callahan. "Father Lindner told me that Dennecker had informed him that his attorney was not having any success with his appeals. Father Lindner suggested he appeal directly to the High Commissioner, and said he would personally deliver the appeal. Dennecker wanted him to contact the judge who sentenced him, insisting that he had made some kind of contract with this man prior to his trial. Father Lindner convinced Dennecker that the High Commissioner, being the utmost authority in Germany at that time—with the exception of God," the priest interpolated with a wry smile, "was the only man with the power to commute his sentence of death."

"Did he know any of the details of the agreement Dennecker referred to?"

"If he did, he never discussed them with me," the priest replied. "But now that I think of it," he went on, gazing at Jack intently, obviously concentrating, "I once asked him that very question. His reply was startling, considering his dislike of people who did not answer questions directly. He told me it was something best not discussed, for the benefit of all concerned, considering the far-reaching implications. Yes, those were his very words."

"And there was no explanation of that phrase?"

"No." The priest shook his head. "If you had known Father Lindner, you would realize how futile it would be to pursue a subject he considered closed."

"Well, father," Callahan said, "thank you for your time and trouble."

"I'm sorry I couldn't be of more help." The priest rose from behind his desk. "But you are a few years late for the information you need." He went over to a small door at the rear of the office and opened it. "If you care to accompany me, we can take a short tour of some of the prison grounds before you leave."

The rear door of the chapel office opened onto a large grassy area, completely enclosed with ten-foot chain-link fencing topped with barbed wire, joining the old prison wall at one end—an obviously recent addition to the prison facilities. Inside the enclosure were two soccer fields, each encircled by a hard-surfaced jogging track, a separate area for weight lifting, with gymnastic apparatus, and at the end closest to the prison wall, an Olympic-size swimming pool.

"It seems as though the prison authorities look after the men's physical well-being in addition to your spiritual guidance," Callahan commented.

"Oh, yes," the priest replied cheerfully. "We have a well-rounded athletic program for the men. The only sport we don't allow is pole vaulting." He laughed heartily at this hoary joke, and Paula and Jack smiled politely.

They walked across one of the soccer fields to a gate near

the entrance to the prison. Paula felt relieved they were not going out the way they had come in; the dysgenic cretin in the guard room had sent chills up her spine. A prison guard snapped to attention and greeted the priest, nodding to Paula and Jack, and opened the gate to allow them passage.

Just outside the gate, off to the right, a small area of high grass, with an abundance of weeds, caught Jack's eye. There was a row of five or six wooden crosses, struggling to be seen above the overgrowth. Jack looked quizzically at the priest.

"Our area of benign neglect," the priest said, lowering his eyes. "Had it not been for Father Lindner's intercession, one of those crosses would be marking the grave of Karl Dennecker. The crosses you see there mark the graves of the men with whom Dennecker was to be hanged. They were the last men to be put to death in this prison. They were hanged on June 8, 1951, unceremoniously, from the rafters on the second floor of a storage shed inside the prison walls."

"Why aren't the graves maintained?" Jack asked impulsively.

"Politics," the priest replied shortly.

"Politics?"

"Yes. Politics. It seems the prison officials do not want to be accused of making martyrs of Nazi war criminals, or of glorifying the past."

"With all due respect, father," Callahan said, "I hardly think caring for these graves could be considered a glorification of the Nazi past."

The young priest stiffened slightly, then said coolly, "It is not difficult for me to understand, Mr. Callahan, why you would be unaware of certain sensitivities of our people, but believe me, they are very real." He studied the graves a moment, then added, "Initially, the families of some of the men requested permission to care for the graves, but the prison authorities, on order from the government officials, strenuously discouraged it."

"That's a shame, father," Callahan said. "Any soldier, regardless of circumstances, who died for his country, right or wrong, deserves some modicum of respect."

The young priest stared thoughtfully at Callahan, considering the statement rather odd, wondering where its roots lay. "Yes, a shame, Mr. Callahan," the priest agreed, still holding his gaze. "Indeed it is."

Jack walked over to the area where the crosses stood and

knelt to read the inscription on one that was less weathered than the rest and still legible. It read simply: OSWALD POHL—1892–1951. There were only a few letters remaining on the other crosses, not enough to make out the names. "Do you know who the others were?"

"I did," the priest answered, "but I've forgotten. They were all members of the SS hierarchy, mostly generals, like Dennecker."

"An ignoble end," Jack said, "for men of such high rank." The priest nodded, still curious about the previous sentiment, finally attributing it to, perhaps, Vietnam.

Jack thanked him again for his time and consideration. The young priest wished them Godspeed.

On the drive back, Callahan put the small Mercedes through its paces, molding the curves of the winding country road at near the car's performance limits.

"We've got all we're going to get here," Paula said, breaking a long silence. "I have a hunch that the key to this Pandora's box is to be found at Oyster Bay."

"Bauer's home?"

Paula nodded.

"When do you want to leave?" Callahan asked, both hands on the wheel, and eyes straight ahead.

"Tomorrow."

"Fine with me." As he rounded a sharp curve, Callahan put his arm across Paula's chest to hold her in place as he stood on the brakes, coming to a screeching halt a few feet from a tractor pulling a hay wagon. Glancing in the rearview mirror as he pulled out to pass, he saw a white BMW sedan round the same curve, narrowly avoiding crashing into the wagon by an adroit last-minute sideways skid.

Callahan pulled away slowly, gazing intently through the mirror. There were two men in the car, and there was no mistaking the heavyset, bull-necked passenger—it was Halek.

Continuing to build speed, Callahan drove as he did before the interruption, watching for just the right stretch of road. "Fasten your seatbelt," he told Paula.

"They're too confining," Paula complained.

"You're going to need it," Jack said firmly.

Paula shrugged and pulled out the retractable shoulder harness, attaching it loosely to the waist strap.

Jack reached over and checked the belt. "Tighter," he said. "As tight as you can stand it."

"What are you planning, loop the loops?"

Accelerating through a long S turn, he pressed the throttle to the floor on the straight stretch that followed, reaching 125 as they approached a long, gentle curve.

Catching a blurred glimpse of what he was looking for, he slammed on the brakes midway into the curve, coming to a howling, bone-jarring stop. Quickly putting the car into reverse, he backed up and swerved into a narrow, secluded farm road leading through the woods, stopping facing out. Leaving the engine running, he watched the main road from the concealed position.

"Callahan, what the *hell* are you doing?" Paula asked, still shaken from the hair-raising maneuver.

"Baiting the trap," he answered. "We have a tail."

"Halek?" Paula asked, feeling a sudden chill.

"And another man . . . probably Candellari. I spotted them back at the hay wagon."

"What are you going to do?"

Jack noticed the edginess in her voice. "Nothing terminal," he said coldly.

"This *isn't* a goddam game, Callahan," Paula flared; the nagging uneasiness that had been with her since the incident at the beer garden came to the surface. "Suppose they have guns? Suppose they try to kill us?"

"If that was their assignment, they've had ample opportunity," Jack said calmly, keeping his eyes on the road. "No . . . they've been instructed to follow us, nothing else. I don't like upsetting you," he added soothingly, "but I have a stake in this, too. Trust me. It'll be all right."

Paula nodded and fell silent. She didn't really doubt his abilities, but Popcorn's fate loomed large in her mind.

The BMW flashed by moments later. Callahan immediately floored the accelerator, and the little car squatted and lunged forward, raising a cloud of dust and a spray of pebbles as it roared from the dirt road, squealing and swerving when the tires bit firmly into the hard surface of the highway. Paula gripped the armrests, her eyes wide, her face tense.

The boxy BMW sedan didn't handle as well in the turns as the low-slung Mercedes, and Candellari wasn't as skilled at the wheel. Callahan was able to close the distance after a few miles.

Candellari maintained ninety miles an hour, and intent on his driving, was unaware of the turn of events as Jack paced him through a series of turns that ended in a straight and level stretch bordered on the right by a large pasture.

Callahan made his move. Shifting into a lower gear, he accelerated into the outside lane, pulling alongside the BMW with ease. The look on Candellari's face was one of complete surprise. Jack grimaced and cut the wheel hard to the right, slamming into the left front fender of the BMW. Candellari lost control, and the car swerved violently, careening off the road and out into the pasture, bouncing and bucking over the uneven surface, coming to a sudden, jarring stop in the middle of a shallow stream.

"There," Jack said, smiling as though unaffected by what he had just done. "That wasn't so bad, was it?"

Paula's face was ashen. "To what purpose?" she asked, visibly shaken by the experience.

Jack reached over and slowly massaged the back of her neck. "To let the hunter know that he can become the prey. It can be very unnerving."

Paula forced a weak smile. "Has it occurred to you that if we uncover a criminal conspiracy—anything that can hurt the people they work for—they'll come after us in earnest?"

Callahan nodded. "I'm counting on it," he said grimly. Taking Paula's hand, he held it as he drove. "I can be earnest myself," he said, squeezing her hand reassuringly. "*Very* earnest."

Paula stared at the confident, capable man she was getting to know, and depend on. Despite her rising anxiety, she felt sheltered and secure with him. He was not a man to boast idly.

Charlie Halek slammed the hotel room door with a force that Candellari thought might split it in two.

"Calm down, Charlie," Candellari said, crossing the room to the dresser. He pressed a switch on the voice-activated recorder and waited for the tape to rewind. "I've put up with your foul mood for the last hour; now, enough is enough."

Halek paced the room like a caged animal. "I'm not runnin' no more! I've had enough of this shit!" He grabbed the bottle of Scotch from the nightstand, filling a water glass to the brim, and took a long drink. Pointing at the ceiling, indicating the room above them, he said, "The next time that son of a bitch comes after me I'm gonna kill him! I don't like runnin' away from people, Phil," he said, flopping in a chair. *"Goddam I don't like it!"*

"I don't like it any more than you do," Candellari said, "but we have a job to do, and if it means we have to do things against our grains, well, so be it."

"It don't make no sense this way," Halek groused. "If they're out of the picture then the investigation's over—kill the head and the body dies with it."

"I believe that's 'kill the body and the head dies with it,' " Candellari corrected.

"Whatever," Halek snapped. "You know what I mean."

"Stopping the investigation isn't the objective," Candellari said patiently. "Cook wants it to run its course, and we're to keep him informed and follow his instructions. There's to be no violence unless absolutely necessary. What Callahan and the girl *think* we did can't be proved, and so far they have nothing damaging, that I can see, on Cook, other than possibly the information in that diary, and we'll take care of that shortly. So they can't hurt any of us, and consequently there's no reason to eliminate them."

"Bullshit! And you know it. That motherfuckin' Green Beret has a roarin' hard-on for us 'cause of his hippie friend and that goddam dog; and I know his type, he's a hard-ass, and he's comin' after us sooner or later—count on it!"

Candellari knew he was right, but now wasn't the time to add fuel to his fire. "That's a definite possibility," he said calmly, "and we'll deal with it if and when we have to."

Halek smiled at the prospect, chuckling to himself. "And I get the broad, too, right, Phil?"

Candellari looked at him askance and nodded. *"If* it's necessary," he said tersely.

The transmitters had fed little into the recorder—a maid humming to herself as she cleaned the suite, Paula making reservations for a flight to New York tomorrow, and her persuading Callahan to take her shopping and to a Mozart concert that evening in the great hall of a nearby castle.

They hadn't been spending much time in their room, and when they returned for the night they had already finished discussing any pertinent issues. But Candellari had picked up a conversation about the diaries at the Froeschmann home that revealed information that had upset Cook. "Get them and destroy them," he had told Candellari. The allusion to a "mystery woman"—Inge something or other (the last name had been lost when the radio was turned on)—intrigued him, and he was hoping to get something more revealing and substantial about her, and the reason for the visit to the prison.

Halek had perked up when he heard the recording of Paula making the airline reservations. "That mean we're goin' back to the States, too?" he asked hopefully.

Candellari nodded. "We'll take an earlier flight and wait for them in New York."

"Good," Halek said. "I don't like these goddam Krauts. The bastards forgot in a hurry who won the war."

"Sometimes I wonder myself, especially when I make a currency exchange," Candellari said, glancing at his watch; they had most of the afternoon left. "Our quarry doesn't require watching anymore today, so let's get the diary, then you can have a night out—find yourself a girl; it might take the edge off."

Halek grunted. "I can't get off on some Nazi bitch shouting orders at me, and besides, most of them are skunks."

Candellari shook his head, laughing softly. "Have I ever told you what a sterling fellow you are, Charlie?"

Halek stared at him blankly. "No," he replied expectantly.

"There's probably a good reason for that," Candellari said straight-faced, clapping him on the back. "Come on, let's go."

Helga Froeschmann's departure less than an hour after they arrived was a stroke of luck; they might have had to stay there all night. From their vantage point at the edge of the woods, Candellari trained the binoculars on her as she got in her car and drove away from the huge stone mansion. They waited until she started down the steep hill to the main road to Fürstenfeldbruck, then came out into the open, moving swiftly toward the house behind the cover of an overgrown hedge. Candellari slipped the lock on the terrace door at the side of the house hidden from view of the road by a grove of trees, and stepped cautiously into the drawing room.

"Damn, Phil. Will you look at this place? Talk about a home where the deer and the buffalo roam. This dump looks like it hasn't been cleaned in years." He shook one of the sheets covering a chair, raising a small cloud of dust. "Old broad must be a mole, livin' with all this filth."

"Let's get to work, Charlie. I want to be out of here before she gets back."

"What the hell's the difference? She's no problem."

Candellari ignored the remark, knowing further explanation wouldn't penetrate his thick skull any more than it previously had. He glanced around the huge, high-ceilinged room, and went over to the doorway to the next room. "The library is in here. Let's get a move on."

"Son of a bitch!" Charlie shook his head in disgust when he saw the floor-to-ceiling bookcases on all four walls of the forty-foot-square room. "There must be a couple thousand books here!"

"At least," Candellari replied. "You start here, and I'll start on the other side."

The first section of bookcases Halek checked contained the volumes of diaries, but the books with the typed labels indicating the years didn't register when he scanned over them—in his simple mind, a diary would say "Diary." An hour later, his eyes watering, irritated from his constant sneezing caused by an allergy to the dust being raised, he turned to Candellari with a practical solution to the problem. "Let's burn this bastard to the ground," he fumed. "We could spend the next three days here and not find those goddam books!"

Candellari considered the heavy-handed idea seriously, somewhat to Halek's surprise. They might get lucky and find the diaries soon, but the old woman could return at any moment and they would have to go back to the woods and wait until she again left . . . or, if they didn't hear her return and she walked in on them . . . Charlie's crude, unsophisticated approach, he decided, was the lesser of the evils. Cook had been explicit in his instructions about destroying the diaries. "All right, Charlie, we'll do it your way."

Halek responded eagerly, tearing down drapes, removing sheets from the furniture and piling them in the center of the room, coughing and gagging as the air thickened with dust. Candellari left the room, returning shortly with two cans of gasoline found in the garage behind the house. Halek tore down more drapes in the drawing room as Candellari saturated everything with gas.

Helga Froeschmann smiled politely and thanked the grocer for carrying her bags to the car. She turned the ignition key and the 1951 Mercedes sedan came to life, purring quietly, as it had for the past twenty-eight years and 255,000 miles. Driving slowly and carefully, both hands on the steering wheel, she still occasionally strayed to the middle of the road. The local residents knew her well and gave her a wide berth when they saw her coming. As she neared the narrow bridge leading out of the town, a local delivery van approached from the other direction. The driver, recognizing her, pulled to the side of the road and waved her ahead. She crossed the bridge at a snail's pace, steering with short, jerky movements of the wheel, smiling and nodding as she passed the van. The driver watched in amusement as she continued along the road, veering off the shoulder and struggling to get back on. Frau Froeschmann had learned to drive at the age of seventy-five, after the death of her husband. She was self-taught and had no driver's license, and because of her cataracts the road was a hazy blur to her, definable only by the contrasting darkness with the surrounding landscape. Her ineptitude was legendary throughout the district. She had never had an accident, but had caused more than anyone cared to remember.

The bumpy dirt road leading to her driveway tossed her gently in her seat, and some of the groceries tumbled from the bags to the floor of the car as she started up the steep hill.

Candellari lighted a corner of the piles of drapes and sheets in each of the rooms, and in a matter of seconds the first floor of the house was engulfed in flames. He ran out the front door as Halek arrived with the car, left hidden off the road a short distance from the house. As he jumped into the car, he saw the old lady's Mercedes turn the corner at the top of the hill and start down the driveway.

Helga Froeschmann saw the blurred figure running from the house, and huge puffs of black smoke billowing from two of the first-floor windows. She pressed the accelerator to the floor; the old engine coughed and sputtered with the effort, but answered the call, roaring loudly with a burst of speed that caused her to lose control as it careened down the driveway, half off the roadbed, crushing forty yards of shrubs before coming to an abrupt halt with its front tires imbedded in the mud of the algae-choked fish pond in front of the house.

"Move it!" Candellari screamed.

Halek sat at the wheel gunning the engine with the transmission in neutral. "Not yet," he answered calmly.

"*Goddammit, Charlie. I said move it!*" he shouted again, shoving him roughly against the door.

"Fuck Cook!" Halek gritted, staring intently ahead. "I don't want no witnesses, and that old broad can identify this car and us."

Frau Froeschmann got out of the old Mercedes, slightly shaken but uninjured. She glanced at the two men in the car and moved as fast as she could toward the house. Halek waited until she was in the center of the driveway, put the car in gear, and stomped on the throttle. The tremendous force of the blow knocked her into the air, across the driveway and patio, slamming her against the side of the house.

"All right, Charlie," Candellari said, turning from the sight of the mangled, lifeless body. "You had your fun. Now let's get the hell out of here before the whole town comes down on us!"

Halek stopped the car and jumped out, running over to the old woman's body. He picked her up, carried her inside as far as the flames permitted, and tossed her into the midst of the roaring blaze. "Loose ends," he said to Candellari as he got back in the car. "Don't want no loose ends."

"No one answers in Fraulein Carlson's suite," the concierge told the short, thin, impeccably dressed young man. "If you like, I will take a message for her." The concierge would have welcomed any excuse to talk to the attractive American woman. If it hadn't been for her companion, he would have introduced himself when she first arrived—under the proper circumstances, of course; creating them if necessary.

With a quick, precise movement, the young man reached inside his leather sport coat, removing a thick envelope. "Please deliver this immediately upon her return," he said officiously.

The concierge looked past him to the bank of elevators across the lobby. Paula and Jack were exiting one of the cars, luggage in hand. "Fraulein Carlson has just entered the lobby," he said, pointing in the direction of the elevators. "It appears they are ending their stay with us."

The young man turned in the direction the concierge had indicated, recognizing Paula instantly from Verity's description. Walking quickly across the lobby, he approached her from behind, tapping her on the shoulder.

Paula startled, dropped her bag and exhaled audibly. Callahan spun around, glaring suspiciously at the unfamiliar face.

"Excuse me, Miss Carlson," he said. "I did not mean to frighten you so." He clicked his heels and made an obeisant gesture somewhere in the middle distance between a nod and a bow. "Karlfried Nordmann, of *Time*. Mr. Verity in New York instructed me to gather certain information for you on his behalf." He handed Paula the envelope.

"Oh, yes, Mr. Nordmann. You surprised me."

"Obviously," Nordmann replied curtly, flashing a quick smile.

Paula took the envelope, placing it in her carry-on bag. "Thank you for getting it to me on such short notice."

Nordmann nodded again. "My pleasure. You will find it most complete. I personally visited the government offices in Ludwigsburg for some of the information, and contacted a reliable source in Berlin for the rest. I hope it is what you require. I could not obtain a current address on the subject," he added, "but I am quite certain she is no longer residing in Germany." Nordmann nodded to Jack, then to Paula. "Good day, Miss Carlson, and have a pleasant journey." He turned quickly, marching out of the hotel.

Jack took Paula's hand; it was cold and trembling slightly. "You okay?"

"Christ, am I on edge!" she said, squeezing his hand.

"Don't let it get to you," he said, smiling confidently. "It'll be all right."

Enroute to New York, seated across from Callahan at a small table in the upstairs lounge of the 747, Paula opened the envelope Karlfried Nordmann had given her. He had compiled a lengthy and thorough report from two sources: the Berlin Documents Center and an organization from Ludwigsburg with a rather long title: the Central Agency of State Administration of Justice for the Prosecution of National Socialist Crimes of Violence. The latter kept extensive files containing biographies and all pertinent information on war criminals, and proved to be the more informative. Inge Bauer, as the report revealed, had had a far more interesting and checkered past than Karl Dennecker.

Inge Bauer, born June 10, 1915, Hannover, Germany. Parents, Werner and Erica Bauer. Brother, Frederich Bauer. Wealthy, prominent family. Toy manufacturers with international market. Brother ran business from South America during war. Parents chose to remain in Germany, killed in Allied bombing raid, 1944. Sketchy information on Inge Bauer's early years; records destroyed during war. Graduated from Berlin Medical School, 1940. Participated in government medical program 1940–1945 (details to follow). Frequent companion of SS Lieutenant General Karl Dennecker. Disappeared at end of war. Believed to be living with brother in United States (unconfirmed).

Paula turned the page and began reading the text. Inge Bauer was originally on the list of Nazis to be indicted along with Karl Brandt in the infamous "medical case" tried by the U.S. government at Nuremberg, subsequent to the International Military Tribunal. The government, unable to find and arrest her, decided to try her *in absentia* in the event she was still alive and would be found later. The charges against her were eventually dropped, either from lack of sufficient evidence to convict, or owing to influence in the right places. She was no longer on the active list of the Ludwigsburg organization.

The "medical case" charged Karl Brandt and twenty-three other defendants with performing medical experiments on defenseless concentration-camp inmates against their will, murdering concentration-camp inmates for the purpose of collecting skulls and skeletons for the Anatomical Institute of the Reich University in Strassburg, and conducting a systematic euthanasia program. Inge Bauer was involved in the heinous euthanasia program.

T-4 was the code name for the program of legalized slaughter of helpless human beings under the guise of medical research, administered from the headquarters at Tiergartenstrasse 4, in Berlin. The objective of the T-4 euthanasia program was *Vernichtung lebensunwerten lebens*—the destruction of lives not worthy of living. The majority of victims were German citizens—the terminally ill, mentally retarded, physically deformed, aged and infirm, and insane. They were all categorized as "useless eaters," people who consumed valuable and limited food supplies, contributing nothing in return.

The ultimate desire of the T-4 program was to develop a fast and economical method of killing their victims, which they accomplished with remarkable efficiency in a relatively short time. They got their subjects from hospitals and asylums throughout Germany.

Paula was amazed to find that only a few of the principals involved in the program were punished severely after the war—those who left T-4 and went to work in the extermination camps. The U.S. government took the position that the euthanasia program was a crime by Germany against its own people and could best be dealt with by the reconstructed German courts at their own discretion. (Paula couldn't believe that piece of convoluted logic, a decision not dissimilar to placing the neurotics in charge of the psychopaths in a mental hospital.)

Inge Bauer's first assignment as a young doctor was at Castle Hartheim, in Alkoven, Austria. This sanitarium, like a number of others in Germany, was used as an experimentation center for the euthanasia program and a training center for the men who were soon to become the commandants of the newly established extermination camps.

In the early stages of the program, the victims at Castle Hartheim were killed by lethal injections, but as the experiments progressed, becoming more sophisticated and efficient, they were gassed to death in the prototype gas chambers which, once perfected to the point of maximum efficiency, would become a horrifying reality to the arrivals at the death camps. The training at the sanitarium also provided the psychological conditioning necessary to inure the trainees to their future assignments. They not only observed the experiments being conducted, but took part in them as well. There is no way of knowing how many people died because of the experiments at Hartheim; the records have never been found. But testimony has been given estimating the figure at forty thousand dead in a four-year period, with an additional three-hundred thousand murdered in the other involved institutions. Toward the end of the war, when the Germans were evacuating the death camps in the east, because of the advances of the Russian army, the Mauthausen concentration camp, near Castle Hartheim, was overcrowded with the arriving prisoners from the eastern camps to the point of being uncontrollable. Countless thousands of prisoners were taken to the nearby sanitarium to be gassed and cremated, greatly increasing Hartheim's death toll.

Inge Bauer was an assistant to the commandant of Castle

Hartheim, SS Hauptsturmfuehrer Christian Wirth. She was later transferred to another of the euthanasia institutions, Castle Brandenburg in Germany, where she served in an advisory capacity. After a few months at Castle Brandenburg, she was transferred to Berlin, probably because of intervention on the part of SS Lieutenant General Karl Dennecker. In Berlin, she worked with Dr. Werner Heyde, a professor of psychiatry from Wurzburg University who was in charge of the entire euthanasia program. She was a member of Heyde's medical committee at his headquarters at Tiergartenstrasse 4 until the end of the war.

The remainder of the report consisted of excerpts from the testimony at the medical-case trial concerning the treatment of the victims before they were killed, involving detailed descriptions of the nature and scope of the experiments conducted. Paula was horrified by what she read, finding it impossible to understand how any sane, responsible person could allow such things, let alone take part in them. She recalled a discussion she had had with Callahan last evening after the concert. He had argued that the reason why the western world, principally the United States, was so fascinated with the Nazi era was a romantic impulse—our last great global crusade, never to be experienced again in the age of the ICBM. World War II had given us a common cause, something we could believe in—the last justifiable war in which killing was honorable, and the most daring and proficient killers were considered heroes, decorated, honored, and paraded. She had disagreed, arguing that it was a morbid fascination with absolute power, with evil, with the almost surreal cruelty of the Nazis. Perhaps it was not unrealistic to consider the possibility of the Nazi specter once again being raised.

Paula glanced over at Jack; he was slumped in his chair, sound asleep. She looked at her watch—three more hours and they would be home.

TWELVE

The Madison Avenue coffee shop was noisy and bustling with its usual frenetic early-morning crowd. Al Verity calmly sipped his tea amid the din and assessed the ruggedly handsome man seated beside Paula in the booth. Callahan was more than muscle, he decided; a bit rough around the edges, not Paula's usual fare, but he seemed a decent enough chap. One might feel comfortable on a midnight stroll through Central Park with him along.

Verity listened attentively as Paula brought him up to date. Bits and pieces of information he had read about T-4 flashed in his mind, and he found it difficult to connect the attractive woman in Dennecker's photograph with the horrors of the euthanasia program. Her appearance was that of a sheltered aristocrat far removed from the blood and guts of things, waiting for her hunter to return from the hill.

"I think the agreement mentioned in the letters, the entries in the diaries, and the reprimand from the High Commissioner support my theory of a conspiracy to have Dennecker hanged," Paula concluded.

"It's plausible," Verity said, "but proving it is another matter. You must not confuse circumstantial evidence with facts. The agreement could be something as banal as a promise to give Dennecker a light sentence if, off the record, he provided them with information on other Nazis, a deal that was reneged on after the trial. And the letter from the High Commissioner doesn't necessarily support your hypothesis of coercion on the part of the OSS man, Cook; the entries in the diaries are subject to interpretation. Froeschmann could have exaggerated and embellished the facts. Cook could very well have threatened Froeschmann with prosecution for war crimes, legitimately so, considering that the lawyer did have some connection with the SS. This could explain his inadequate efforts on behalf of his client." Verity paused, shaking his head. "If it weren't for the continued surveillance and the seemingly related incidents in Aspen, I would have serious doubts about the merits of pursuing this, Paula. But Cook, and presumably the others, is worried about something; why else the extraordinary efforts to keep tabs on you?"

"The one constantly nagging problem I have with this is ... why?" Paula said. "Why would they conspire to hang a Nazi general? There's nothing to indicate that it was a personal vendetta, and I can't accept righteous indignation over Nazi atrocities. There has to be a profound motive."

"And when you find the motive," Verity counseled, "we're going to need watertight facts and a reliable witness who participated in or has firsthand knowledge of what they did and why. Without that, we can't print the story or we'll be in litigation up to our ears. And I assure you," he added, "accusations aren't going to make Senator Hill and the others step forward and confess their guilt. It's going to have to be proven conclusively, and I imagine they'll still fight us every inch of the way."

"Inge Bauer may be the solution," Paula said. "It looks as though she was with Dennecker during that time period. They were both in Berlin at the end of the war, and they both went into hiding; my guess is together. If she's still alive, she's our best bet."

"I suspect that she is alive," Verity said. "After your call from Munich, I called the Bauer residence at Oyster Bay." He paused, smiling at Paula. "Sorry, you know how difficult it is for me to postpone immediate gratification. The maid told me that Frederich Bauer was out of the country and would be back within the week. I asked her if there were any other members of the family I could talk to, perhaps Inge Bauer; she hesitated a moment, then told me none too convincingly that she didn't know of any Inge Bauer and that Mr. Bauer lived alone."

"Do you think she was really there?" Paula asked.

"I don't know, but I think you should get out there before her brother returns to bolster the line of defense. She may be your only living link with what happened in Nuremberg in 1947. And I wouldn't call again if I were you; you might spook her before you have a chance to question her effectively."

"We'll leave immediately," Paula said, gulping the last of her coffee.

"There might be someone you'd like to talk to before you do," Verity said, with a smug smile.

"Who?" Paula asked.

"Oliver Granger."

"Who's Oliver Granger?"

"A judge who was on the panel with Judge White at Dennecker's trial; retired and living at 480 Park Avenue, right here in the Big Apple."

"You have been busy," Paula said with admiration.

"I thought that might please you."

"We'll call on him first, then go out to Oyster Bay."

"Good hunting," Verity said, rising. He extended his hand to Jack. "Mr. Callahan, it's been a pleasure. Keep in touch," he said to Paula.

Outside, immersed in the constant pedestrian stampede, they sidestepped and wove their way up Madison Avenue.

"That Verity is a nice fellow," Callahan said. "An old flame?"

"Why do you ask that?" Paula asked with a quizzical look.

"It's written all over his face. He wears it well, but whatever you once had, he'd like to have again."

"That was a long time ago," Paula said with a shrug. "We're just friends; good friends."

Paula found Judge Oliver Granger to be a man who defied all the stereotypes of old age. At ninety-five his thought processes were lucid and his mind capable of astounding quantum leaps. He had total recall of the trial and the men involved and gave them a fascinating detailed account of the events, often anticipating their areas of interest and answering their questions before they had a chance to ask them. Unfortunately, he had no idea why Judge White had so aggressively pursued the death penalty for Dennecker. Before entering final deliberations to determine the actual verdicts and sentences, they had held a series of preliminary deliberations during which each of the judges expressed his views on the defendants and cast tentative ballots indicating how they would vote. Judge White had been intractable on the issue of Dennecker's sentence, much to the amazement of Judge Granger and the third judge on the panel. They believed that Dennecker should receive a prison sentence of not more than ten years, but Judge White would not hear of it. The test ballots showed that Judge White and the third judge also wanted to condemn to death two other defendants Judge Granger felt should receive lesser sentences. If he wanted White's support on the two other defendants, who had played very minor roles in the SS, he would have to compromise on Dennecker and arrange a tradeoff. He decided the two-for-one trade was the best he could do, with White hell-bent for his pound of Dennecker's flesh. He told Paula and Jack he had not been surprised to hear of the commutation of sentence by the High Commissioner.

They accepted Judge Granger's invitation to have lunch with him and chatted away the better part of two hours with this charming and brilliant man. By the time they were ready to leave they felt as though they had attended a seminar on the crosscurrents and undercurrents of the politics of World War II.

"May I again inquire as to the nature of your investigation?" Judge Granger asked as he showed them to the door, remembering they had evaded the question previously.

"We believe that certain events at the time of the trial are the impetus for criminal activities that have occurred recently," Paula said vaguely.

"What manner of criminal activities?" the judge asked.

"Possibly murder," Callahan answered. Paula could have kicked him.

"Oh, dear!" Judge Granger said, genuinely shocked. "I can't believe that Judge White would have any involvement in anything like that."

"We're not suggesting that he has," Paula interjected quickly. "And we have no evidence to that effect."

"I should think not," the judge said. "Very unlikely, *very* unlikely."

Once inside the elevator, Paula looked at Jack and shook her head. "Callahan, don't say things like that, at least not without qualifying your statements. We have no proof that

Judge White has done anything illegal, let alone being involved in a murder that we can't prove is a murder!"

Callahan nodded. "It just came out," he said apologetically. "I was thinking of Popcorn at the time."

Paula put her arm through his. "Promise me something, Callahan," she said affectionately.

"What's that?"

"Don't ever enter politics. You'd be a disaster."

Judge Granger walked haltingly back to the living room and picked up the telephone. Preposterous! he thought. White was an honorable man, a bit obstinate, but kindly and amiable. Young people today are so irresponsible. If memory served him, White lived in Cincinnati.

Judge White finished the last of his ten laps, hauled himself out of the water, and sat on the edge of the pool. The swim had relaxed him somewhat, but the anxiety was still there. He had lost ten pounds in the short time since the meeting with the Senator and Cook, and he hadn't been able to sleep more than two or three hours a night. He was totally preoccupied with nightmarish thoughts of disgrace and ruin; he could sense the undeniable inevitability of it. The journalist and her friend were on the right track; it was only a matter of time. The face he saw in the mirror each morning seemed to age before his eyes. He had deep circles under his eyes and a gaunt, haggard look. Carla hadn't noticed, but then she never noticed anything other than the balance in her checkbook. The only relief from the chronic anxiety was periods of low-grade depression and flattened emotions that gave him some measure of inner peace when he was physically exhausted and emotionally drained. He had come to welcome these brief respites and at times even tried to induce them.

A car came up the driveway and continued around the house to the parking area in the rear. A few minutes later Carla appeared on the flagstone walk leading to the pool, dressed in a scanty golf skirt. The judge had asked her not to wear those short skirts; her thighs had the consistency of cottage cheese and it wasn't a very appealing sight. She had spent the morning at the club with her friends, and from the wobble in her gait, the judge surmised they had spent most of their time in the bar.

Carla was unusually attentive today, offering to make him a drink and a sandwich. He interpreted this behavior as an indication that she wanted something outrageously expensive. She brought the sandwich and drink from the pool-house kitchen and sat beside him.

"How much do you want?" the judge asked flatly.

Carla bristled. "Oh, Ed, you're such a boor!"

"How much?" he repeated.

Carla got up and started toward the house. "Five thousand dollars; transfer it to my checking account."

"It'll be in your account tomorrow morning," he called after her.

Carla stopped and turned toward him. "Just before I came down to the pool there was a call for you ... a Judge Granger; the number is on your desk in the library."

Granger ... Granger, the judge repeated to himself. The name was familiar but he couldn't place it. Then—Nuremberg—Dennecker's trial.

The judge's skin turned cold and clammy; he began to tremble uncontrollably. Stumbling up the walk, he entered the house through the sun porch and hurried straight to the library, finding the slip of paper on which Carla had written the telephone number. His hands shook so badly he had to redial twice.

Judge White sat slumped in the chair, unable to move, shocked and frightened by what Granger had told him. He mustered his reserves and picked up the address book from the desk, finding John Cook's number. Cook's secretary put the call through immediately in response to the judge's urgent demand.

"What the hell's on your mind, Ed?" Cook asked impatiently. "I'm in the middle of an important meeting."

"I know what you've done!" the judge lied, his voice shaking. "I won't be a party to this! I'm going to the authorities and wash my hands of the whole affair! I'll take what's coming to me for the Dennecker mess, but I will not condone *murder!*"

Cook's mind raced frantically. How the hell had he found out? Hill didn't know. *"Shut your goddam mouth!"* Cook bellowed. "I will not discuss this any further on the telephone!"

"Why? Why, in the name of God? How *could* you?"

Cook decided it might be best to try to talk some sense into the judge before hanging up. "Look, Ed. It was totally unavoidable, believe me. We had no choice. We're in this thing up to our necks and halfway measures just won't cut it. It's either sink or swim, and I don't intend to sink at this late date."

The judge felt faint at hearing the confirmation. "I want no part of this . . . this madness," he sputtered, almost at the point of hysterics. "I want out!"

"You're in too deep, Ed. Any confession to the authorities at the eleventh hour might cleanse your soul, but it sure as hell wouldn't save your ass. Now get control of yourself. I'll come to Cincinnati tomorrow and we can talk this thing out."

The judge broke the connection and collapsed into the chair, quivering. The confirmation of his hideous suspicions had drained his last ounce of strength. He sat there, numbed, abject, for hours, his mind a hazy swirl of memories: how he had rationalized sentencing Dennecker to hang; how convincing Hill and Cook had been, arguing that all the top SS officers were vicious, murdering animals that deserved to die; how easy, in the end, it had been for him to do something so alien to his character. Carla. Carla was his motivation, his weakness and his strength. How wonderful it was going to be to give her everything she wanted. How happy they were going to be. He remembered Dennecker's face as he stood in the prisoner's dock to hear his sentence, proud and cold, no trace of emotion when he heard his fate—complete betrayal of the promises that had been made to him. He had looked directly into Judge White's eyes, and it was as though he had spoken aloud: "You are worse than we are. At least we had a cause we believed in, however distorted or evil."

The judge at last regained some of his strength and willpower and decided what he must do. He went upstairs and put on his best business suit, carefully selecting an appropriate tie, and returned to the library. He took a sheet of stationery from the desk drawer; when he had finished writing, he reread a short passage from a Greek tragedy he had been reading that morning:

> Better to die and sleep the never-ending sleep, than
> linger on and dare to live when the soul's life is gone.

He removed one of his shotguns from the cabinet near the door and sat down at the desk. Placing both barrels of the gun in his mouth, he pulled the trigger.

*　　*　　*

John Cook's secretary interrupted the board of directors meeting for the second time that day. This time it was an urgent call from Senator Hill. Cook took the call in his office.

"Ed White blew his brains out this afternoon," Senator Hill said gravely. "My aide got it off the wire service."

Cook remained silent for a moment, then breathed an inaudible sigh of relief. "Could be a blessing in disguise," he said callously. "The little twit called me earlier today, blubbering like an hysterical old woman. He said he was going to take the whole story to the authorities," he hedged. "I'm relieved he took the easy way out."

"I called a friend of mine with the Cincinnati police," the Senator said. "No suicide note was found, but I want you to get out there and make certain the son of a bitch didn't leave any written confession lying around. Talk to his wife. Do whatever's necessary to get her fullest cooperation."

"I'll be there in a few hours," Cook said. "Call you after I've talked to her."

Cook arrived in Cincinnati early that evening and took a taxi to the judge's home. He had the driver park at the rear of the house and told him to wait. As he walked toward the kitchen entrance he noticed a young girl with long chestnut-brown hair sitting on the lawn at the edge of the hill overlooking the river. She seemed unaware of his arrival. Carla answered the door and told him she was not feeling up to talking to any more reporters. Cook explained who he was and that he and Senator Hill were business partners of the judge's. Carla nodded knowingly and invited him in.

"I thought I might get a visit from either you or the Senator," Carla said with a trace of arrogance. "You needn't worry. It's in my best interests that Ed's final pathetic outburst of emotional diarrhea doesn't become public knowledge."

Cook stared at her momentarily and smiled to himself. He thought he, too, might prefer a quick death to life with the hardnosed bitch standing before him. There wasn't a trace of grief to be seen. Cook guessed that she was most concerned with the social embarrassment her husband's suicide might entail. "Then he did leave a note?"

"More like a goddam spiritual enema," Carla said disgustedly. "I was upstairs changing when I heard the gun go off. I found him in the library at his desk, with half of his face

166

missing. There was a three-page confession of his past sins on the desk. I burned it before I called the police. You and the Senator might well be grateful to me."

"I can assure you that we are most grateful, Mrs. White. Most grateful."

"And you will express that gratitude by promptly agreeing to purchase the six hundred thousand worth of stock my husband held in your company—at a premium, of course. Let's say fifty percent above current market value."

The smile left Cook's face and his eyes grew hard. "I'm certain that can be arranged. If you will have your attorney contact me in the morning we can have the transaction completed within a few days."

"That will be fine, Mr. Cook. And that will be the last you will hear of the matter."

"That would be advisable, Mrs. White," he said, seeing from the look on her face that they understood each other. "Most advisable."

"If you will excuse me," Carla said as though dismissing an uninvited guest, "I have some funeral arrangements to attend to."

Paula and Jack drove a few miles north of the town of Oyster Bay and crossed the causeway to Center Island. They followed the main road past well-groomed estates to a private drive at the southernmost tip of the island. The property was heavily wooded, and a sign on one of the stone pillars marking the entrance to the driveway read: PRIVATE ROAD—NO TRESPASSING—F. BAUER. They took the drive for a half mile or so until it ended in a parking area in front of a large Georgian mansion. They rang the doorbell a number of times, but there was no response. The house and gardens were surrounded by a high, dense hedge, impossible to see through, but Callahan found a gate off to one side that led into the garden. A well-tended path took them to where a huge expanse of open lawn rolled gently for nearly a hundred yards to the crest of a small hill that overlooked the bay. Jack could make out an informal grouping of furniture at the edge of the hill, and it looked as though someone was sitting there. As he started walking in that direction he saw a black dog get up from in front of the chair where the person was sitting. It had a wedge-shaped head and pointed ears, and stood stiffly, staring intently at him. Paula continued walking across the lawn; Callahan caught her by the arm, telling her to stand absolutely still. The dog raised its nose and stretched its neck, moving its head slowly from side to side, testing the air for a scent.

"What is it, Callahan?"

"I think that dog spells trouble."

"Oh, don't be silly. He's just standing there looking at us. Besides," Paula said, pulling him ahead, "I have a way with dogs. They all love me."

"If I'm not mistaken, that's a Doberman, and I don't think he loves you. Trained Dobermans have been known to dismember people they feel are threatening them and theirs. And he's taking the same posture that Boomer does when he's about to challenge someone."

No sooner had Jack spoken than the dog started moving toward them, slowly at first, single-tracking, then quickening its pace, and finally, when it was certain they were intruders, breaking into an all-out run at an amazing speed.

Jack dragged Paula along behind him as he sprinted toward a large oak tree near the terrace. Cupping his hands, he made a stirrup for her foot, boosting her high enough to grab one of the lower limbs and swing up into the tree. A quick, agile move of his own put him out of danger only seconds before the huge dog slammed into the tree and bounced off in a snarling rage. He stood at the base of the tree braced for attack, making the most terrifying sounds Paula had ever heard. The godawful noise seemed to start in his bowels as a low grumble and work its way out through a respiratory amplification system that finally released it as a roaring, hyperventilated snarl.

A woman appeared and spoke sharply to the dog. "Quiet, Otto! Sit down and be quiet." The dog did so immediately. Callahan couldn't see the woman very well from his precarious perch in the tree, but guessed it was the same person who had been sitting at the edge of the hill. She looked up at them and said, "You may come down now. Otto will not harm you unless I tell him to." Paula recognized her immediately; it was Inge Bauer.

Jack helped Paula to the ground, jumping down behind her. Otto growled menacingly but held his position, his watchful eyes flicking from Paula to Callahan. Jack slowly removed his tweed sportcoat, wrapping it tightly around his forearm so as to be prepared in the event the dog decided to attack.

"That will do you no good," the woman said flatly. "Otto is trained to attack vital areas. You will please remove it before you anger him."

Callahan reluctantly did as she had instructed.

With cold, lucent blue eyes, she gave each of them a swift, appraising glance. Paula didn't know which was more frightening, the dog or the woman controlling him. She looked remarkably like the picture taken of her thirty-seven years ago, still an exceptionally handsome woman at the age of sixty-four, tall and slender, with an air of cool sophistication.

"Who are you and what are you doing here?"

"I'm a journalist," Paula said, extending her hand. "My name is Paul Carlson, and this is Jack Callahan."

She ignored Paula's outstretched hand. "I do not speak to reporters. You will leave immediately. You had no right to trespass on my property and violate my privacy."

"I apologize for that, Miss Bauer," Paula said, "but it is imperative that we talk."

Inge Bauer's tone became more hostile. "We have nothing to talk about, Miss Carlson. You *will* leave this instant, or Otto will enforce my demands."

Callahan believed she meant it. "Let's go," he said firmly, taking Paula's arm. "This isn't the time or the place."

"Just one moment of your time," Paula persisted, reaching into her shoulder bag and removing the report the stringer had given her in Munich. "Please read this."

Inge Bauer hesitated, but took the report, reading quickly, her face expressionless. "Judging from the completeness of this, Miss Carlson," she said tonelessly, handing her the stack of papers, "there is no need for us to talk."

"I believe that there is, Miss Bauer. If enough exposure should be given to these facts and your presence in this country," Paula said, setting the stage, "a certain ethnic faction in this country would bring pressure to bear to have you extradited and brought to trial in Germany; I'm sure you're aware that the statutes for prosecuting war criminals are still in effect and in most cases actively pursued."

"I'm well aware of that, Miss Carlson," Inge Bauer said, her lithic stare wavering.

"However," Paula continued, "if you are willing to help us with another matter, that need not happen. Of the three people who know of your whereabouts, none of us is interested in you or your sullied past."

"Then what?" Inge asked suspiciously.

"SS Lieutenant Karl Dennecker," Paula replied.

At the mention of Dennecker's name, Inge Bauer's entire demeanor changed, as though a page in a photo album had been turned to an image of another day, another mood. A vulnerable look came into her eyes and her voice softened as she asked, just above a whisper, "How do you know of my relationship with Karl?"

Callahan noticed for the first time that her light, cultured German accent gave her voice a very feminine, almost sensual quality.

Paula again reached into her shoulder bag, this time removing the photograph of Inge and Dennecker, and handed it to her.

Inge smiled fondly as she looked at the old snapshot. The cherished memories came rushing back, nearly overwhelming her with their emotional impact. She blinked and sniffled and tossed her head in an attempt to hold back the tears welling in her eyes. When she spoke her voice was husky with emotion, but she wasn't speaking to Paula and Jack; it was directed inward to someone who used to be and things that might have been. "Such a wonderful holiday. In the fall. Yes, the fall, just about this time of year." She seemed to slip back in time, unaware that she was not alone. "We went to the opera. We danced under the stars. We loved. It was such . . ." She stopped abruptly. "Where did you get this photograph?"

"When Dennecker died earlier this month I found it among his possessions," Paula said.

Inge stared at her with a pained, puzzled expression. "You must be mistaken. Karl died in 1955 in Landsberg prison, in Germany."

"I'm sorry," Callahan said gently, "but Karl Dennecker died of a heart attack a few weeks ago, in the mountains near Aspen, Colorado. We found his body and took it back to town."

Inge stood silently for a few moments, then looked at Paula and Jack. "Come and sit with me. We must talk." Calling Otto to her side, she led them to the chairs at the far end of the lawn. Otto stood tense and alert, glaring at Paula and Jack until they were seated, then he curled up at the foot of the chair Inge had taken. He sensed that his mistress was upset, and rested his head on her knees in a gesture of comfort.

In response to Inge's questions, Callahan told her what little he knew of Dennecker's life in Aspen for the past twenty-four years. Paula sparingly explained that their investigation centered on the period in Dennecker's life immediately following the war when he was captured and tried as a war criminal; there were three men involved in his trial who possibly conspired to have him hanged.

Inge nodded knowingly, but remained noncommittal, saying nothing.

Callahan observed something he had been too preoccupied to notice before: Inge displayed all the symptoms of a chronic alcoholic in an advanced stage of the disease. It became obvious to him that she was trying her best to hide it, but it manifested itself in spite of her best efforts. Her hands trembled as she attempted to light a cigarette; she fumbled with the lighter; tipped over a glass and her reflexes were too slow to keep it from falling. This seemed to upset her more than it should. Jack had assumed she was sipping water from the glass, but he now guessed it was gin or vodka. Other telltale signs would have been impossible to conceal: the dilated blood vessels on her face and neck, looking like tiny blue spiders; the whites of her eyes streaked with red; her flushed face and slightly slurred speech that came and went with a will of its own. Jack guessed that though she was still lucid, she spent a good deal of time in a foggy, alcoholic haze.

Inge looked again at the photograph she was holding in her lap and said, "It is comforting to know he kept it all these years." This time she was unsuccessful in her attempt to hold back the tears. Callahan glanced at Paula and knew she must be wondering, as he was, how in the name of God this woman, who seemed to have a full range of normal emotions, could have been involved in something as twisted as the Nazis' euthanasia program.

Inge regained her composure with difficulty and said to Paula, "I would like very much to keep this photograph. It would mean a great deal to me."

Paula nodded imperceptibly to Jack. He shrugged; it was only one of the prints. "Of course," Paula said. "By all means keep it."

Inge smiled gratefully. "Thank you. Thank you very much."

"I have something I must ask you, Miss Bauer," Paula said

hesitantly, still not certain that the threat she had made had had its desired effect, "and I mean no disrespect." She paused to phrase the question as diplomatically as possible. "It's very apparent that you and General Dennecker loved each other very much at the time that photograph was taken, and you obviously still love him. I understand why you wouldn't have looked for him, believing him to be dead, but for the past twenty-four years he has been within a day's travel from you. Why didn't he come to you?"

Inge smiled sadly to herself. "I have lived in this house with my brother since 1948. I believe I have left the property less than a dozen times. Being familiar with my past, you can readily understand why I am so private a person. I am not proud of what I have done, Miss Carlson. Oh, there was a time when I was, but the passions and unquestioning belief of that era have gone with my youth, and I most certainly do not want to draw attention to myself or my 'sullied' past, as you put it. However, had my brother not lied to me about Karl's death, for whatever reason he may have had, I would have gone to Karl without hesitation. As to why Karl did not come to me . . . that is part of the story you came here to get."

"Are you going to tell me?" Paula asked.

Inge forced a weak smile. "The prospects if I do not are very unappealing to me at this stage of my life, Miss Carlson; I shouldn't think I have a choice. Is that correct?"

Paula held her gaze and said nothing.

"In that case, I believe I have the answers you want." She removed the stopper from a crystal decanter on the table, refilling the glass she had spilled. She took a long compulsive swallow, and from the expression on her face, Callahan decided it was definitely not water.

"I have relived those last few years with Karl over and over in my mind for the past thirty-one years. They are the only treasured moments of my life. There has been nothing since."

As she began to talk, she seemed again to drift back in time, reliving each incident with the telling. . . .

Berlin—April 10, 1945

The huge truck rumbled slowly away from the WVHA head-quarters toward what remained of Berlin. Karl Dennecker grimaced as he drew closer to the heart of the once proud and

172

vital city. Thick plumes of black smoke billowed from the countless scattered fires, reminders of last night's raid. The incendiary bombs continued to take their toll long after the planes that dropped them had gone. The center of the city had been hardest hit; as he approached the Tiergarten he rolled up the windows of the cab in an attempt to keep out the foul sulfur smell. People were beginning to emerge from their underground shelters and basement hovels, many wearing mufflers and goggles against the masonry dust and fine particles of soot suspended in the air. They seemed to be functioning well in spite of the devastation surrounding them, no signs of panic or confusion. The effects of the constant day and night raids were awesome; skeletons of blackened, twisted steel that had once been magnificent buildings were everywhere. The city would have been unrecognizable to anyone who had not seen it since the war began. Every day thousands of homeless refugees from the east streamed through the city heading westward, away from the Russians. They were the innocent victims of war, ragged, destitute, carrying what was left of their meager possessions on their backs, or pulling it along in handcarts.

Dennecker drove carefully and slowly through the all but impassable streets, skirting bomb craters and avoiding piles of rubble and debris. They have not yet had the worst of it, he thought. The Russians are still to come. The Red Army would only have to contend with poorly equipped and untrained old men and children. It would be a nightmare.

The drive from Dennecker's office to Tiergartenstrasse 4, under normal conditions no more than a fifteen-minute trip, took almost two hours because of the detours necessitated. Inge was standing in the entrance to the T-4 headquarters waiting for Karl to arrive. She, too, had spent the night working, destroying files and films of the organization's programs and experiments. Seeing the truck approach, she ran out to meet him, leaping in before it came to a complete stop. Kissing him passionately, she put her arm through his and held tightly.

"Oh, Karl, it will be so good to get out of this death trap. Did things go well with General Gluecks?"

Karl opened a small briefcase, showing her the contents. He had obtained bogus military orders with the Reichsfuehrer's signature, ordering him to transport top-secret SS files to Bavaria for safekeeping, travel authorization for her as his administrative assistant, and false identification papers for both of them when they reached their destination. Their primary concern now was not the enemy but the German roadblocks and patrols looking for deserters and stopping all unauthorized travel in restricted areas.

Before leaving the city they stopped at the apartment they shared in the Wilmersdorf district, picking up two trunks packed with personal belongings. Karl weaved his way through the cluttered streets of the outlying districts until he reached Reichsstrasse 96. He then headed south, away from the battered, smoldering ruins of the dying city.

The four-lane highway was lined with columns of refugees also going south, but except for an occasional staff car or supply convoy speeding back to the city, the traffic was light. The previous week the road had been clogged with endless convoys of trucks heavily laden with office equipment, filing cabinets, furniture, and the personal possessions of the party officials and administration agency staffs and their families who were fleeing the city. Karl was stopped at an SS roadblock near Zossen, where the German High Command headquarters were located. The officer in charge, seeing Karl's insignia of rank, waved him through after a cursory examination of his papers. They continued south through the dense pine forest for another thirty miles to Luckau, and then drove southwest in the direction of the Elbe River. Karl felt sure that the advance American units would not have reached this section of the river as yet. Gluecks had said they were in the vicinity of Magdeburg. Karl chose the town of Torgau as his point for crossing the river, then drove farther west and south, putting as much distance between them and the Russian lines as possible. They saw no Americans.

Karl told Inge about a copy of a map Gluecks had seen in Reichsfuehrer Himmler's office, a map summarizing an Allied plan called Operation Eclipse which had been captured from the British during the battle of the Ardennes. The Allies planned to partition Germany into zones of occupation at the end of the war. The Russians would occupy the territories east of a line drawn roughly from Lübeck in the north to Schweinfurt in the center of Germany. West and south of that line the country would be divided in half, the British controlling the north and the Americans the south. France was to be given a zone in Austria. Karl had chosen their destination based on that information. Bavaria was to be in the American sector, and Karl believed their chances would be better there. The Americans were inexperienced conquerors.

"Do you think I, too, will be on the war criminals list?" Inge asked.

"Not at first," Karl replied. "The T-4 programs were not widely known even to our own people. Perhaps after they finish investigating the party leaders, and the concentration-camp system, they will get around to some of the other programs, but if we are lucky, you will escape their attention. Time is on our side; time and the fact that the most incriminating documents and records have been destroyed." He put his arm around her and kissed her gently on top of her head. "Don't worry, my love. We will leave Germany as soon as we can make the necessary contacts."

Karl left the main road a few miles east of Leipzig and skirted the heart of the city to the north, then continued in the direction of Weimar. A short distance from Weimar he was stopped at another roadblock set up by the field police. Beyond the roadblock the roads leading from Weimar were jammed with vehicles of every description, and hordes of soldiers trudged wearily along beside them. The German army was in full retreat. A young sergeant approached the truck and politely asked to see their travel authorization. When he noticed that Karl's destination was Bavaria, he told him he should not go any farther west but to turn south immediately. Patton's Third Army had taken Weimar and had liberated the Buchenwald concentration camp, and the Americans were in an unusually vengeful mood. "God only knows what they might do to an SS general," he said to Karl. Dennecker thanked him for the information, turned around, and retraced his route until he found a secondary road leading through the forest a few miles from the roadblock.

His progress was slowed considerably by the narrow, bumpy, winding road, but the trees formed a canopy overhead, providing excellent cover from strafing attacks by Allied fighter planes. Karl occasionally stopped on high ground to reconnoiter any American units in the area, but the immediate countryside was peaceful and empty. They passed along the edges of a number of small farming villages, and Inge commented on the variety of makeshift flags of surrender displayed at the windows of the homes. The Americans would be greeted with an array of undergarments, bed sheets, and towels put out by frightened people who wanted to save their villages from unnecessary destruction.

They continued south through the deep forest and mountains of the region west of Saalfeld. Inge suggested they stop for lunch, and Karl pulled the truck into a wooded section of towering pines far enough off the road to be hidden from view of anyone driving by. Inge brought the picnic basket she had prepared, and they walked deeper into the woods, their footsteps muted by the thick carpet of pine needles, until they found an idyllic spot along the banks of a mountain stream. Inge placed a bottle of white wine in the icy water to chill, and they sat propped against a large tree, listening to the soft murmur of the forest, enjoying a scene a world away from the anguish they had left behind in Berlin.

The overcast skies were breaking up and the sun's warm rays filtered through the trees to the forest floor. Inge stretched out on the bed of pine needles beneath the tree and lay her head in Karl's lap. "Oberhof is not far from here," she said, smiling up at him. "Do you remember Oberhof?"

"Yes. I was thinking about Oberhof, too." He ran his fingers through her hair. "The scent of the pines brought it back to me."

"We took steaming baths together," Inge remembered fondly, "and we made love in front of the fireplace in our room. And you, my dearest Karl, were—"

Karl bolted upright and stared at the edge of the woods on the other side of the stream. Inge turned her head to see what had startled him. His eyes were wide in disbelief. He thought at first it was a ghostly hallucination, but as the barely human figures crossed the stream and drew nearer, Karl knew they were real—and he knew, too, where they had come from.

There were seven of them, all in the most wretched physical condition imaginable. Their bodies were mere skeletons, and the tattered and filthy blue-and-gray-striped jackets and trousers they wore had more substance than the bodies from which they hung. The tall man leading the group across the stream had a large frame, capable of carrying well over two hundred pounds; Karl doubted that he weighed as much as a hundred. They all carried crude weapons; some had wooden clubs, others kitchen knives and axes.

Inge held Karl's arm tightly, staring at the faces of the men as they approached. They were deathly pale and gaunt, their skin covered with open sores, their sunken eyes like hollow sockets. "Jews," Inge whispered, "from Buchenwald."

Karl nodded. He knew; he had seen enough of the wretched creatures when he had accompanied Gluecks on inspection tours of the camps. He opened the flap of his holster and removed his pistol. The Walther PPK held seven rounds of ammunition. He had loaded it that morning before leaving his office. One for each of them, he thought grimly.

The tall one leading the group stopped about ten feet from where Karl and Inge were sitting; the others stood on either side of him. His eyes held Karl's for a moment with a blank gaze, the look of one who had seen the worst and was now drained of all emotion. His eyes raised slowly upward to the skull-and-crossbones insignia above the peak of Karl's cap. Karl released the safety on his pistol.

"Give me your gun, Herr General," the tall skeleton said in a flat tone, "and we will not harm you."

Inge began to shake with fright. Karl raised the barrel of the gun to point at the man's head. "I will not hesitate to kill you if you do not leave at once," Karl said calmly.

The man smiled, revealing decayed and broken teeth. "We have no fear of death, general. We have lived with death for years; it came as a welcome guest to us." He took a few steps foward, and the others followed. "If we attack you in unison, you may kill one of us, possibly two, but the rest of us will deal with you and your companion."

Inge screamed as the men began walking toward them as a group. One of them raised an ax in the air, and Karl fired. The bullet struck him just above the bridge of the nose, killing him instantly. The group surged forward, breaking into a run.

Before Karl had a chance to select his next target and fire, the cries of anger from the charging men were drowned out by the deafening roar of machine-gun bursts that seemed to come from all directions. The ragged group was literally cut to pieces before his eyes; a fine mist of blood, bits of flesh, clumps of earth, and a flurry of pine needles flew through the air amid the hail of bullets. The uproar ended as quickly and mysteriously as it had begun. Karl was too stunned to move.

The eerie silence following the carnage was pierced by a shrill whistle that came from behind an outcropping of rocks near the edge of the stream, about ten yards to the left of Karl and Inge. Men began to appear all around them from behind trees and thickets. In their camouflaged uniforms and helmets they were almost indistinguishable from their surroundings. Karl estimated that there were about twenty of them. They walked among the scattered, mutilated corpses and kicked at them, making certain they were dead. A tall, lanky young captain walked briskly toward them. He had striking blue eyes and light-blond hair and wore his uniform cap at a jaunty angle. Stopping a few feet from where they sat, he clicked his heels, snapped to attention, and saluted. "Captain Hans Ackerman," he announced, "of the SS Gebirgs Division Nord. Forgive me for intruding, Herr General, but it appeared you might be in need of assistance."

Karl helped Inge up and smiled at the flamboyant young officer, returning his salute. "The intrusion is most welcome, Hauptsturmfuehrer," he replied. "We would probably have been killed had it not been for your timely assistance."

"Glad to be of service, Herr General," the captain said with a neat, elegant bow from the waist. "My men and I were a few hundred yards from here when we heard your truck stop and pull into the woods. We thought it best to investigate." The captain's expression changed as he noticed, for the first time, the Knight's Cross with Oak Leaves and Crossed Swords Karl was wearing around his neck. He stiffened slightly, then, as a matter of justifiable pride, as opposed to empty vanity, opened the top of his parka, displaying his own Knight's Cross with Oak Leaves. Karl smiled and nodded in recognition.

Inge invited the captain and his men to join them for lunch, going back to the truck to get four more bottles of wine, handing them to the captain to distribute among the men. Moving far downstream, away from the site of the slaughter, they sat in a clearing near a small waterfall. The Waffen SS men and the captain ate their rations, supplemented with a large block of cheese and a basket of salted rolls Inge passed among them; she and Karl, having lost their appetites, listened as the captain told them of the latest developments on the western front. He explained that he and his men were all that remained of their company. Their division had been badly beaten and overrun by Patton's Eleventh Armored Division south of Worms. They had been separated from what was left of their division and were making their way north to Dessau to the headquarters of the German 12th

Army Group. Karl told him about the Americans' capturing Weimar and warned him to stay well east of that area. The captain considered asking Karl about Inge, the contents of the truck, the reason for their journey, and their destination, but decided against it. There were a great many deserters throughout the country, quite a few high-ranking officers included, but it was inconceivable to him that a Waffen SS General, holder of the Knight's Cross, would be deserting his comrades. He concluded that whatever the general's reason for being there, it was with official sanction. The captain and his men left after eating, and not wanting to risk another encounter with liberated camp inmates, Inge and Karl were on the road within minutes.

They continued south, passing to the east of Sonneberg, and penetrated deeper into the Bavarian forests, then drove southeast past Bayreuth and Weiden and due south again through the peaceful forests and hills of the Bayerisherwald. The isolated country roads were time-consuming and treacherous in spots, but were well suited for the clandestine journey. A few hours of night driving were all that Karl could manage after a long day, and thirty miles south of Regensburg he pulled the truck into the far corner of a field, where they slept until dawn. That day, shortly before noon, they reached their destination.

The town of Waging and the nearby lake were in the foothills of the Bavarian Alps, near the Austrian border, fifteen miles northwest of Salzburg. The area had remained as Karl remembered it from a visit before the war. Other than the absence of vacationers and the young men who had gone off to fight, life in the picturesque resort continued as though the war did not exist. Inge was enchanted with the small chalet on the shore of the lake. The setting was magnificent, with its views of the water and the Alpine peaks in the distance. It had belonged to Karl's brother, who had been killed during the battle for Stalingrad. The chalet was in a secluded spot, the perfect place to sit out what was left of the war and plan their escape from Germany.

After removing the trunks they had packed with personal belongings and taking them inside, they spent most of the rest of the day unloading the truck and stowing the contents in a culvert behind the chalet, carefully concealing the hiding place with branches, leaves, and the trunk of a tree felled by a winter storm. Karl's brother had left an old Mercedes sedan, covered with a tarp, parked under the rear portico, and after a few hours of tinkering Karl had the car working. That night, with Inge following in the Mercedes, Karl took the truck away from the lake and sent it over a steep embankment on one of the mountain roads.

In the days that followed, the pleasant surroundings lulled them into a sense of security and well-being. They walked the miles of footpaths around the lake in the mornings, read in the afternoons, and at night listened to the radio for news of the outside world. The pace of events quickened as the war neared its end. Within a matter of weeks, the Germany Karl and Inge knew no longer existed. Hitler committed suicide, Berlin fell to the Russians, and Germany signed an unconditional surrender. It was more final and catastrophic than the armistice ending the First World War.

The war now ended, Germany was in complete chaos. Millions of uprooted, homeless civilians roamed the country, scavenging for food. It was easy for the top Nazis to escape, swallowed up by the hordes of refugees and the ruins of the bombed cities. The search for them was concentrated in two areas: in the north between Hamburg and Flensburg, and in the south between Munich and Berchtesgaden. Karl had no way of knowing when he chose Waging as a refuge that he would be in the center of the area many other Nazis on the war criminals list would choose to go into hiding. The manhunt was relentless. Photographs and descriptions were distributed to all Allied barracks, displaced-persons camps, prisoner-of-war camps, and refugee centers. Karl's photograph was among them.

One morning during the last week of May, Inge returned from the grocery store in the village with some sobering news: Himmler had been captured at a British checkpoint somewhere near Hamburg and had been taken to an interrogation center, where he committed suicide with a poison capsule secreted in his mouth. Captured with him were Otto Ohlendorf, Karl Brandt, and Karl Gebhardt, all high-ranking officers of the SS. Ohlendorf had been in charge of extermination squads in the east, and Brandt and Gebhardt had been involved in the SS medical programs using concentration-camp inmates for their experiments. They were all sent to Nuremberg to be imprisoned until they could be tried for their crimes. Karl knew these men well, and felt that their capture would be sure to draw more attention to himself and his department. It was now imperative to make contact with someone who could help them get out of the country. They decided that Inge should go to Salzburg to see some of her family's influential friends and find out if there was an underground organization active in that area. She left the following morning.

The trip proved unsuccessful. Inge's friends were unable to help. They had heard rumors of an organization formed to help arrange escapes, somewhere in the Aussee region of Austria, but knew none of the details, if indeed the organization actually existed. They told her the Americans had heard the same rumors and were searching the region for the wanted Nazis. Inge said she would contact them later and asked them to make further discreet inquiries about the escape organization.

The summer months seemed to drag on endlessly. Karl prudently confined himself to the chalet and occasional walks around the lake. Inge shared his routine except for her weekly trip to the village for food and newspapers. The feelings of relief and relaxation they had felt when they first reached the lake soon changed to tedium and restlessness.

In November the International Military Tribunal began the trial of the Nazi Party hierarchy in Nuremberg. Karl followed the newspaper accounts of the proceedings with a morbid fascination and was dismayed when the IMT declared the SS a criminal organization. There was no doubt now that all officers in purely administrative positions would be tried for war crimes. The papers said the Americans were preparing their own war-crimes trials to be held subsequent to the IMT.

"The Americans are weaklings and fools," Karl told Inge. "They have neither the courage nor the resolve to do what must be done—cull the worthless parasites and insidious, dissenting traitors for the greater good. Criminals, are we? The Jew and the communist, if allowed to attain influence, will soon take advantage of their naive, sententious benefactors; then the Americans will understand, too late."

By spring of the following year, Karl could no longer tolerate the close confinement and inactivity. In the past few weeks he had become irritable and argumentative, taking his daily walks alone and often spending the days in a room separate from Inge. When she tried to comfort him, he would erupt into fanatical tirades about the international Jewish conspiracy and the American idiots, blinded and lulled by the clever, treacherous Jew.

Inge again went to her friends in Salzburg. They told her that there were no well-organized escape organizations at that time. Two names were usually mentioned, Der Spinne and ODESSA, but upon further investigation they proved to be more myth than reality. They had heard that Colonel Hans Rudel, a much-decorated Luftwaffe pilot and a diehard Nazi to the end, was in the process of putting together an organization called the Kameradenwerk to aid fellow Nazis in getting to South America, but they had no idea how to contact him. Oddly enough, they told Inge, Karl's best chance was from within the Catholic Church. They had learned the name of a Jesuit priest who was helping hunted SS officers to escape by hiding them in a monastery in Austria until arrangements could be made to get them out of the country. There were also a number of similar "safe havens" in monasteries in Italy. The main escape route was from Austria to Italy and then a final destination of either South America or the Arab countries. Her friends offered to contact the priest and told her she and Karl should arrange to be in Salzburg within a week. Inge was pleased with the plan and agreed to stay for lunch and a few hours of conversation. Her hopes were high; perhaps their long wait was almost over. Her friends also told her that her brother Frederich was trying to locate her. He had called last month, having learned of the death of their parents, he wanted to take Inge to America with him; she was all the family he had left. Inge begged them not to tell him of her whereabouts; she would contact him once she and Karl were out of Germany and settled.

Karl was on the last leg of his habitual walk around the lake. He breathed deeply, enjoying the fragrance of the warm spring air. His thoughts were on a newspaper story he had read about Ernst Kaltenbrunner's testimony at the trial in Nuremberg. The former head of Reich Security was denying knowledge of programs and activities over which he had had direct control. The prosecution had no difficulty proving his complicity and participation, making his defense seem ludicrous at best. Some of the defendants were weeping openly in court; the once powerful and arrogant leaders of the "thousand-year Reich" were begging for mercy at the feet of their conquerors. Karl was appalled by the accounts of their behavior.

As he left the footpath and entered the clearing in front of the chalet, he saw someone move quickly out of sight in the direction of the portico. Stepping back into the shadows of the trees, he knelt in the underbrush, watching silently for a few minutes, but saw no further movement and decided to approach the chalet from another direction. He began to make his way slowly through the woods along the edge of the clearing toward the rear of the house. Suddenly he heard a metallic click, and felt the pressure of cold steel at the base of his skull.

"You take one more step, you kraut bastard," a gruff voice said, "and I'll splatter your goddam brains all over the woods. Now put your hands on top of your head and turn around. Slowly."

Karl did as he was told and found himself face to face with an American officer holding a .45 pointed directly between his eyes. "What is the meaning of this?" Karl demanded.

"Shut your mouth, Dennecker," the American said, removing a photograph from his breast pocket, looking at it for a moment, then studying Karl's face. "I'm Major Hollis of 15th Army Intelligence, and you're under arrest, you bag of garbage. Start moving toward the house, and if you even look like you're thinking of running, I'll drop you and bury you right here."

Karl considered denying his identity and using his false identification papers, but he knew it would be hopeless. The major ordered him to a jeep parked under the portico and told him to sit in the front passenger seat. Two American sergeants appeared from behind the chalet and sat in the back of the jeep. Both were armed with machine guns. The major climbed in and started the engine.

"I am Karl Dennecker, SS *Gruppenfuehrer* and lieutenant general of the Waffen SS," he said with as much dignity as he could muster, "and I expect to be treated accordingly."

The major laughed, and the sergeants joined in. "Oh, you'll be treated accordingly," the major promised. "Don't worry about that."

Inge had stopped in Waging for groceries on her return from Salzburg and was walking back to where she had parked the car when an American colonel stopped her and attempted to start a conversation. Inge tried to step around him, but he persistently blocked her path. Placing a hand on her shoulder in a friendly gesture, he politely asked her to have dinner with him that evening. Inge declined the invitation, but decided, since he wasn't being offensive, that a few minutes of casual conversation would be the most graceful way out of the situation. If the right questions were asked, she might even get some useful information out of him. The colonel carried her bag of groceries as they walked toward an outdoor café at the far end of the street. She smiled coyly, amused by his clumsy German, then, much to his relief, spoke to him in English.

Inge didn't notice Major Hollis's jeep turn the corner near the cafe and continue up the street at breakneck speed, nor did she see Karl looking back, the scene etched indelibly in his mind.

The owner of the grocery store in Waging told Inge what had happened to Karl. A group of American military police had arrived at the village that morning, inquiring about the location of their chalet. The American colonel who had waylaid her that day had been watching the main road into the village and had followed her when she returned from Salzburg. The grocer apologized for not warning her, but he had not known until after she was seated at the café with the colonel.

Inge's friends in Salzburg told her that the Americans had taken Karl to 15th Army Headquarters at Bad Tolz for interrogation, then transferred him to the Nuremberg Detention Center for further interrogation and to await trial.

"Your brother is here," her friend said, handing the phone to him.

"Inge, you must come with me," Frederich said. "It is far too dangerous for you to remain in Germany."

"Not now, Frederich. Please, not now. I must go to Karl. I will contact you later." With that, she hung up quickly.

Disregarding the personal risks involved, she decided to go to Nuremberg to try to see Karl. She had a friend there, a woman who had attended medical school with her, with whom she could stay.

Inge hardly recognized the once beautiful and charming ancient walled city. The former medieval center of culture and commerce had been reduced to piles of rubble. Many of the magnificent buildings, gabled houses, and stone bridges crossing the Pegnitz River had been leveled. What remained was blackened, pockmarked, and scarred from the saturation bombing and the fires that followed. During Hitler's reign it had been the center of the National Socialist Party, and the site of the annual September celebration of the Nazis, a pagan festival at which tens of thousands of hysterical patriots worshipped at Hitler's shrine. It was here that the Nuremberg Laws had been decreed, stripping the German Jews of their rights and their humanity. Inge considered it a twisted form of poetic justice that the International Military Tribunal should choose this city for the war-crimes trials.

She shared a one-room basement apartment in a bombed-out building with her friend, Hannah Graber. Hannah told Inge that all the prisoners were being kept in the prison behind the Palace of Justice, where the trials were being held, and to her knowledge they were allowed no visitors other than their attorneys. Hannah suggested that Inge might try some of the reporters in the press room at the courthouse. They would probably be able to give her some information about Karl.

The Palace of Justice had been hastily repaired to accommodate the trials, and the main courtroom had been enlarged by knocking out a wall of an adjoining room to provide space for the press and a visitors' gallery. Inge talked with a reporter from a Zurich paper and learned that Karl's trial would probably not start for at least another six months, but that he was scheduled to appear as a witness for the prosecution at the International Military Tribunal in a few days. The reporter also told her that Karl's attorney was Ernst Froeschmann, who was acting as co-counsel for former Foreign Minister von Ribbentrop, now on trial. Inge spent the day in the visitors' gallery listening to the proceedings, and when the court recessed for the day, she waited outside for Ernst Froeschmann.

Froeschmann told her it was impossible for her to visit Karl, but he would gladly deliver a message. Inge told him to tell Karl simply that she was there and would be waiting for him, no matter what. Froeschmann said that he would be talking with Karl the day he was to testify. She should contact him after that.

Inge was in the visitors' gallery the day Karl was called.

She watched him enter the courtroom through a small door behind the prisoners' dock, guarded by military police. He looked pale and drawn, but seemed composed. He spent most of the day in the witness box, evasive and uncooperative. The defendants, witnesses, prosecutors, defendants' counsels, and judges all wore headsets that were connected to a central interpreters' booth for instantaneous translation to French, Russian, German, and English. The speakers were asked to speak slowly to ensure adequate time for a precise translation. Inge smiled inwardly as she watched Karl deliberately wait for the translation of the questions asked him by the American prosecutor at the lawyer's lectern; fluent in English, he needed no translation, just time to formulate his answers. His responses were rapid, causing flashing red and yellow lights to go on in the interpreters' booth, signaling him to slow down. But he continued to speak swiftly until the prosecutor gave up in disgust and dismissed him.

Inge waited anxiously for the court to adjourn, then hurried outside to wait for Froeschmann. His expression, when she saw him, was grave.

"I'm afraid I do not have very good news for you," he said. "Karl does not want you to contact him, ever again. No matter what the reason."

Inge was dumbstruck. "I don't understand, Herr Froeschmann. Why would he say such a thing?"

Froeschmann avoided her eye for a moment, then looked directly at her. "The day he was captured he saw you in town with an American officer." Froeschmann hesitated, not liking what he had to say. "To be brutally frank, Fraulein Bauer, he believes you betrayed him. The American interrogator told him that he was captured through information provided by a Frederich Bauer—your brother, I believe."

Inge gasped. "But that is madness!" she protested. "Absolute madness. I would never be a party to such a thing. He knows that! You must make him believe that! My brother must have acted on his own. . . . Oh, God. Didn't he realize what would happen to Karl?"

Froeschmann shook his head. "I am sorry, Fraulein Bauer, but there is nothing I can do. He has forbidden me to mention your name again. There is one more thing: He said if you betrayed him in another matter, one about which he was not specific but said you would understand, he would reach out from the grave for revenge."

Inge was shaking visibly. She closed her eyes and took a deep breath to gain control. "You may tell Karl that I do understand what he is referring to and I will not *and have not* betrayed him." Tears streamed down her face.

Froeschmann handed her a handkerchief and put a consoling arm around her. "I am truly sorry I had to be the bearer of such bad news, but there is little else I can do. I would suggest you write him, but he is not allowed contact or correspondence with anyone other than myself. However, I give you my word," he said reassuringly, "that I will make him listen to your reply to his allegations, and if it is any comfort to you, *I* believe you are telling the truth."

Inge explained about her brother's efforts to get her to leave Germany, believing that that was his motivation. "Please, you must tell Karl I love him and will not give up hope."

"I will tell him," Froeschmann assured her. "And now I must go. Good luck to you, Fraulein Bauer, and let us both pray for Karl's deliverance."

Inge walked across the Adolf Hitler Platz in the center of the old city on her way back to the apartment, still numbed by what Froeschmann had told her. The late-afternoon sun cast abstract shadows across the square through the hollow shells of buildings. The Frauen Kirche still stood defiantly among the ghostly ruins, the facade intact but the interior gutted by fire. She stopped midway across one of the old stone bridges, feeling weak and sick to her stomach. She looked down into the river, its mirror image shattered by the rubble that had fallen into it. Her world was a void and she felt desperately alone. Her life, all that mattered, was here in Nuremberg. She decided to remain for Karl's trial and hope against hope that he would be acquitted so they could be reconciled and resume their life together.

She saw Ernst Froeschmann the following week. He told her that Karl had listened but had said nothing in return.

The trial of the Nazi leaders ended on October 1, 1946, four months after Karl's capture. Inge had been in the visitors' gallery prior to the sentencing of the prisoners, the day Sir Hartley Shawcross, the British chief prosecutor, gave his final speech to the tribunal. Shawcross quoted Goethe: "Years ago Goethe said of the German people that someday fate would strike them because they betrayed themselves and did not want to be what they are. It is sad that they do not know the charm of truth, detestable that mist, smoke and the berserk immoderation are so dear to them, pathetic that they ingenuously submit to any mad scoundrel who appeals to their lowest instincts, who confirms them in their vices and teaches them to conceive nationalism as isolation and brutality. With what a voice of prophecy he spoke," Shawcross said, raising his voice dramatically and pointing directly at the prisoners in the dock. "For these are the mad scoundrels who did those very things."

The death sentences handed down by the tribunal demonstrated that the judges categorically agreed with Shawcross's estimate of the German character and the inherent evil of the leaders of the Third Reich. Inge feared that the mood and the temper of the court did not leave much hope for Karl.

Eleven months later her worst fears were realized. Karl's trial began on January 13, 1947, and on August 11 the U.S. Military Tribunal sentenced him to hang. Ernst Froeschmann assured Inge that he would exhaust all the avenues of appeal and there was an excellent chance of a commutation of sentence. She asked if he would smuggle a letter to Karl, but he explained that even if he could, Karl was still adamant about any mention of her name.

When Karl was sent to Landsberg prison, where he was to be held until his sentence was carried out, Inge returned to the chalet on the lake near Waging, to sort out what remained of her life. Froeschmann had promised to contact her with any news of the appeals. She spent her time reading and walking in the woods, fighting the loneliness and desolation that filled her days. After two weeks of the oppressive isolation she realized she needed human companionship if she was to maintain any semblance of sanity, and decided to visit her friends in Salzburg.

She spent the morning packing and shortly after lunch went outside to take some photographs of the chalet and the scenery around the lake to commemorate the place where she and Karl had spent their happiest days. It was late afternoon by the time she had finished photographing their favorite spots. As she walked through the woods toward the chalet she heard a vehicle coming up the road. As it rounded a bend and came into view she recognized the markings of the U.S. Army on the sides of the huge truck. She instinctively moved out of sight behind a large tree and watched as the truck continued up the road to the chalet and parked in the rear, behind the portico, partly in the woods. Two men got out and walked toward the chalet. One knocked on the rear door while the other looked in the first-floor windows. Inge caught only glimpses of them from where she was hidden. They were both dressed in civilian clothes; one was tall and broad-shouldered, the other shorter and slighter. When they had satisfied themselves that no one was home they went back to the truck, and removed a shovel and a rake from behind the seat of the cab. They walked slowly through the woods, carefully scanning the ground in front of them until they found what they were looking for. They stopped at the exact spot where Karl and Inge had hidden the crates brought from Berlin. Inge had a clear view of them now, recognizing them immediately. The broad-shouldered man she had seen nearly every day for the past eight months in the courtroom in Nuremberg. He was the man who had prosecuted Karl. The other man she had seen occasionally at the prosecutors' table, usually supplying facts and figures to the broad-shouldered man when he questioned the defendants and witnesses.

Inge watched as they removed the fallen tree and raked away the leaves and branches concealing the crates. She had only one thought in her mind: Karl must not think she was in any way responsible for what was happening. She checked the film indicator on the camera; there were fifteen exposures remaining on the roll. She was approximately thirty yards from where they were working, but the 135mm lens was sufficient to record in detail what they were doing.

After they had loaded the last of the crates on the truck and driven swiftly out of sight, Inge hastily finished packing and left for Salzburg. The following week she took an extra set of prints of the photographs to Ernst Froeschmann in Fürstenfeldbruck. She handed them to him in a sealed envelope and instructed him to get them to Karl, unopened, as quickly as possible, impressing him with the urgency of the matter. Froeschmann promised to deliver the envelope to Karl the following day.

Inge spent the next six months in Salzburg, with no word from Froeschmann about the appeals. When she finally called him, he told her to prepare herself for the worst. Karl's appeals had been denied and he would probably be executed. In the weeks that followed she began drinking heavily, and her friends, worried about her health, decided to get in touch with her brother in the United States.

". . . and I have been here ever since, all this time believing that Karl had died in 1955. After first denying his culpability, my brother admitted that he had made a deal with an American general—Karl, and a large sum of money for my safe passage to the United States and no prosecution for alleged war crimes. I read in a German magazine that Karl's sentence was commuted, but my brother told me that he died of a heart attack shortly after that, while still in Landsberg Prison."

"As you can well imagine," Paula said, sitting on the edge of her chair, "I have two very important questions to ask you. Do you still have the photographs, and do you know what was in the crates?"

Inge refilled her glass from the nearly empty decanter and looked from Paula to Callahan. "I not only have the photographs, I have also the negatives, and a manifest listing the contents of each of the crates." She stood up, a bit wobbly but needing no assistance. "If you will come inside with me to the library I will get them for you."

The photographs were clear and sharp. Paula recognized Senator Hill, thinner and younger but incontestably the Senator, and identified John Cook from the photograph she had seen in his file at the National Records Center. Callahan noticed some stenciling on some of the crates stacked near the back of the truck. Using a magnifying glass that was lying on the desk, he examined the photograph closely. The markings became legible: TREBLINKA, SOBIBOR, AUSCHWITZ-BIRKENAU.

"Christ!" Jack said in a hushed voice.

Paula came over to where he was standing and looked through the magnifying glass. "Oh, my God, Callahan!"

Inge removed the manifest from where she kept it hidden in a large volume on the top shelf and handed it to Paula. "The SS accumulated their vast wealth in a number of ways," she said, sinking into the chair behind the desk. "Many industrialists gave large grants to them, either for business reasons or because they truly believed in the cause, or in some cases because they had been suborned into doing so. Another main source of income was from the Jewish businesses they took over. When a Jew was sent to the camps, the

SS confiscated his business and ran it for their own profit. They would bring in their own administrator, and all proceeds went to the SS general fund, not to the state. They also made enormous amounts of money from the concentration camps, hiring out slave labor to large industries, and by selling war materials—clothing, combat gear—made by camp inmates and sold under contract to the state. It was almost clear profit, because of course no labor cost was involved."

Inge got up from behind the desk and went over to a cabinet near the entrance to the room. She came back with a bottle of bourbon and a shot glass. Taking a quick swallow, she continued. "However, the contents of these crates came from an altogether different source. When the Jews arrived at the camps they carried with them whatever valuable and easily portable possessions they had, concealing them in the most ingenious ways, sewing currency and gold coins into the lining of their clothes, inserting capsules containing jewels inside their bodies. They were unaware of their fate, and many believed they could buy their way out of the camps. After they were gassed, there were special squads that went through the clothing and examined the bodies, removing the valuables, including any gold bridgework. Millions in gold, jewelry, and currency were recovered each month. It was all sent to a central depot at the Oranienburg concentration camp near Berlin, then transferred to the SS Economic and Administration Headquarters in Lichterfelde to be inventoried and taken to a special vault at the Reichsbank for storage. Karl and General Gluecks supervised the inventory and the shipments to the Reichsbank."

Inge gestured toward the manifest Paula was holding in her hand. "The contents of those crates and the crates that General Gluecks took with him were the last shipments to arrive from the death camps in Poland, just before the Russians liberated them. The SS driver who was to deliver the shipment to the Reichsbank was killed in a bombing raid the day before Karl and Gluecks left Berlin. Oswald Pohl, the head of the SS Economics and Administrative Offices, had fled the city the previous week, and Karl and Gluecks were the only ones with knowledge of the shipment, other than Pohl. They divided the crates between them."

Paula handed Callahan the manifest, and he read the list of contents in Karl's crates, mentally converting the figures into dollars:

```
        $2,600,000 in Swiss francs
        1,850,000 in English pounds
        1,250,000 American
          100,000 in gold coins
          100,000 in diamonds (approx.)
           75,000 in gold bars
TOTAL $5,975,000
```

Jack looked up from reading the list and caught Paula's eye. It was no longer a mystery why Senator Hill and the others wanted to see Dennecker hang.

"I would like to keep the photographs, the negatives, and the manifest," Paula said.

"If you must," Inge replied. "But is there anything you can do to them after all these years?"

"As far as criminal prosecution is concerned, probably nothing," Jack answered. "The statute of limitations would exclude that. But with the evidence you've given us, and further investigation into what they did with the money, Paula will be able to print her story and expose the conspirators publicly. And believe me, Miss Bauer, that's a severe punishment indeed, considering the positions of the men in question and the repercussions that will follow.

"There is one more thing," Jack said as an afterthought. "When we have all the loose ends tied together we would appreciate a deposition from you as background for the photographs and the manifest."

"What does that require?" she asked stiffly. "You assured me that if I cooperated with you I would be kept out of this." She glanced suspiciously at Paula.

"A deposition can be taken in the privacy of your home," Jack said. "And whatever you say to the attorney taking it is privileged communication. I assure you it will not involve anything other than what we have just discussed, and we can omit any references to your brother's deal to get you off the hook."

Inge stared off in the distance, slowly shaking her head. "Is this absolutely necessary, Miss Carlson?" she asked bitterly.

Paula nodded, knowing it was not, but wanting the added weight. "Yes, but that's the end of it. We won't bother you again."

"You will please bring a lawyer who is not Jewish and who is not from this area," Inge said.

Paula agreed.

As Inge escorted them to the front door, Paula remembered something important she had forgotten to ask. "Does your brother know about the men who came to get the crates?"

Inge thought for a moment and then answered, "No, I never told Frederich about the crates, or the men who came for them. When he brought me to the United States I made him promise never to ask me about the war years or anything connected with them. He kept his promise and has never questioned me, even when I asked him to inquire about Karl's fate."

Paula reassured her about the deposition, telling her that she would get back to her in a few days with the arrangements.

Inge watched them drive away, then returned to the library, to her only source of solace and peace, refilling her glass with bourbon and settling back in a chair with her memories.

"If we delve deep enough into the financial backgrounds of Senator Hill and the others," Paula told Al Verity, "we'll find the rest of the answers, I feel sure. Then we can give all the physical evidence and the information we've gathered, along with a deposition from Inge Bauer, to the Attorney General."

Verity held the phone in place with his shoulder as he lit a cigar. "You do realize that there is nothing the Attorney General can do about a crime committed thirty years ago outside the territorial limits of this country?"

"I think there *is* something," Paula replied. "The Internal Revenue Service has a three-year statute of limitations on auditing tax returns *unless* they have evidence to indicate there may have been a fraudulent return and substantial amounts of unreported income. Then there is no limitation on how far back they can investigate the financial records of the person in question."

"And of course Senator Hill and the other two men brought the money from Dennecker's crates into the United States," Verity said.

"What else?" Paula replied. "And an amount of money that large has got to show up somewhere. I called a friend, Marsha Talbot; she's with the international department of Chase Manhattan. She's going to see what she can find on the business dealings of Hill, White, and Cook. She should be able to find anything that's there, and know how to interpret what she's looking at."

"I'd sleep lightly until you've turned your evidence over to the Attorney General," Verity said. "If Hill and the others are aware of what you have, they're bound to come after it."

"Once I've made duplicates of everything and written my story I'll give it to the Attorney General, but not before. I'll be damned if some clown in the Justice Department is going to leak my story to a Washington correspondent. I'd rather die."

"My, dear Paula," Verity said gravely, "that's within the realm of possibility."

"We'll be careful," Paula said, feeling a sudden chill from the reminder of the shadowy menace. "It won't be much longer. I think I know pretty clearly what happened. Let me go over it for you so you can collar the powers that be and get back to me with a firm offer."

Paula read from the outline she had been working on. "John Cook was an interrogator at the Nuremberg detention center. He interrogated Dennecker. Dennecker was frightened by the death sentences being handed down by the International Military Tribunal and offered to turn over the contents of the crates to Cook in return for a lenient sentence. Cook took the proposition to Hill, then they both went to Judge White. All three of them must have talked to Dennecker at some point, to assure him the deal was acceptable to them. That was the 'agreement' Dennecker mentioned in his letters to his attorney. They probably insisted on knowing the location of the crates before Dennecker was sentenced, and Dennecker had no alternative but to tell them. When they reneged on the deal and sentenced him to hang, there was nothing he could do. But when he got out of prison and went to Aspen, my guess is that he planned to blackmail them. He probably blackmailed them for years. I don't know if we can prove the blackmail, but it really isn't necessary to have that nailed down before printing the story. It's not Dennecker we're after. We have enough hard evidence to ensure against a successful libel suit. The only thing remaining to be proved is that Senator Hill, Judge White, and John Cook kept the money and did not turn it over to the army. Common sense tells me that the possibility of that's having happened is so remote it's not even worth considering, but before I submit the story, we'll check it out thoroughly. Marsha and her contacts at the bank should be able to help us establish that by showing us where to look for evidence of how they brought the money into the country and what they did with it. If we

194

draw a blank, then at least the Justice Department will be able to prove that the money was not given to the army. Actually, the matter of what they did with the money, as long as they kept it, is of no consequence to my story. I have what I need to expose them publicly, and the IRS can make its own determination about criminal prosecution. I must admit, though, my vindictive side wants to see them in prison as well as financially ruined and disgraced. I have very little doubt that they were responsible for the death of Callahan's friend."

Verity considered what Paula had said and then asked, "If Dennecker was blackmailing them, why, when he made his initial approach, didn't they simply arrange to have him killed?"

"We know from our meeting with Inge Bauer," Paula said, "that Dennecker had a set of prints of the photos she had taken, and I imagine he had other means of convincing them they'd be exposed if anything ever happened to him. Karl Dennecker was by no means a babe in the woods, and Hill and the others had to realize he had them over a barrel."

"I'll get back to you tomorrow," Verity said. "I suggest you put your evidence in a safe deposit box immediately."

"As soon as I've made duplicates. Talk to you tomorrow."

Paula and Callahan were about to leave the apartment when Verity called back.

"So soon," Paula said. "I thought you'd at least feign disinterest to bring the price down," she quipped.

"Something just came across my desk," Verity said. "Judge Edward T. White committed suicide yesterday at his home in Cincinnati,"

"Damn!" Paula said.

"For the sake of the impact of your story, I do hope the others don't follow suit," he said dryly. "Get the deposition from Inge Bauer, and write your story as soon as possible."

"We're meeting with Marsha at the bank first thing in the morning," Paula said. "I'll call Inge Bauer now and set it up for tomorrow afternoon."

"What was that about?" Callahan asked when Paula hung up.

"Judge White committed suicide."

Jack smiled grimly. "So the chickens have come home to

roost." He patted the inside pocket of his sport coat where he had placed the packet of evidence. "This goes wherever I go," he said. "And there's only one way they'll get it."

"You want them to try, don't you, Callahan?" Paula said, looking directly into his eyes. "You really do, don't you?"

"Let's go to dinner," he replied. "I'm hungry."

THIRTEEN

"Good work, Phil," Cook said cheerfully. "You have a bonus coming for this."

"Thank you, sir," Candellari replied. "How do you want me to deal with these latest developments?" he asked, knowing the answer.

"The Bauer woman is an eyewitness," Cook said, "and the negatives, photographs, and manifest are damaging in and of themselves; that doesn't leave us much choice, does it?"

"No, sir. And the girl and Callahan?"

"They're no threat to us without documented evidence. Treat them accordingly," Cook said firmly.

"I'll do my best, sir. But if there are complications . . ."

"Do what you must," Cook said tersely. "By now you know the stakes. And I want the Bauer woman questioned thoroughly before . . . just make certain she has nothing more of interest to us."

"Charlie's quite good at interrogation," Candellari said. "If she has anything else, we'll find out."

"Call me the moment you have things under control," Cook said, breaking the connection abruptly.

Halek grinned as Candellari turned to him. He had the sense of the conversation. "Now, Phil?"

"Now," Candellari confirmed.

Halek laughed in a low monotone and gulped what remained of his beer.

Inge Bauer's eyes filled with tears as she stared at Otto's body lying near the steps to the terrace—a stream of blood gushed from the bullet wound in the dog's head.

Halek strapped her hands tightly to the arms of the wrought-iron chair, while Candellari bound her legs to the base.

Halek saw her wince as he removed the long steel needle from its case, laughing softly as he rotated it slowly between his thumb and forefinger. "You vill tell me vhat I vant to know," he said mockingly.

Candellari glared at him. "Get on with it, Charlie."

"Put the gag in place," Halek said, waiting until it was done and Candellari securely held her shoulders.

Kneeling before her, Halek pushed her skirt up to her thighs and grasped her kneecap, feeling for the exact spot he wanted. Finding it in a matter of moments, he shoved the needle a fourth of its length into the terrified woman's knee.

Inge's body went rigid, and the muted cry of pain escaped as a low, gurgling groan.

"Miss Bauer," Candellari said softly, "it would be best if you talk to me now. Charlie enjoys his work."

Inge stared straight ahead; the initial shock had subsided, but the pain persisted with the needle left in place. Taking a deep breath, she shook her head defiantly.

Halek held her leg firmly, and this time moved the needle in further at an upward angle, eliciting another muted cry accompanied by an involuntary shudder and labored breathing.

Again, she shook her head in response to Candellari's request.

Halek grinned. "Tough old Nazi bitch, ain't she? The next one'll do it."

Grasping her leg tightly below the knee, he shoved all but the last two inches of the needle roughly into the joint.

The seemingly endless hollow groan was higher in pitch, her eyes bulged in their sockets, and her mind reeled from the excruciating pain. Visions flashed before her in rapid succession—a small room in the basement of Castle Hartheim—faces; anguished, tortured faces; desperate faces—running blindly against the walls; clawing maniacally at the observation window in the airtight door; screaming, wailing, moaning.

"It only gets worse as we continue," Candellari said calmly. "What did the reporter and her friend want, and what did you tell them?"

Halek gritted his teeth as Inge once again shook her head.

With the needle firmly imbedded in the knee joint, he grabbed the exposed tip, shaking it forcefully.

The violent convulsions and spasms tore the gag from her mouth. A bilious yellow gruel erupted from her, followed by a shrill, soul-born scream; then another, and another, until she slumped exhausted, barely conscious, unable to endure any more. Slowly, almost imperceptibly, she nodded her head.

Comparing what she told them with what they knew, Candellari determined that there was nothing that concerned Cook now in her possession. "Take care of her," he told Halek. "I'll be in the car."

Marsha Talbot greeted Paula warmly and shook Callahan's hand, understanding Paula's attraction to him at first glance. He actually looked as though he spent at least a few hours a year outdoors; not like the pasty, spangled, singles-bar-hopping fops she had to contend with.

"I've collected some information for you," Marsha said, offering them chairs, "but I don't know how helpful it'll be. The head of our loan department explained to me that up until a few years ago there was a national clearing house where member banks could get in-depth information on each other's customers, but that's been declared unethical and illegal and is no longer in existence. And under the new law banks are only required to keep records for three years, making it virtually impossible to get information through normal channels prior to 1976. He compared my chances of getting records from 1947 to finding photographs of the actual crucifixion of Christ."

"What was he able to get?" Paula asked.

"A line on Allied Electronics," Marsha replied, "the corporation controlled by one of the men you mentioned, John Cook. It ties him in with the others. One of the principal stockholders in his corporation is Janet Hill, wife of Senator Hill; she owns twenty-five percent of the stock, and Edward T. White of Cincinnati owns twenty-five percent. The corporation was founded in 1948. A rough estimate of the initial investment at the time was about half a million each. Good enough?"

Paula smiled. "If the IRS can establish the amount invested by them, and Cook, and compare it to their previously declared incomes and assets, they'll have no difficulty nailing their hides to the wall."

"Good. Is there anything else I can do for you?"

"Excuse me, Martha," Callahan said.

"That's Marsha," she corrected him good-naturedly, "but that's all right; you can call me anything, just call me." She tossed her long auburn hair theatrically and flirted with her vivid green eyes. "Sorry," she said jokingly to Paula, "but it's a jungle out there."

Callahan laughed heartily. He couldn't imagine the woman before him having any problem attracting men. She was a bit overweight, but still attractive and sexy, with a disarmingly pleasant disposition, and, he suspected, a great sense of humor.

"What is it, Jack?" Marsha asked.

Callahan handed her a slip of paper on which he had written: JOCHEN—038-193862.

"Does that combination of a name and number suggest anything to you?"

Paula leaned over and glanced at the paper, giving him a questioning look.

Marsha shrugged. "Nothing immediately comes to mind."

"They were part of a code," Callahan said. "Two sets of numbers after a list of names that didn't make any sense when decoded in the same manner as the names. Chemical tests indicated they were written with a different pen and ink and probably at a later date. The first set of numbers, if decoded with the same key as the names, gives us the letters J-O-C-H-E-N or I-O-C-H-E-N. Jochen is a man's name, so let's assume for the moment that Jochen is what was encoded. The second set of numbers are meaningless when decoded, so let's assume they were written as numbers."

"What are you getting at?" Paula asked.

"Since I first saw them," Jack said, "that combination of a name and number was hauntingly familiar to me. I just realized why. I think it's a bank-account number; probably from a Swiss bank."

Paula raised an eyebrow.

"A friend had one," he answered her unspoken question.

Marsha looked again at the slip of paper. "Yes. I see what you mean. You're more than just a pretty face, Callahan," she said, getting a smile from him.

"According to Kurt," Jack said to Paula, "Dennecker left

Aspen once each year. You believe, and I agree with you, that Dennecker was blackmailing Senator Hill, Judge White, and John Cook. We aren't certain why Frederich Bauer's name was included, but we have a pretty good idea. So let's again assume, for the sake of my theory, that they paid Dennecker once a year and met him personally to give him the payment in cash—the only way an intelligent person would accept blackmail payments. Dennecker didn't live above his means in Aspen, so it stands to reason he would have immediately deposited the money in a bank."

Marsha removed a book from the top drawer of her desk and thumbed it to the section she wanted, running her finger down the lefthand margin, stopping near the bottom of the page. She looked at Callahan and smiled. "038 is the bank identification number for the Ottawa branch of the Swiss Credit Bank." She glanced at the numbers Jack had written down. "It fits," she said. "A nine-digit number. The first three are the bank identification number and the last six are the account number."

"Didn't Kurt Bierman say that Dennecker occasionally went fishing in Canada?" Paula asked. Callahan nodded.

"What about the name, Jochen?" Paula asked.

"I'm not certain," Marsha replied, "but it could be a code word set up with the bank by the depositor as a means of ensuring proper identification. And, if that's the case, it would suggest that this is a numbered account, which isn't surprising, considering what you told me about the source of the money being deposited."

"What are the chances," Callahan asked, "of finding out the current balance and a schedule of deposits and withdrawals?"

Marsha drummed her fingers lightly on the desk, considering the question. "It depends on the system of safeguards this Dennecker arranged with the bank about giving out information regarding the account. Common sense tells me that if it is a secret account, no one other than Dennecker and a limited number of officers of the bank would have access to any information. But if Dennecker made arrangements to have information given to him over the telephone, we may have a chance at it. We have the account number and what appears to be a code word, so it just might be worth a try. I'll have to bend the banking rules a bit, but . . ."

"Just for the record," Callahan said, "let's say this is my account and I'm considering transferring it to this bank."

"Fair enough," Marsha said. She looked up the number of the Swiss Credit Bank in Ottawa and dialed the call, pressing a button on the console, enabling Jack and Paula to hear the conversation on a remote speaker. She told the switchboard operator who answered that she wanted information on an account, and she rang the appropriate office.

"This is Mr. Hofer speaking," a man said in clipped, lightly accented English. "May I help you, please?"

"Yes, thank you," Marsha replied. "I need some information concerning an account."

"What is the account number, please?"

Marsha read the numbers the way Jack had written them. "038-193862."

"And the information requested?" asked the toneless Mr. Hofer.

"The current balance," Marsha replied, "and the dates and amounts of the last three deposits and withdrawals."

"One moment please," came the reply; Marsha heard a click as she was put on hold.

Paula and Jack sat quietly, waiting for Hofer to come back on the line. Marsha covered the mouthpiece with her hand and said, "So far, so good." She heard another click and then Hofer's voice.

"Do you have additional means of identification?" Hofer asked.

Marsha held up crossed fingers to Paula and Jack and said, "JOCHEN."

There was a brief silence, then Hofer read the information he had gotten off the computer. "Current balance—$4,600,000. The last three deposits were: October 5th, 1976, $200,000; October 5th, 1977, $200,000; October 5th, 1978, $200,000. There are no withdrawals of principal on record for that period of time. However, the annual interest rate of two percent has been withdrawn each of the aforementioned years. Is there anything else I can help you with?"

"Thank you, no," Marsha replied. "Not at this time."

"Very well. Good day, madam."

Paula began scribbling on a note pad. "If we include Frederich Bauer as a contributor to the payoffs, that means each man paid $50,000 a year, and if they collectively paid $200,000 a year since 1955, that comes to exactly the amount of the current balance." She thought for a moment and then asked out of curiosity, "Why did the bank pay such a low interest rate all these years?"

"That's not unusual," Marsha replied. "The Swiss bankers have been known to investigate the people requesting secret accounts, and to set their interest rates according to the liability of their client; it's gotten so bad today, with the currency fluctuations, that they have taken to charging negative interest on many of their foreign accounts. In Dennecker's case, as an ex-Nazi general, they probably decided to penalize him with a low interest rate to make it worth their while in the event he ever became an embarrassment to them—if the funds were later proved to have been obtained illegally and the bank was to become involved in litigation."

"Prudent little devils, aren't they?" Paula said.

"Always," Marsha replied.

The attorney Paula had called was waiting for them at a restaurant near the causeway to Center Island. After a brief conversation, he followed their car to the Bauer home.

Paula had never seen Frederich Bauer before, but at once noticed the family resemblance in the man who answered the door. He was quite handsome, tall and lean, with a high forehead and thining gray hair combed straight back. He stood silently in the doorway, his steel-gray eyes questioning her.

"I'm Paula Carlson," Paula said, then introduced Callahan and the attorney. "Inge is expecting us." She smiled warmly, but got no response from Bauer. "You must be Inge's brother Frederich?"

Bauer nodded slightly, but remained silent.

"Please tell Inge we are here," Paula said.

"That will not be possible, Miss Carlson. My sister died last night."

Paula was so shocked she spoke without thinking. "Died or was murdered?"

Bauer's expression changed instantly. "I don't understand, Miss Carlson. What are you saying? I arrived home this morning to learn that Inge had died last night. The police said it was an accident; a fall."

Paula looked at Callahan, then lowered her eyes. "Oh, God!"

"What do you know of this?" Bauer asked, with a pained expression.

"I think we'd better talk, Mr. Bauer," Paula said.

The attorney left, his presence no longer required, and Paula and Jack followed Frederich Bauer to the library.

"Why do you think my sister may have been murdered?" Bauer asked.

Paula told him, sparingly, about their investigation and of their visit with Inge.

"The men who have been following you," Bauer said harshly. "You must have led them here!"

"No," Callahan replied. "I took precautions against that. No one followed us."

Bauer sat silently staring across the room, through the terrace doors to the crest of the hill beyond. "Perhaps she has found some peace now," he said, his voice a hoarse whisper.

"How did the police say it happened?" Jack asked.

"If you will come with me, I will show you." He led them outside to the terrace and across the lawn to the edge of the hill overlooking the bay, and to the top of a steep path, not far from where Paula and Jack had sat talking with Inge. The steps were simply small uneven stones set into the side of the hill in switchback fashion, leading to the beach below. Anyone who lost his balance while descending would drop nearly forty feet, almost straight down.

"This is where it happened," Bauer said, pointing to the steps. "She must have been going down to the beach and fallen. The police said she struck her head on that large rock near the bottom. A couple walking on the beach around midnight found her."

Jack started down the path and found that he had to stop with both feet on each step before going on to the next. "I can't imagine your sister attempting this," he said, walking back to where Bauer was standing.

"My sister was not always in possession of all her faculties," Bauer replied softly. "She was an alcoholic."

Callahan nodded, realizing the futility of further discussion. If Candellari and Halek had killed her, without an eyewitness it would be impossible to prove.

As they walked back toward the house, Jack realized what had been bothering him. Something was missing. "Where's Otto?" he asked.

Bauer stared at him blankly. "My God! With all that's

happened I've completely forgotten about Otto. I haven't seen him."

"Did the police or the people who found Inge mention him?" Paula asked.

Bauer shook his head. "He never left Inge's side. Perhaps the police had to have someone subdue him before they could get to Inge. Strange, though, that they didn't mention it. I'll call them immediately."

"I doubt that they saw him," Callahan said. "My guess is that whoever subdued him did it permanently, while your sister was still alive."

"If you have any evidence that my sister's death was not an accident," Bauer said, "I would appreciate it if you would inform the police."

"I doubt there is any evidence," Callahan said, "but when we've finished our investigation I'll give them what we have."

"If you don't mind, Mr. Bauer," Paula said, "it would be helpful if you answered a few questions for us, about Karl Dennecker."

Bauer looked away, staring at the ground. "What is it you want to know?"

"Why have you been paying Dennecker fifty thousand dollars each year for the past twenty-three years?"

Bauer rubbed his eyes wearily. "So you know about that, do you?"

"Why was Dennecker blackmailing you?" Paula prodded. "What leverage did he have?"

Bauer hesitated, then said, "I see no reason not to tell you now. He's dead, and it's finished with. I was responsible for General Dennecker's being captured after the war. I made an arrangement with the Americans—him for Inge's freedom and immunity from prosecution; the details are of no consequence. When he was released from prison in 1955, he came to see me. He believed that Inge was a party to my complicity with the Americans, and I let him continue thinking so. I didn't like him and I believe he would have brought my sister nothing but sorrow. He had incriminating evidence about Inge's work during the war, and threatened to turn it over to the West German authorities and the Israelis and have her arrested as a war criminal if I didn't pay him. I had no choice. I am a businessman with many Jewish customers, owners of large department stores. Their accounts are worth millions to me. If Inge's past was known to them it is possible they would no longer deal with me, and I assure you it would cost me a great deal more than fifty thousand dollars a year."

"Did Inge know he was blackmailing you?"

"No. I told her he had died in prison, rather than have her know what he was doing. She had enough pain to live with."

"How were the payments made?" Paula asked.

Bauer hesitated again, then, "Every year on October 5th, according to General Dennecker's instructions, I went to Ottawa and placed fifty thousand dollars in cash in a locker in the bus terminal. I then went to a park near the capitol building and taped the key under a bench. I assume he picked up the money later, although I can't be certain. I never saw him once in all the twenty-four years."

"You followed the same routine this year?" Callahan asked.

Bauer nodded.

"I imagine your money is still in the locker," Callahan said. "Dennecker died before October 5th."

"Thank you. I'll see to it." He stared at Paula for a moment and then asked, "Will Inge's past be exposed in the story you are writing?"

"No," Paula replied. "There's no reason for it to be."

"Thank you," Bauer said softly. "I appreciate that."

"Did you ever meet any of the other men on Dennecker's list when you were in Ottawa?" Callahan asked.

Bauer shook his head. "I didn't know he had a list until today."

"My condolences, Mr. Bauer," Paula said as they reached the gate leading to the driveway, "and thank you for your time."

"My sister's activities during the war," Bauer said, his tone apologetic, "taken out of context, are not representative of all that she was. She was a decent woman, impelled by the madness of the times into a situation as alien and distasteful to her as it would be to you."

Others faced with the same dilemma had chosen to resist, or leave the country, Paula thought, but saw nothing to be gained by pointing it out. "They were difficult times, Mr. Bauer," she said halfheartedly. "I suppose she handled it as best she could."

"They've got to come after us," Callahan said, taking the suitcases from the closet and tossing them on the bed. "And you're far better off in Aspen with me than you would be here in this apartment alone. What we have is enough to expose Hill and Cook, and they must know it; Inge Bauer's deposition would have been nothing but icing on the cake. I don't want you out of my sight until you've finished writing your story and the evidence is in the hands of the Attorney General."

"Why are you assuming that they know we have the negatives and the manifest?" Paula asked.

"If they killed Inge Bauer, and I have no doubt that they did, they probably questioned her first. We have to assume she told them everything. Believe me, they'll come after what we have, and I'd rather meet them on home ground."

Paula shuddered at the thought. "I want you to promise me you'll put the evidence in a safe place."

"I will," Callahan said. "I'll put it in my safe deposit box until we're ready to duplicate it and turn it over."

"You know, Callahan," Paula said, putting her arms around him and resting her head on his chest, "now that this is almost over, I'm frightened as hell. I suppose I have been ever since what happened to Popcorn, but I was able to control it much better than I can now. I begin to come unglued if I allow myself to dwell on it."

Jack held her tightly. "You write your story; I'll take care of the rest." He glanced at his watch. "Let's get to the airport. If the flight to Denver arrives on schedule, we'll just make the last flight into Aspen this evening."

FOURTEEN

The flight from New York arrived late, necessitating an overnight stay in Denver, and Paula and Jack got to Aspen the following morning. Driving a circuitous route, taking care they were not being followed, Callahan went to Kurt Bierman's house, arriving just as he was about to leave.

Kurt was eager to hear all about the investigation, but had a meeting at the shop with a rare-book dealer in ten minutes. He suggested they get together that evening for dinner, with Professor Girard included. They could put the packet of evidence in the wall safe in his den, transferring it to Jack's safe deposit box the following morning. Paula was reluctant, but agreed, not wanting to disappoint Kurt.

Boomer was elated to be back in his own home. He thumped joyously through the house, handling the cast on his leg as though it were an integral part of him. After a triumphant stomp through each room, carrying his oversized rawhide bone, he settled into a corner of the sofa with it, gnawing and grumbling contentedly.

Outside, a damp, chill fall day threatened an early snowstorm. Paula sat cross-legged on a thick wool throw rug in front of the fireplace, a legal pad in her lap, structuring her story, while Callahan tended the fire to a cheerful blaze. Within the hour the wind picked up, sweeping in the dark, moisture-laden clouds from the north, and a heavy, wet snow began falling, accumulating rapidly, blanketing the ground and frosting the trees.

Jack spent the afternoon reading and working on a new pair of skis he had bought to replace those that were stolen, meticulously filing the edges and adjusting the tension on the release bindings. Having completed one of the skis, he propped it against the living-room wall. As he returned to work on the other binding, the ski skidded down the wall, colliding with a large framed print hanging above the sofa, sending it crashing to the floor, startling Boomer from a sound sleep and causing him to leap up growling menacingly, looking in all directions for the source of the disturbance.

"Christ, Callahan," Paula said, rolling her eyes upward. "You damn near gave me heart failure."

"Sorry," Jack said. "I wish I had a dollar for every time that happened." Reaching behind the sofa, he retrieved the print. Seeing that the glass was unbroken, he checked to make certain that the wire on the back was still intact. The moment he saw the flat, perforated disk-shaped object attached to the back of the frame, he knew what it was. "Goddammit! *Goddammit!*"

"Did you cut yourself?" Paula asked, looking up from her work.

Callahan removed the small transmitter, holding it for her to see. "They have us wired!" he said angrily. "The bastards have us wired! How could I have been so stupid? They've probably had us bugged from the start; your apartment, the hotel in Munich; they know every . . ." he stopped abruptly in midsentence, realizing the full implications.

Paula's face turned ashen. "Kurt . . ."

Callahan dashed to the phone on the kitchen wall, glancing at the clock. It was almost five; Kurt should still be at the shop. He punched out the number, waiting nervously as the phone rang.

"Aspen Bookstore," a woman's voice answered.

It was Betty, the young girl who helped out when Jack was off. "Let me speak to Kurt," Jack said anxiously.

"That you, Jack?" she asked.

"Yes, where's Kurt?"

"He just left a . . ."

Callahan hung up, threw open the kitchen door, and ran to the jeep; Boomer bounded after him, leaping into the back of the jeep as it roared down the driveway.

The snow had accumulated to a depth of four or five inches,

and twice Callahan nearly lost control of the ungainly vehicle on the slick surface as he sped toward town.

Kurt always walked home, and if he didn't have too much of a head start, Callahan had a chance of stopping him before he reached the house. The jeep leaned precariously on two wheels as Jack ran a stop sign and rounded the corner at the post office.

Kurt turned up the collar of his topcoat and shoved his hands deep into his pockets as the now light, powdery snow swirled and gusted about him. Hunched against the wind, he crossed the street, passed the Hotel Jerome, and walked toward the west end of town. He slowed his pace, partly because his hip ached more than usual, and partly to enjoy the first heavy snowfall of the season. Aspen thrived on snow, exuding a special charm not to be found in the lethargy of the short-lived summers. There would be no trace of the snow by noon tomorrow, but it heralded the change of seasons. Soon the scent of piñon wood, burning in thousands of fireplaces, would fill the air, and hordes of exuberant skiers would descend, whipping the town to a frenzied pace.

Callahan saw the lonely figure, huddled against the cold, walking haltingly past the library. Turning onto a side street, he skidded to a stop and leaped from the jeep, startling Kurt as he ran toward him.

"You can't go home right now," Jack told him. "There's no time to explain; just give me the keys to your house and go back to the shop. I'll call you later."

Kurt handed him the key ring. "What is it, Jack?"

"Later," Callahan shouted as he jumped into the jeep.

Candellari sat calmly in the leather wingback chair in the corner of Kurt Bierman's den, hidden from view of anyone entering the cozy paneled room. He had cocked the hammer of the snub-nosed .357 magnum when he heard the front door creak, and waited patiently as Callahan slowly made his way from the entrance hall, through the living room, to the doorway of the den.

Upon entering the room, Jack saw him out of the corner of his eye, but too late to get out of the line of sight of the pistol aimed at his head.

210

"Come in, Mr. Callahan," Candellari said. "All the way in. Hands in your pockets, and sit in the chair facing me at the other end of the room." He glanced at his watch; it had been fifteen minutes since Halek had called him, alerting him to Jack's discovery. "I suppose you found the old man on his way here?"

Callahan sat quietly, staring at the pistol.

"Don't even consider it," Candellari said, smiling. "I'd put two between your eyes before you got out of the chair." He gestured with the pistol to the smoldering ashes in the fireplace. "All for nothing, Callahan."

Jack turned his head slowly toward the wall. The painting that concealed the wall safe was lying on the floor, and the safe was open, the evidence removed.

"That was never my concern," he said flatly.

Candellari nodded. "Your hippie friend? We had no choice."

Jack placed his foot under the small stool in front of his chair, deciding that kicking it at Candellari was his only chance. If he was lucky it would distract him long enough for him to try for the gun; if not, he was dead anyway. He angled his body slightly to get more leverage for his right leg. The appearance of Kurt in the doorway shocked him as much as it did Candellari.

Kurt's face was chalk-white with fright, his body tense; an incongruous sight with a pistol in his hands.

Candellari reacted instinctively, pointing and firing at Kurt. Callahan was on him before he could recover, wrenching the pistol from his hand, breaking his wrist in the process.

Candellari aimed a kick at Jack's groin that thudded against his thigh, diverted by a stiff forearm blow.

Cocking the pistol, Jack stepped back. "Blink, and you're dead."

Candellari slumped in the chair, holding his broken wrist.

Kurt lay on the floor, one hand gripping his blood-soaked shoulder, his face twisted in pain. When Jack looked in his direction, Candellari lunged from the chair.

It was a foolish and fatal mistake. Callahan fired, his aim true to the mark; the bullet entered Candellari's left eye, blowing away the back of his skull, driving him against the wall, into a crumpled heap.

Kneeling beside Kurt, Jack quickly removed his topcoat and jacket and tore his shirt away from the wound.

"Am I dying?" Kurt asked, almost resignedly.

"You'll be fine," Jack said, folding a piece of the torn shirt into a compress. "It's only a flesh wound. Hold this against it," he said, putting the compress in place. He stared incredulously at the pistol lying at Kurt's side: a World War II vintage Luger—and the clip was missing.

"Kurt, that goddam gun isn't even loaded!"

Kurt smiled valiantly through the searing pain. "He didn't know that."

In spite of the circumstances, Callahan had to laugh. "You're right, Kurt; he sure didn't. You fooled the hell out of him."

"Just after I gave you the keys, Betty drove by and stopped to tell me about your call to the shop; she said it sounded urgent. She tried calling me at home, and the line was busy. No one was supposed to be here, so . . . I thought you might be in danger."

Callahan lifted him in his arms. "If you hadn't arrived when you did, you'd be saying Kaddish for me."

Kurt saw the open wall safe as Jack carried him from the room. "Your evidence?"

Callahan shook his head. "In the fireplace; nothing but ashes."

Kurt glanced apprehensively at Boomer as Jack sat him in the jeep.

"Your allergies are the least of your worries right now," Jack said, noticing his expression. "We'll be at the hospital in a few minutes."

Paula placed another log on the dwindling flames and returned to staring out the window, watching the wind swirl the snow in lacy wisps among the trees, feeling helpless and frustrated. She should have followed her instincts and put the evidence in Callahan's safe deposit box, but Professor Girard and Kurt were entitled to a thorough briefing, including exhibits. If anything happened to that sweet old man, she'd never forgive herself.

Her back was to the kitchen door when it opened and Charlie Halek entered, puffing from his trek through the woods, his hair matted with snow.

Paula startled at the sight of him. "Do you always walk

into homes without knocking?" she asked edgily. "If you're looking for Callahan, he isn't here."

"I know," Halek replied, brushing the snow from his head and the shoulders of his parka.

"What is it you want?" Paula asked, believing him to be a friend of Callahan's who had stopped by.

Halek walked toward her. "The name's Charlie," he said, grinning. "Charlie Halek."

The name sent shock waves through her. Instantly realizing her vulnerability, she was gripped by a paralyzing fear. She tried to reach for the poker lying on the hearth, but her body wouldn't respond.

Halek pulled a pistol from an inside pocket of his parka. "The bedroom!" he commanded gruffly, motioning to the hallway with the barrel.

Paula steadied herself on the arm of a chair, feeling weak, about to collapse. "Oh, God!" she gasped. "No! I will not!"

Halek grinned. "We can do this easy, or we can do it hard," he said in a low monotone. "You wouldn't like hard."

Paula began to tremble; she was terror-stricken, on the verge of losing all control.

"No! *Please* no!" Her mouth was dry; she tried to swallow but couldn't.

A sick, twisted smile spread slowly across Halek's face. "Oh, yeah; I like that; I like it when you beg. *In the bedroom!*" he snarled through clenched teeth. *"Now!"* Grabbing her arm, he pulled her toward him, shoving her roughly into the hallway.

Paula stumbled to the entrance of the bedroom; another shove forced her through the doorway and sent her sprawling onto the bed.

Halek sat in a chair opposite, propping his feet on the edge of the mattress. "If you do what I tell you, little lady, and do it right, I'll let you die quickly and painlessly. Give me any shit, and before I'm through, you'll wish you were dead a thousand times. Take off your clothes!"

"Callahan will be back any moment," Paula tried desperately, her voice shaking. "He'll kill you if he gets the chance."

Halek let out a short harsh laugh. "Your boyfriend ain't comin' back; we have all kinds of time—days, maybe. Now you got thirty seconds to get naked. Do it!"

The thought of Callahan's being dead drained her last

ounce of strength. She stood at the far side of the room to disrobe, her back to Halek. She was past the point of offering any resistance; fear permeated every fiber of her being.

Halek took great pleasure in watching her undress, his excitement mounting with the removal of each article.

"Come over here!" he commanded.

Paula stood before him, naked and trembling. She glanced at the pistol lying on the table beside the chair; it was within reach, but she hadn't the will to attempt it.

Halek saw the focus of her attention. "You do anything stupid an' I'll break your fuckin' arm—for starters."

Paula began to sob convulsively.

"Stop it!" Halek shouted, saliva spewing from the corners of his mouth. "I want the same things Callahan got; the same sounds, too. I really get off on that. I used to play them tapes over and over, ya know?" He stood and grabbed a fistful of hair, throwing her on to the bed. *"Understand?"*

Kurt had faded into unconsciousness by the time they reached the hospital. Callahan, afraid that he had gone into shock, ran, carrying him in his arms, into the emergency room.

At the doctor's insistence, he left the room and waited in the reception area. He had just settled into a chair when a sudden realization brought him quickly to his feet. *Paula!* Paula was alone and Halek was unaccounted for. He burst through the door and sprinted to the jeep. Boomer nearly tumbled from his seat as Jack tore away from the emergency entrance.

Concealed from view, Callahan quickly circled the house from the edge of the woods. The curtains in his bedroom were drawn, but he soon determined that there was no one in the other rooms. He carefully and quietly worked his way around to the front of the house. Cautiously opening the door, he entered the kitchen, giving Boomer a hand signal to remain outside. Standing silently just inside the door, listening, he heard muted sounds drifting down the hall from the bedroom.

A second hand signal brought Boomer to his side, and another dropped him into a down-stay, his head cocked in the direction of the sounds.

Placing an open hand in front of Boomer's muzzle—the

signal for him to stay—Jack quietly edged his way along the hall to the half-open bedroom door. Callahan had never had a wide range in the area of flexibility of response, and something snapped inside his head at the sight before him.

Paula lay on her stomach, spread-eagled, strapped to the four posts of the king-size brass bed; her body was covered with welts and scratches; one of her eyes was swollen shut, and what appeared to be small bites on the insides of her thighs trickled blood.

Halek, his back to the door, knelt behind her, a burning cigarette in his hand.

Callahan saw the pistol on the nightstand, within easy reach; picking it up, he cocked the hammer, pointing it at the back of Halek's head. He held it for a long moment, breathing deeply, getting control of himself. Then, *"Halek!"* he bellowed.

The squat bear of a man started and turned toward the door, staring dumbfounded down the barrel of the pistol now pointed directly between his eyes. Moving slowly off the far side of the bed, he crushed the cigarette out and glared at the enraged man in the doorway.

Callahan fought the urge to pull the trigger. No! That would be too easy; he'd never knew what hit him.

Halek stared at him, watching his eyes, and read the soul of the man before him; knowing that he wasn't going to shoot; he wanted a piece of him. He smiled and squared his stance. "That's the only way you'd take me," he taunted, gesturing toward the gun. "You mick son of a bitch." He smiled, glancing at Paula. She was half conscious, emitting a barely audible whimper. "She loved it; they all do."

Callahan calmly placed the gun back on the nightstand. Halek came at him instantly, diving across the bed. A perfectly timed knee came up to meet him as he reached the other side, slamming into his jaw, breaking it in two places and shattering his teeth. The lightning-fast blows that followed were equally devastating: One fractured his nose, splattering his face with blood; another, a well-placed kick to the groin, landed solidly, doubling him over in excruciating pain.

Halek's barroom brawling tactics were no match for Jack's expertise at hand-to-hand combat; he could have killed the clumsy man quickly, had he chosen to.

Halek struggled agonizingly to his knees, leaning on an arm, staring at his attacker in disbelief.

Jack grabbed the outstretched arm, twisting it behind Halek's back, forcing his shoulders to the floor. "You're out of your class, asshole," he muttered, and with a quick, forceful upward motion, snapped the arm at the elbow. Halek cried out in pain, collapsing on the floor. Dragging him across the room, Callahan propped him in a sitting position against the dresser, stepped back, and drove another kick into his groin.

Untying the straps that bound Paula, he wrapped her in the bedspread and carried her to the living-room sofa. Boomer had held his position on the kitchen floor, whining at fever pitch, eager to get to the bedroom, but too well trained to break a command.

Taking a pitcher of cold water with him, Jack returned to the bedroom, dousing Halek, reviving him considerably. Halek gazed up at him, his face twisted in pain.

"That's a .32," Jack said, pointing to the pistol on the nightstand, "the same caliber they removed from my dog's head. And I see you had a nasty bite on your upper arm," he added, staring at the naked, beaten man, his eyes blank, his voice emotionless. "That's where Boomer always hits first when he's worked on a gun. Quite a coincidence; let's see if he remembers you. Boomer, *come!*" Jack commanded.

The huge dog thumped up the hall and into the bedroom, overshooting his mark, backing up to sit alertly at Callahan's side, his attention riveted on Halek, his hackles up, his eyes glaring, red-streaked slits.

"Watch him, Boomer!" Callahan whispered, eliciting a menacing snarl and a show of teeth. Halek grabbed the top of the dresser, pulling himself to his feet with one arm.

"Take him high!" Jack commanded.

With that, Boomer charged, leaping up, sinking his teeth into the side of Halek's face, tearing away most of his cheek with a toss of his massive neck. Halek's scream was inhuman. He struggled to remain on his feet, using his undamaged arm to clamp a viselike grip on the crazed animal's throat, but to no avail; Boomer pulled free, biting deeply into Halek's chest.

"Low!" Callahan shouted above the snarling and screaming.

Immediately releasing his bite on Halek's chest, Boomer dropped to all fours and lunged, tearing savagely into the lower abdomen. Driving his muzzle deep, his canine teeth slashing, he clamped down tightly, and with a powerful twist of his head, ripped away a section of the stomach wall. He ravaged the same spot again, this time removing a piece of the large intestine. Halek shrieked insanely and slid to the floor, his body limp.

"Hold!" Jack commanded.

Boomer sat obediently, staring down his bloodstained muzzle at the writhing figure lying at his feet.

"No more," Halek pleaded. "No . . . more," his voice weak, his words barely discernible.

Callahan gazed at him coldly and stepped out into the hallway. *"Finish him!"* he told Boomer, and closed the door.

A bloodcurdling scream filled the house; another and another; then a prolonged silence, and Jack knew Boomer had ended it with a final attack to the throat.

"Have the police tied you to the two men that the Green Beret killed?" Senator Hill asked.

"I had a visit from someone with the Arizona attorney general's office," Cook replied, "concerning an inquiry from the Colorado Bureau of Investigation. I told them that I had dismissed Candellari three weeks ago because of unstable behavior and unauthorized use of corporate aircraft and that I had never met or employed anyone by the name of Halek, nor was I familiar with any investigation being conducted into the death of Karl Dennecker. It'll hold up," Cook said confidently. "No one has seen Candellari around here since Dennecker's death."

"You're positive everything has been destroyed?" the Senator asked.

"Absolutely. Candellari called me the moment he had it in his hands; he was watching it burn as he talked to me."

Senator Hill propped his feet on his desk, finishing what remained of his Scotch. "Well then, a celebration is in order. Have you taken delivery on the new yacht you've been telling me about?"

"Last week," Cook replied. "But I haven't had time to get down to see it."

"How about a shakedown cruise?" the Senator said cheerfully. "A little fishing off Mazatlán; a stop at Acapulco?"

"Sounds good," Cook said. "The new contract has been accepted and signed, and things are moving along well here. Why not?"

"I have a new lady for you to meet," the Senator said. "I could have her bring a friend."

"No thank you, Tom. I'll pass on that," he said, remembering the last cultural dwarf the Senator had brought him. "I prefer scouting something up along the way—makes it more sporting."

"I'll meet you at the club in L.A. Monday morning."

"Monday morning will be fine," Cook confirmed.

After a brief stay in the hospital and a few days relaxing with Callahan, and soaking in the hot springs, Paula was ready to return to New York.

Callahan checked her bags and joined her in the airport lounge. "I know we've been over this," he said, "but I still think the IRS would hear you out."

"No," Paula said. "They might look into it, but I'm sure Hill and Cook will have some way of accounting for their money." She took his hand and squeezed it gently. "I think it was Erasmus who said, 'In great things it is enough to have tried.' We did our best." She removed her sunglasses—the swelling around her eyes was gone, but some discoloration remained. Their eyes met and held; she reached up, touching his face. "I love you, Callahan."

"The offer still stands," he said, kissing her tenderly on the forehead. "You can stay if you want, for as long as you want. . . ." He hesitated, realizing that he had never before said what he was about to say. "We could get married; we'd be good for each other."

Paula embraced him, kissing him passionately. "I know; I know," she whispered, holding him tightly. "I have a few weeks' work waiting for me at home. When I'm finished, I'll take a few months off. We'll try."

Jack smiled, pleased with the concession. "You promise?"

"I promise."

At the announcement of her flight, Jack walked with her to the boarding gate, his arm around her shoulder. "I'll bet with a little extra effort you could get that work done in a week."

Paula laughed, raising her head to kiss his cheek. "I'll bet you're right."

Paula was near the door at the end of the ramp when she stopped and called to Jack. "Do you think you can keep Boomer from climbing into the shower with me?"

A passing stranger cast a wide-eyed glance.
Jack smiled and shrugged. "I'll talk to him about it."
Paula nodded and threw him a kiss.

Epilogue

The manager of the Ottawa branch of the Swiss Credit Bank reread the cover letter on the file which his secretary had placed on his desk that morning. The instructions were unusual, to say the least, but he reminded himself that it was not the bank's policy to question its client's stipulations regarding arrangements it had previously agreed to honor. He made a note to transfer the balance in the Dennecker account to the Central Bank of Uruguay in Montevideo, to be credited to the account of one Ricardo Galenda. He glanced at his watch. It was 10:30. His secretary had said the man from the Russian embassy would be expecting him at eleven. Removing the sealed envelope from Dennecker's folder, he put it in his briefcase and left the office.

"Good morning, Mr. Hautmann," the burly, heavyset Russian said, leaning over the top of his desk and grasping the banker's delicate hand in a crushing grip. "I am Yuri Polichenko, chief of security here at the embassy."

"Good morning," Hautmann replied, flexing his fingers after the Russian released his hand.

"Please be seated," Polichenko said, gesturing to a chair in front of his desk. "It is not often I get to talk to a Swiss banker," he said jovially.

Hautman was not a man given to idle conversation. He got straight to the purpose of his visit. Polichenko pressed a small button hidden along the molding inside the kneewell of his desk, activating the recording equipment.

"One of our clients," Hautmann said, "has left instructions regarding a sealed envelope he left in our care. In the event this client did not notify us to the contrary, in person, each year within ten days of a specified date, we were instructed to deliver this envelope by hand and unopened to a security officer at the Russian embassy." Hautmann removed the envelope from his briefcase, handing it to Polichenko. "Our client did not make his intentions known to us this year, and I am therefore complying with those instructions. As you can see, the seal is intact."

Polichenko took the envelope and examined the seal carefully. "Who is your client?" he asked.

"I am sorry," Hautmann replied, "I am not at liberty to disclose that. Our obligation is fulfilled once the envelope is in your possession." Hautmann stood up, extended his hand, thought better of it, and bowed instead. "If you will excuse me, Mr. Polichenko. I have a pressing schedule."

After Hautmann left, Polichenko opened the envelope, spreading the contents across the top of the desk. He examined the series of photographs of men he didn't recognize, men carrying crates, stacking them behind a truck with U.S. Army markings, and loading them into the truck. He could barely read the letters stamped on the crates, and got a magnifying glass from his desk to examine them more closely. The names were familiar to him and piqued his curiosity. There were individual photographs of the same men at a bus station, putting packages in a locker, and another series of each of them sitting on a bench in a park he recognized as being near the capitol building in Ottawa. One of the photographs taken in the park held his attention. The man had one of his hands beneath the park bench and appeared to be holding a roll of tape in the other. The tall, gray-haired, distinguished-looking man was familiar to him, and after a few minutes he recognized him as a well-known United States Senator.

There were three cassette tape cartridges with labels noting the recorded material: CONVERSATION WITH HILL, JULY 3, 1955; CONVERSATION WITH COOK, JULY 10, 1955; and CONVERSATION WITH WHITE, JULY 14, 1955.

Polichenko set the tapes aside and read the thirty-page

handwritten explanation of the contents of the envelope. There was a brief biography of each of the men. He took particular note of a line about John Cook—"a former OSS officer in World War II, now involved in top-secret defense work for the U.S. government." The pages that followed gave a detailed accounting of Dennecker's arrest, interrogation, trial, sentencing, imprisonment, and eventual release, ending with his arrival in Canada and the contact and subsequent blackmailing of the three men.

Polichenko fully realized the potential value of the information in his hands. He put everything in his attaché case and placed a call.

"I would like reservations for tonight's flight to Moscow," he said, settling back in his chair, smiling with a deep sense of anticipation.

GREAT ADVENTURES IN READING